"D...s
for y...d?"

"I—" Her th... ...ed out.

Reverend Pollock cleared his throat. "I now pronounce you husband and wife." In finishing, he raised his voice to cover the whispers from the congregation behind them. "May God bless you both and keep you safe in the shelter of His love. You may kiss the bride," he added in a lower tone.

Leah waited in an agony of nerves for Thad to touch her. She blinked hard and then Thad's mouth settled gently over hers, his lips warm and firm. It lasted but an instant, but Leah's breath knotted beneath her breastbone.

It was over. Thad's hand held hers just tight enough to keep her feet anchored to the earth. If she skipped down the aisle, as she felt like doing, she would float away.

Together they started toward the church door, and only then did Leah become aware of the heavy, disapproving silence that greeted them. She kept her head up and tried to smile at the sea of stony faces. Not one person would meet her eyes....

* * *

Smoke River Bride
Harlequin® Historical #1147—August 2013

Dear Reader,

When you picked up your Harlequin Historical book this month, I'm sure you will have noticed that we've had a little makeover! But, rest assured, inside you'll still find the timeless stories you know and love and, yes, those deliciously sexy heroes—be they Regency rakes, Viking warriors or rugged, honest-to-goodness cowboys. Fall for every one of these men as they find love with spirited, unconventional heroines—and watch as they break all the rules!

We're proud of our beautiful covers here at Harlequin Historical and hope you like this fresh new take on them as much as we do. Drop by www.Harlequin.com to let us know what you think.

Don't miss this month's fantastic reads:

SMOKE RIVER BRIDE by Lynna Banning

NOT JUST A GOVERNESS by Carole Mortimer
(A Season of Secrets)

A LADY DARES by Bronwyn Scott
(Ladies of Impropriety)

TO SIN WITH A VIKING by Michelle Willingham
(Forbidden Vikings)

Happy Reading!

Linda Fildew
Senior Editor
Harlequin Historical

SMOKE RIVER BRIDE

—

LYNNA BANNING

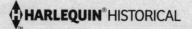

HARLEQUIN® HISTORICAL

Recycling programs
for this product may
not exist in your area.

ISBN-13: 978-0-373-29747-4

SMOKE RIVER BRIDE

Printed in U.S.A.

Avail

Wildwood #374
Lost Acres Bride #437
Plum Creek Bride #474
The Law and Miss Hardisson #537
The Courtship #613
The Angel of Devil's Camp #649
The Scout #682
High Country Hero #706
One Starry Christmas #723
"Hark the Harried Angels"
The Wedding Cake War #730
The Ranger and the Redhead #773
Loner's Lady #806
Crusader's Lady #842
Templar Knight, Forbidden Bride #914
Lady Lavender #1027
Happily Ever After in the West #1039
"The Maverick and Miss Prim"
Smoke River Bride #1147

For Suzanne Barrett

Author Note

The inspiration for this book came from a photograph of a young Chinese girl taken by Arnold Genthe, which I found in the book *San Francisco's Old Chinatown*. The struggles of the Chinese in the nineteenth century touched me, and I felt drawn to the difficulties a young woman of a totally foreign culture might have experienced in a small Western American town. As a nation, we have not always shown tolerance toward those who are "different" from us; I pray we are becoming more enlightened.

LYNNA BANNING

has combined a lifelong love of history and literature into a satisfying career as a writer. Born in Oregon, she has lived in Northern California most of her life. After graduating from Scripps College she embarked on a career as an editor and technical writer, and later as a high school English teacher.

An amateur pianist and harpsichordist, Lynna performs on psaltery and harp in a medieval music ensemble and coaches in her spare time. She enjoys hearing from her readers. You may write to her directly at P.O. Box 324, Felton, CA 95018, U.S.A., or at carolynw@cruzio.com. Visit Lynna's website at www.lynnabanning.com.

Chapter One

The day Leah arrived in Smoke River it was snowing. She stepped off the train from Portland and peered into a cloud of swirling white flakes, unable to see a foot ahead. Her feet were freezing inside her black leather slippers and she could think of nothing but reaching the squat whitewashed station house and folding her blue fingers around a cup of hot tea. She stumbled blindly forward, lugging her small valise.

A white mountain loomed in her path, and before she could stop, her face smacked into something furry at nose level. It turned out to be the beaver trim on the front of a man's jacket. A large man, taller than her father by at least six inches.

"Sorry, lass," he rumbled.

She clutched her floppy silk hat and looked up. Through the mist of falling snow she saw a man's square jaw and a trim mustache that reminded her of Father's. He was tall and broad-shouldered and towered over her like a sturdy tree. Instantly she lowered her eyes as she had been taught.

"Might watch where you're goin'," he grumbled.

"And the same to you, sir," she said before she could stop herself. She should not have spoken out like that. Her mother would have scolded her.

She moved to step around him, but a large, long-fingered hand encased in a leather glove gripped her arm. "You just come in on the train from Portland?"

"Yes, I did." She pulled out of his grasp and resumed her path toward the station house and the prospect of hot tea.

"Did you see a woman, maybe with red hair and a Scots burr, on the train?"

She turned to face him, and this time she did meet his eyes. He was good-looking in a craggy sort of way, with steady, sky-blue eyes that seemed to look right through her. "I was the only woman on that train, sir. And I do not have red hair."

"Ye're not Scots, then?"

"I am half Scottish. Of what interest is that to you?" She could almost see her mother's scowl for being so forward.

"None, I guess. I'm waitin' for my new bride. She's supposed to be comin' from San Francisco, but I've never laid eyes on her before, and I wouldn't recognize her."

Leah's heart dropped into her ice-crusted shoes. Oh, no. *She* was the woman he was waiting for. He thought she would be a Scottish woman because of her name, Cameron. She swallowed twice. Such a mistake was a very unlucky sign.

Ten days ago she had replied to a notice in the San

Francisco newspaper. "Rancher with young son needs wife. Educated, honest, hardworking."

Mr. Thaddeus MacAllister had answered immediately and enclosed the train fare. He had never seen her, and she had never seen him.

And we are to be married in twenty-four hours!

She couldn't do it. She'd thought she could marry a man she had never seen, but she just couldn't. What had she been thinking?

She had *not* been thinking, of course. She'd just had to escape the ugly situation she'd found herself in. Now she thought she would be sick all over this man's beaver jacket, and *that* would be even *more* unlucky.

The tall man bent toward her. "Her name is Leah Cameron. Do you know her?"

"Oh, yes," she said, her voice resigned. "I do know her." She drew in a big gulp of air and let it out slowly. "I am Leah Cameron."

His eyes widened. "What? You don't look Scottish to me!" He brushed back her silk bonnet and scanned her face. "Don't look Scottish at all!"

Leah raised her chin but kept her eyes lowered. "I am half Scottish, as I said. My father's name was Franklin Cameron. He died of cholera a month ago."

The man grabbed her by both arms and pulled her forward until her nose grazed a jacket button.

"And the other half?"

"The other half is…" She reached up and pulled her floppy hat completely off so he could see her face.

His eyes went even wider. "Good God, you…you're a Celestial!"

"I am half Chinese. My mother's name was Ming Sa. She is now dead, as well."

He kept staring at her, his mouth hanging open. Finally his jaw clicked shut. "Look, miss, I placed my notice because I need a…well, a wife. I never figured you'd be a…a foreigner."

"According to the Immigration Authority, I am not a foreigner. My father was an American citizen, a missionary living in China, so I am American, too."

"Well." The man cleared his throat. "I never expected this. I mean, you."

Not a good sign. "You mean you expected me to be a white woman. Caucasian." It wasn't a question. She knew how the Chinese were regarded in the West. The tales she had heard of the treatment of "Celestial" railroad crews made her cringe.

Leah watched his expelled breath puff into a foggy white cloud. "Yeah," he muttered at last. "I guess I did expect you to be…well…" His voice trailed off.

Heavenly Father, he would send her back! She could never return to San Francisco. Not now.

"Wait," she said. "I can cook and clean and care for a child. I have had experience at the Christian mission orphanage in Canton. And I can sew and embroider…."

But she could not return to China. Never. Third Uncle would lose face, and besides, there was no longer any place for her there. In China, she was not half Chinese, she was half White Devil. She no longer knew where she belonged.

She watched him look away, then back to her. "It's not that I think you're not qualified, miss. But—"

"You need not explain, Mr. MacAllister. It is clear that you no longer want me." She had half expected such a reaction, but now what was she to do?

She hefted her valise and started moving slowly toward the station house entrance.

He caught up with her in two strides. "It's not that you're a Celestial, not exactly." He lifted the suitcase out of her hand and fell into step beside her.

"Then what *is* it, exactly?" She sneaked a look at him.

His mouth tightened. "Aw, hell, I don't know. The folks here in town might not—"

"Would you protect me?"

"Well, sure, but—"

"Mr. MacAllister, I cannot go back to San Francisco. It took me eight days to escape from my host lady. She was a very bad woman. I will not go back."

He pulled open the door of the station house just as the train gave a high, throaty toot and chuffed on down the track. "Come inside, miss. You look like you could use some—"

"Tea," she supplied without thinking. "Yes, please."

He frowned down at her, then stamped the snow off his boots. "You might let me finish a sentence now and then, Miss Cameron."

"Oh! I beg your pardon, Mr. MacAllister. Father and my teachers always said I was impulsive and outspoken. They were right."

His rust-brown eyebrows waggled. "You've been to school, then?"

"Of course. I can read and write in two languages.

My father headed a mission school in China. I was educated there until..." She bent her head.

He waited. "Until?"

Leah clenched her jaw until the urge to cry passed. "Until Mother and then my father died of cholera. Papa saw to it that I was well educated."

"Aye, I can see that. You talk right proper."

"Thank you."

"Me, I know farming—cattle, and this year I'm trying some wheat. Nobody in these parts grows wheat, but... Let's see, where was I? I know how to build a barn and a house and I can read and write. That's what I want for my boy, and more."

He guided her to a stool at the counter. "Tea for the lady," he said. "Coffee for me, with a shot of— Aw, skip it, Charlie. Just coffee." Charlie was the manager, the telegraph operator and the ticket seller for the small Smoke River station.

The short balding man leaned over the counter. "This yer, uh, new bride?"

Thad purposefully cleared his throat. "Mind your own business, Charlie."

"Hell, ever'body in town knows you sent away for..." He focused on Leah's face and his voice trailed off. "Oh, I see."

"Oh, you do?" Thad challenged.

"Yeah, I do," Charlie said quietly. "Won't be easy, Thad. Good luck to ya." He clomped over to the black potbellied stove in the center of the small reception room and tossed a small log into the fire.

Within minutes the room was toasty warm. Leah

sent the stationmaster a grateful smile, stood up and shrugged out of her ankle-length wool coat. Thad stood, as well, grasped the coat and strode off to hang it on the coatrack by the door. When he turned back to Miss Cameron, the floor tilted under his boots.

Jehosephat, she was a looker! She wore some kind of silky blue-green trousers and a matching long-sleeved tunic with frog loops down the front. But what he noticed most was how the smooth fabric curved over her breasts and hinted at her hips. She was small and slim, built like a China doll, but she sure looked womanly.

And she'd come to Smoke River to be a bride and run a home? Hell, she looked too delicate to hang out the laundry, let alone boil sheets and dungarees in a tin washtub.

"Listen, Miss Cameron, you sure you want to live out on a ranch? To be honest, it's a hardscrabble life out here in the West, and some years it's harder than others. Summers can be scorching, winters are—"

"Snowy," she interrupted. "I understand. It snows in China, too, Mr. MacAllister."

He walked a slow circle around her. Huh. She'd blow over in a stiff wind. And he sure couldn't see her down on her hands and knees scrubbing the kitchen floor. Or anything else, come to think on it.

"Miss Cameron, you don't know how hard ranch life can be."

She spun toward him. "I am not afraid of hard work. I fear only being alone and unprotected in a big city where I know no one."

"Like San Francisco?" He was fishing, but he had

to know something about her. "What scared you in San Francisco that wouldn't scare you here in Smoke River?"

She was quiet for a long minute. "It was not safe in that city," she said softly. "Especially for a Chinese girl. I...I had to get away."

Thad frowned. Something didn't add up. "How come?"

She twisted away from him so he couldn't see her face. "When I left the ship, two men laid their hands on me. They wanted me to come with them. I showed them my papers, but they laughed and tore them up."

"Good grief," Thad muttered. "I never thought about... Sit down, Miss Cameron. Have some more tea."

She sank back onto the stool at the counter and wrapped her slim fingers around her teacup. "Those men dragged me into a carriage, but I escaped through the other door and ran down an alley and kept running, but they caught me."

"Did you get away?"

"No," she said shortly. "Nothing happened to me before I got free, but I cannot go back, do you understand? Hard work does not frighten me." She gave an involuntary shiver. "But bondage does."

Thad took a long look at her thin shoulders, her creamy neck and the delicate-looking hands. She appeared small and kind of lost, like a kitten. The least he could do was give her a home. She could teach Teddy. And she could keep house and cook and...

"Charlie? Look after Miss Cameron for five minutes, will ya?"

Charlie poked his head out of the ticket window across the room. "Where ya' goin'?"

"Up the street to the mercantile. Gotta get her some ranch duds."

For the third time, Carl Ness dusted off the display of kerosene lamps, watching out the corner of his eye while Thad MacAllister pawed through boy-size flannel shirts and jeans. Too big for his seven-year-old son, Teddy; too small for any adult he'd ever seen in town.

"Find what yer lookin' for, Thad?"

"Nope," the tall Scotsman snapped.

"What *are* you lookin' for, anyway?"

"Work clothes."

"You hire somebody to help out at the ranch?"

Thad paused and gave the diminutive mercantile proprietor a hard look. "Yeah, you might say that." He held up a blue plaid shirt with buttons down the front, then snagged two more—one red and one green—and piled them on top of the three pairs of dark denim jeans he'd laid over his forearm.

"Kinda small for a ranch hand," Carl observed. He patted the pile of garments Thad laid on the counter.

"Yup."

Carl just shook his head. "You know, gettin' more than three words out of you since your wife… Well, you know. It's like squeezing a hen's egg. You press too hard and you end up with egg yolk all over your hand."

"Yeah."

Carl started to wrap up the shirts in brown paper. "Anything else, Thad?"

"Yeah. Bottle of brandy. Make it a big bottle." Thad dropped some coins on the counter and gathered up his paper-wrapped parcels. He could hardly wait to see Miss Cameron's reaction to his purchases. Maybe the sight of the rough work clothes would convince her ranch life could be a killer. It had killed Hattie, his wife. It could kill a delicate woman all too easily.

Leah sat huddled over her tea, watching the station-master behind the ticket cage. He could sell her a train ticket to…well, to anywhere. But where could she go? Not back to the city. Not to Portland, either, which was just another big city where she would know no one. One small town was probably as good as another, and here there was a man who noticed her heritage but acted as if he did not care much.

"Mr. Charlie?" she called across the room.

"Yes, miss? What can I do for you?"

"Is…" She could scarcely get the words out. "Is Mr. MacAllister a good man?"

"He's the best kind there is, miss. Leastways he used to be."

"What happened to him?"

"Lost his wife a year ago in a train wreck. Ain't been the same since."

"Is he…cruel or violent?"

The stationmaster laughed. "Thad? Nah. He's gone kinda crazy over this wheat-growing idea, and once he gets his mind made up, he's hard to move. Sure, he gets hot under the collar sometimes, but I've never seen him do anything mean."

Leah turned back to her tea. Everything would work out. It *had* to work out; she had no place else to go.

The front door banged open and there stood Mr. MacAllister, snow frosting the shoulders of his jacket and dusting the wide brim of his gray hat.

"Come on, Miss Cameron. Time to take you home."

Chapter Two

Mr. MacAllister snagged Leah's gray wool coat off the stand and held it out to her. "Ready to head to my ranch, Miss Cameron?"

Leah stared at the tall, muscular man. She had not thought this would be so hard to do. To be honest, she had not thought at all; she was so grateful for a way to escape Madam Tang in San Francisco, she had seized the money Mr. MacAllister had sent and boarded the first train north. Now, facing the prospect of actually living with this man, becoming his wife, she was frightened.

"Are we not to be married first?" she asked.

"Uh, sure." But now that he was facing it he had to admit he wasn't over Hattie yet. Yeah, he needed someone to keep house and mind Teddy, but maybe he wasn't ready for another marriage.

Still, she needed someplace safe, and she was educated. She probably knew some about the history of the world, and about books. Most of the Smoke River folks hadn't been schooled past sixth grade, and he wanted Teddy to know about literature, about poetry. Maybe even Scottish writers, like Robbie Burns and Sir Walter Scott.

Well, hell, nothing came for free. If he wanted all these things for Teddy, he should be prepared to pay the price. And the price was marriage.

"Gettin' colder outside, Miss Cameron. Might make better sense to go on home where it's warm and discuss this further." He stood with the wool coat draped over one arm, looking at her expectantly.

"No." She said it quietly, but she meant it. It would not be best at all. She remembered the few days she had spent at Madam Tang's in San Francisco. No male servant had been allowed near her. *If a man touch you before, your price will be less. You are virgin. Virgins must be careful.*

Leah clasped her hands in her lap. She was a stranger in a land she did not know, among people she did not yet trust. She must be extra careful or she would end up a concubine, not a wife.

"I cannot go to your home tonight. Not until we are married."

"Huh?" His expressive brown eyebrows shot up. "You mean—"

"Yes, I do mean. I am sorry, but I cannot come before we are married. It would not be proper."

His blue eyes snapped with impatience. "Proper! Hell, Miss Cameron, I'm just offering you shelter."

Leah shook her head. "If I go with you now, there will be harm. Not of your making, perhaps, but…"

She kept her voice calm, but her nerves had begun to scream. Would he change his mind about marrying her if she refused to do what he asked?

"Explain," he ordered.

She sucked in a shaky breath. "I am an outsider in your country. I cannot afford to be compromised."

"Compromised!" He snorted. "I don't aim to do anything but feed you some supper and—"

"Please, Mr. MacAllister. I will eat supper at the hotel. You may come for me tomorrow and then—" she straightened her spine "—then I will become your wife."

"I, uh, I didn't exactly expect… I mean, it isn't that I don't want you to stay—I do. But, well, I wasn't expecting to marry this soon. And I guess you did. Do."

"Yes," she said, her voice quiet. "I do."

His face changed. Desperation faded into resignation, and then he nodded decisively.

"Okay, we'll get married right away. Save your reputation and help me raise my son. More than I bargained for, but…like it or not, there it is. There's an old saying out here—in for a penny, in for a pound. Guess I'm in for the pound."

"Do you wish not to marry me because I am half Chinese?"

"No," he said shortly. "There's other reasons, but makes no matter now."

She slid off the stool, lifted her coat off his arm and shrugged into it. "I will go now to the hotel."

"What? Oh, sure, the hotel." He looked as if he'd been hit over the head with a coal shovel. He rebuttoned his overcoat and started to pull on his gloves but stopped suddenly and peered down at her hands.

"You got any gloves?"

"No. I read a book about the West. About California. It said the sun shines every day."

Again, he peered into her face, and this time his eyes softened into a blue like the sea. "I reckon you didn't read about Oregon."

"No. I never expected to come to Oregon."

His face changed. The soft blue eyes grew distant, and the lines around his mouth deepened. His jaw sagged for a moment until he snapped it shut and thrust his brown leather gloves into her hands. "Life's like that. Always what you don't expect."

A dart of sympathy pricked her. She had lost her parents, but he had lost much more—his wife, his partner in life. The mother of his son. Poor man. He was big and strong and probably fearless about things that would terrify a weaker person, but she saw how he ached inside in his grief. Inside, this formidable man was just like any other human being.

Leah pulled on the offered gloves. They were so large the fingers drooped at the ends and she had to curl her hands into fists to keep them from falling off.

They entered the hotel lobby together. It smelled of cigar smoke and coffee, and instantly all conversation ceased. In the unsettling silence Leah made her way to the portly desk clerk and laid her gloved hands on the counter. The clerk's squinty eyes widened.

"I would like to engage a room," she said.

"Sure thing, ma'am." He did not look up, but kept his gaze on her oversize hands.

She began to tug off the gloves. "Only for tonight," she added.

The shiny-faced clerk picked up a pen and absent-mindedly turned the hotel register toward her. "If you'll just sign here, ma'am, I'll—"

He looked into her face and stopped short. "Just a minute, there. I'm afraid this hotel is full."

"But it was not full two minutes ago," she protested.

Thad strode over to the desk and positioned himself behind her. "No, it isn't full, Sam," he said in a flat voice.

"Sorry, Mr. MacAllister," he mumbled. "We don't cater to…to Celestials."

Thad's bare fist came down hard on the polished oak counter. He leaned over it and spoke in a tone as clear and hard as ice. "This lady is as American as you or me, and tomorrow she's gonna be my—" he took a breath "—my wife. You'll cater to her *now,* understand?"

The clerk goggled at him. "I h-heard ya, Mr. MacAllister, but—"

"How much is the room?"

"Dollar and a half," Sam choked out. "But—"

Thad slapped four coins onto the counter. The clerk flinched, reached to one side and dropped a room key into Thad's deliberately extended palm. "Third d-door on the right."

Thad bent to retrieve Leah's battered leather valise, grasped her elbow and ushered her up the stairs.

Instantly conversation buzzed in the smoke-filled lobby. "My Gawd, didja see that?"

"Never thought a Celestial…"

"Hell, Thad's bit off more'n he can chew this time."

"Celestial or not, didja see her face? She's down-right pretty!"

Leah followed Mr. MacAllister down the musty-smelling hallway and waited while he unlocked the door to her room. He stood aside, and she edged past him.

The room was small, with one lace-curtained window overlooking the main street, a coverlet-swathed bed, a tall oak armoire and a washstand with a blue-patterned china basin and water pitcher. The place smelled oddly of both dust and furniture polish.

Mr. MacAllister shifted from one foot to the other and finally spoke from the open doorway. "I'll be back in the morning, Miss Cameron."

Leah turned toward him. "I will be ready, Mr. MacAllister."

For a long minute he didn't move. "One last thing I've got to say," he grumbled.

She braced herself. She knew it! He didn't want her. In the morning he would send her away.

"You do not want me because I am—"

"Nah, not a bit of it, Miss Cameron. Don't you mind what people say. I—I'm glad you came."

She studied the tall man in the beaver coat. His gaze seemed direct; laugh lines wrinkled the corners of his eyes and his mouth could change from a grim line into a smile in a single heartbeat.

She liked him. She couldn't say why, exactly. He was

gruff, his manners untutored, but she sensed a steadiness about him. He was like Father but not so disapproving. Father had always worried about her Chinese half, even though he had braved Third Uncle, Ming Sa's guardian, to marry her mother. The Chinese did not respect the White Devils, but she knew Father had loved Ming Sa.

"I am glad I came, as well," she said softly. And God knew she needed to belong somewhere safe, even if it was a farm on the rough, uncivilized Oregon frontier.

Thad tipped his hat, backed into the hallway and turned to leave. "Whatever happens, it should be interesting." He tossed the remark over his shoulder.

Leah jerked as if bitten by a horsefly. "Wait!" she called. "Your gloves." She pressed them into his large hand. To her surprise she found his fingers were trembling.

In that moment she guessed what lay beneath his gruff exterior. Underneath, he was as frightened as she was. But, being a man, he would never, never admit it. *Never show fear,* Father had said.

When the door closed behind Mr. MacAllister, she let her heavy wool coat slide off her shoulders onto the scuffed hardwood floor. She undressed by the light seeping through the lacy curtain, poured water into the basin and rapidly sponged off the travel dust and soot from every inch of her body. Then she shook out her silk tunic and trousers and hung them in the armoire along with her coat.

Ravenously hungry, she unwrapped her last dried

bean cake, pulled on her pink silk sleeping robe and crawled into the welcoming bed.

She had been fortunate in America thus far—except for those terrifying days imprisoned at Madam Tang's. Leah had finally escaped in the horse-drawn laundry cart that came each morning and found her way to a church. Now, after a day and a night on the train from San Francisco to Portland, and another half day to Smoke River, here she was. Tired to the bone, but safe in the biggest, softest bed she had ever slept on. God was surely looking out for her.

She stretched luxuriously, nibbled the edge of the hard bean cake and listened to the street noises below her window. Horses clip-clopped down the main road, harnesses jingling. Dishes clattered in the restaurant across from the hotel. Men's raucous voices drifted from the saloon next door. Oh, it all sounded so…American! What a strange and wonderful land this was!

Thank you, Lord, for this place of safety and for this man. She would be a good wife to him.

Nodding over the uneaten bean cake, she curled into a ball and fell asleep listening to the sound of a woman's voice from the saloon below, singing a song about a train and a round mountain.

Chapter Three

Seven-year-old Teddy MacAllister looked up at his father accusingly. "Where ya been, Pa? I had to shoo the chickens inside the henhouse all by myself, and keep the fire goin', and…" His voice trailed off. His father was not listening, as usual.

"What? Oh, I've been in town, laddie. Tomorrow I'll have a surprise for you."

Teddy's blue eyes lit up. "A horse, Pa? Is it a horse of my own?"

Thad regarded his son with eyes that saw only a small part of the boy's eagerness. "Nope, not a horse. Something better."

"Ain't nuthin' better than a horse," the boy grumbled.

But Thad did not hear. He busied himself at the woodstove in the kitchen, heating the kettle of beans he'd set to soak before he'd left to meet the train. His gut felt as if it were tearing in two directions. On the one hand, he wanted to give Teddy someone who could fill the gap left by his mother's death. Someone to keep house and bake cookies and knit socks for the boy.

On the other hand, he did not want Miss Cameron, no matter how capable or understanding she might be, to replace Hattie. Thad and she had grown up together in Scotland, and later, when he had settled on the Oregon frontier, she'd come out from New England to marry him. Her upbringing hadn't prepared her for the hardships on a ranch; in fact, she had disliked living so far away from the life she had grown used to. But Hattie had said she loved him, and she had given him a son.

Teddy dawdled near the dry sink, still stacked full of plates and cups from last night's supper. "Kin we have biscuits?"

"What? Biscuits take mixin' up."

"Then kin I mix 'em? I learned real good from Matt, uh, Marshal Johnson," he amended. "I even know how to bake them on a flat rock!"

"Got a good oven right here." Thad thumped one leg of the nickel-trimmed stove with his boot. "Build up the fire some, Teddy. Need these beans to cook."

"Yes, Pa." He moved to the wood box near the back door, stacked an armload of small oak logs along one arm and staggered to the stove.

"Guess what?" he said as he chunked one piece into the fire box.

Thad didn't answer.

"Pa?"

Thad spooned some bacon grease into his bowl of flour and stirred it up, paying scant attention to the boy. Usually, he thought about his dead wife, or worried about his new wheat field—was some insect nibbling the shoots? Would the snow stunt the sprouts? But this evening, he couldn't get his mind off tomorrow morning.

Miss Cameron wasn't at all what he'd expected. The fact that she was part Chinese had come as a shock, but what had really knocked him off his pins was how young and how damned pretty she was. She had shiny black hair, like a waterfall of satin, and large gray-green eyes that shone when she was pleased. For some reason, she made him nervous.

She hadn't been pleased when he'd suggested she come home with him tonight. He'd meant no disrespect, just wanted to be practical. Hell, he'd never accost a woman, especially one under his care. In the morning he'd make it all proper at the church, and then she'd be here permanently. He'd show her the ranch and the wheat, the experimental crop he was trying to grow on the back three acres, and the springhouse he was building, and…

Teddy turned away with a sigh and tramped to the pocked wooden table in the far corner of the kitchen. "You want me to set out the plates, Pa?"

Again lost in his thoughts, Thad did not answer. With a shrug his son lifted two china plates from the painted wood shelf along the wall and plopped them down on the table.

Thad spoke abruptly from the stove. "You go to school today?"

"Nah. It's Saturday, remember?"

No, he didn't remember. How could he forget what

day of the week it was? Especially Saturday. Hattie had died on a Saturday. He gazed out the window over the sink, suddenly unable to see. She'd wanted that window so she could look at her pink roses sprawling along the back fence. Two summers had come and gone since then; the roses looked awful straggly.

He blinked away the stinging in his eyes and focused on his reflection in the glass. Who was he now that Hattie was gone?

"Pa? Pa?"

"What, Teddy?"

"You're gettin' that funny look again."

Thad drew in a long breath. "Sorry, son. Guess I was thinkin' about—" Hell, he didn't really know what he'd been thinking about except that it was about Hattie. It usually was.

"You hungry, son? Beans are 'bout ready and my biscuits must be near done."

Teddy nodded and settled onto one of the two ladder-back chairs drawn up at the table, then leaped up to retrieve two forks from the cutlery drawer next to the sink. His father laid a basket of hot biscuits in front of him and ladled beans onto his plate.

"What did you say you learned in school today, son?"

Teddy stared at his father, pinching his lips together. Ever since his mama died, Pa hardly even noticed him. Without a word, he turned sideways and pressed his face down on his folded arm.

The wagon rattled to a stop in front of the Smoke River Hotel. Thad looped the reins around the brake handle and climbed down from the driver's bench. Morning had dawned with clear blue skies and bright sunshine, though the air was cold enough to freeze ice cream. Kinda odd weather for November, but he didn't fancy getting married on a rainy, gray day like the one when Hattie…

Hell, he couldn't think about that today.

His son sat beside him, his face shiny from a morning bath and his red-brown hair neatly combed. "Wait here," Thad ordered.

The boy fidgeted but obeyed, wondering what the promised "surprise" would be. Seemed like a hotel was a funny place to buy a horse, but lately Teddy had been surprised by a lot of things his father did. Getting all spiffed up this morning, for instance. Sure, it was Sunday, but Pa never attended church. Besides, a man didn't need to dress all fancy just to buy a horse. Didn't need to take a bath, either.

Inside the hotel, Thad tapped on Miss Cameron's door. When it swung open, all his breath whooshed out. She was a sight, all right. Like something out of a dream. He knew his jaw was gaping open, but at the moment he couldn't remember how to close it.

From head to foot she was enveloped in a pajama-like outfit of scarlet silk that clung to her gently curving body like a second skin. On her head she wore a shimmery gold crown made of what looked like foreign coins that tinkled softly when she moved. Hell, she looked like an exotic princess from his son's fairy-tale book.

"I am ready," she announced.

Thad snapped his jaw shut. *But maybe I'm not.* What

was he going to do with this fragile-looking creature on his hardscrabble ranch?

"This is my wedding-day dress. It belonged to my mother and to her mother before that. Do you like it?"

Yeah, he liked it. All of it. He couldn't take his eyes off her shiny, shoulder-length black hair or the flawless ivory skin or the faint pink blush of her cheeks. All at once what was happening seemed so unreal he felt dizzy.

He had come to escort her to the church to be married, but now that he stood before this delicate creature his mouth was so dry he couldn't utter a word. But he'd offered her marriage in exchange for her presence in his house and his son's life, and come hell or high water, Thad MacAllister always kept his word.

She gestured gracefully at her valise and the wool coat draped over the bedstead. Thad opened his mouth, then closed it and nodded. Carrying the coat and luggage, he followed her down the stairs.

Leah stepped slowly down the stairs to the hotel desk and returned the room key. The lobby was jammed with people—ranchers, visitors, even a circuit judge; the jangle of voices died as suddenly as if someone had puffed out a candle. No one uttered a word.

People stared at the slim woman in red. She held her head high, but her face had gone white. Thad took her elbow, swept her out of the hotel and over to the wagon, where Teddy waited.

The vision in red silk looked up at his son and smiled. Teddy's eyes popped wide open. He made a strangled sound in his throat and scooted across the bench as far away from Miss Cameron as he could get.

Preoccupied, Thad handed her up, strode around to the driver's side and swung himself onto the bench.

"Teddy, here's the surprise I promised."

Teddy just stared at Leah. Finally he cleared his throat. "I thought it was gonna be a horse, Pa."

"Well, it isn't a horse. It's a woman. Her name is Leah Cameron and we're going to the church to get married."

"You're already married," Teddy shouted. "You're married to Momma!"

Thad lifted the reins and clicked his tongue at the mare. "Your mother is dead," he said in a gruff voice. "Now you're gonna have a new—"

"Friend," Leah quickly interjected. She turned to Thad's son. "No one can ever replace your mother."

"How would *you* know?" Teddy muttered.

Leah settled herself carefully on the bench and folded her hands in her lap. "I know because my own mother died just a month ago. No one can ever take her place in my heart."

The boy glared at her slantwise, but said nothing. When they pulled up in front of the Smoke River Community Church, he bolted off the bench, stumbled over Leah's legs and dropped to the ground.

"I ain't goin' into the church," he announced.

Thad wound the reins around the iron brake handle with short, jerky motions. "Nothing you say or do is gonna stop what I'm set on doing, son. We need help on the farm and you need a…well, a mother."

The boy's face went stony. "I don't neither."

Leah laid her hand on Thad's arm. "Don't force him," she said quietly. "It will only make it worse."

"Yeah, guess you're right." He helped her down from the wagon, folded her hand over his forearm and started up the steps of the small whitewashed church.

"You comin'?" he called to Teddy.

"No. I'm not gonna ever speak to her. She'll never be my momma. Never!"

Thad stopped in front of his son. "Nevertheless, Teddy, this lady *is* going to be my wife."

"I hate her!" the boy screamed.

"But," Thad said quietly, "I don't. I like her. I think she will be good for both of us."

Leah looked up sharply at the big man at her side. He liked her? A thousand doubts vanished at his words. But his son…

She tightened her fingers on Thad's forearm. First things first. First she must be a good wife to this man. Later, perhaps, she would learn how to be a mother to his son.

The congregation had not yet arrived for the Sunday service, but Reverend Pollock took one look at them and frowned. "There won't be enough time for a wedding before my flock arrives for church this morning."

Thad's return stare could scorch. "There's plenty of time. Unless you want us living in sin, Reverend, I suggest you marry us right quick." His voice was like cold steel.

"Ah." A shaky smile lit the minister's shiny face. "I believe you might be correct, Thad."

He led them to the altar and lifted his Bible. But he

did not open it. Instead, he gave Leah a long, penetrating look.

"Are you a Christian?"

"I am. My father was a minister, like you, only it was in China and he was a Presbyterian."

Reverend Pollock blinked and studied her face. "China," he echoed. "Of course." He frowned again. "Well, then, shall we begin?"

Chapter Four

Leah had never seen a prettier church. The Protestant mission churches in China were drab structures of weathered gray wood or stone, and she gazed in admiration at the lovely interior before her. Four tall windows punctuated the white-painted walls, two on each side. Sunshine poured through the glass into the sanctuary, spilling warm golden light over the wood floor. She smelled furniture polish and something lightly lemon-scented.

Two large bouquets of red camellias banked the altar. Flowers? In November? Mother would say that was a lucky omen.

The minister disappeared through a small doorway, then returned a moment later draped in his black clerical robe. A smiling young woman followed him to the altar.

"This is Mrs. Halliday," Reverend Pollock announced. "Mrs. Halliday grows lavender on her farm. She will serve as your witness."

Leah stole a glance at the slim, dark-haired woman,

relieved to find her smiling. She moved forward and lifted Leah's hands into hers.

"Welcome. You must be Thad's bride. From San Francisco, *n'est ce pas?*"

"I come from China, Mrs. Hal—"

"Oh, please call me Jeanne."

"My name is Leah Cam—"

"Leah MacAllister," Thad interjected firmly.

Jeanne laughed. "Mrs. MacAllister, then. Your wedding garments are very beautiful," she whispered.

"They were my mother's," Leah murmured. "I brought them from China."

The minister cleared his throat. "We'd better get on with it, folks. The church is beginning to fill up for the morning service." He waited a half second, cleared his throat once more and opened his Bible.

"Dearly beloved…"

Leah sensed people entering the sanctuary and seating themselves on the pews behind them. She also heard their gasps of surprise and the sudden silence that followed.

The ceremony passed in a blur. "Do you, Thaddeus MacAllister, take this woman…?"

Thad's low "I do" rumbled close to her ear, and she realized he had bent his head down to her level to speak his vows.

"And do you, Leah Cameron, take this man…?"

While the minister waited for Leah's response, a woman's shrill voice cut through the quiet. "God save us, she's a Celestial!"

Jeanne Halliday reached out and quietly touched

Leah's arm. Reverend Pollock looked up from his Bible with a frown and repeated the question. "Do you, Leah, take Thaddeus for your lawful wedded husband?"

"I—" Her throat clogged. "I do," Leah choked out.

Reverend Pollock cleared his own throat. "I now pronounce you husband and wife." In finishing, he raised his voice to cover the whispers from the congregation behind them. "May God bless you both and keep you safe in the shelter of His love. You may kiss the bride," he added in a lower tone.

Leah waited in an agony of nerves for Thad to touch her. Instead, he suddenly dug in his vest pocket and produced a wide gold band. "Forgot the ring," he murmured. He slid it onto her finger. "This was my grandmother MacAllister's."

Then he placed his hands on Leah's shoulders and turned her to face him. She could feel his fingers tremble.

He drew her toward him, and for some reason tears flooded into her eyes. She wasn't frightened. Or unhappy. She was moved by something deep inside that she could not explain. She blinked hard and then Thad's mouth settled gently over hers, his lips warm and firm. It lasted but an instant, but Leah's breath knotted beneath her breastbone. She opened her eyes and smiled into his face.

He looked surprised, but she was too giddy to wonder at it. Jeanne Halliday hugged her, and Reverend Pollock shook Thad's hand, then Leah's, then Thad's again, and turned them around to face the swelling congregation.

It was over. Thad's still-shaking hand held hers just tight enough to keep her feet anchored to the earth. If she skipped down the aisle, as she felt like doing, she would float away.

Together they started toward the church door, and only then did Leah become aware of the heavy, disapproving silence that greeted them. She kept her head up and tried to smile at the sea of stony faces. Not one person would meet her eyes.

A shard of disquiet knifed into her belly. They disliked her, but why? Because she was Chinese? Because Thad's son, Teddy, sat outside on the church steps, sulking in obvious displeasure? Because some other woman had wanted to be Thad MacAllister's wife?

She began to count the steps to the last pew. The women glared at her with animosity, and some of the men ogled her with undisguised interest. Only when she was safely outside the church could she regain her equilibrium. At least she would try.

They emerged into the crisp midmorning sunshine to find Teddy still slumped on the bottom step, a sullen scowl on his face. A dark, cold shadow spread over Leah's entire being, carrying with it an odd sense of foreboding. She had never expected to feel such disapproval on her wedding day.

Thad kept her hand in his, and with the other he ruffled Teddy's hair and grasped his shoulder. "Come on, son. Let's go home."

Teddy shrugged off his father's hand and trailed behind them, dragging his feet until they reached the wagon. Thad lifted Leah onto the bench. Teddy clambered up, but scooted his small body as far away from her as he could get without toppling off.

Thad cracked the whip over the mare's head, then had to wonder at his action. He'd never used the whip before, but he'd explode if he didn't do something to dispel the tension gripping his belly.

"Why'd you do that, Pa?" Teddy accused.

"Dunno, son." He glanced at the boy. "Just felt like it."

"Is it 'cuz you got married?"

"Well, kinda. I guess I'm feeling a little nervous."

"How come?"

Thad chuckled. "You'll understand when you're older."

"No, I won't," Teddy yelled. "I won't ever, ever understand."

Leah said nothing. To Thad's dismay she uttered not one single word the six miles out to the ranch, just studied every tree, every grassy meadow and cultivated field, even the shallow spot in Swine Creek where they forded. Was she homesick for China?

Or maybe she was wondering what she'd gotten herself into? Given the frosty reception of the townspeople at the church, maybe she regretted marrying him.

Thad was surprised in a way that *he* did not regret it. He knew it was the right thing. He had given her his name and his protection, and by God, he would give her a home and all the comforts he could afford in this lean year, starting with the boy's trousers and shirts and work boots he'd purchased yesterday at the mercantile. She sure couldn't do housework in that silky red outfit.

Ah, hell, maybe it would work out just fine. He was respected in Smoke River, known as a steady and resourceful man, and she seemed to be good-natured. And—he felt his face grow hot—she sure was pretty.

What could go wrong?

He drew rein at the front porch and watched Leah study the small house he'd built, the barn, and the barely sprouted three-acre field of winter wheat he'd gambled his savings to plant. He'd put his whole life into this farm; he hoped to goodness she liked what she saw.

The minute she walked into the cabin and gazed at what was to be her home, his heart shriveled.

Leah stared at the plank floor, sticky with something that had spilled but never been mopped up. A tower of pots and skillets and egg-encrusted plates teetered in the dry sink. The bare log walls were chinked with brown mud and a grimy, uncurtained window over the sink looked out on the withered remains of what had apparently been a kitchen garden. Another bare window beside the front door suddenly resembled a yawning face, laughing at her.

Were all the houses in Oregon like this, so carelessly kept? Or was it only *this* house?

The room smelled of dust, wood smoke, stale coffee and rotting food, the latter odor drifting from a slop jar that she fervently hoped was intended for a pig. She closed her eyes and tried not to breathe in.

"Guess it could use some cleaning up," Thad said with a catch in his voice. "Hattie always said…" He left the thought unfinished.

"I am sure she was right," Leah said evenly. She

could not imagine how difficult living here must have been for Thad's wife. She could also not imagine how she herself could manage to live in this filth and clutter.

Thad lifted her valise. "I'll just put this in the bedroom."

Bedroom! Heaven help her, she had avoided thinking about what marriage would mean at night. "Is...is there— How many bedrooms are there?"

"Just the one," Thad muttered.

"Where does Teddy sleep?"

"In the loft up there, over the front room. Says it's warmer at night. I planned to sleep up there, too."

Thad lifted his head. "Oh, I almost forgot. Yesterday I bought you some work clothes. Should make do until you can get to the dressmaker's in town."

"The dressmaker's?"

"Sure. Don't you want some dresses like the other women wear?"

No, she did not. Having a Western dressmaker poke at her and criticize her comfortable silk trousers and tunics made her stomach heave. But she was starting a new life in America, and she knew she must fit in.

"Could I not make my clothes myself? Did Hatt—" At the stricken look on his face, Leah couldn't bring herself to speak her name. "Did your wife own a sewing machine?"

Thad ducked his head and started toward the closed door of what she assumed was the bedroom. "Yeah, she did have a sewing machine," he said over his shoulder. "Brought her mother's fancy Singer with her from Virginia. But she never learned to sew on it."

"Perhaps I could use it?"

The puzzled look in his eyes almost made her laugh out loud.

"Uh, well, sure, I guess so. It's probably out in the barn somewhere. I'll—I'll have to find it."

He flung open the bedroom door, plopped her valise in front of a tall chest of drawers and motioned to a square paper package on the bed. "I brought some duds from the mercantile for you."

"But I brought clothes from—"

Thad cut her off. "That red outfit's too fine to wash dishes in. Same for that pretty blue shirt thing you wore yesterday. Silk, wasn't it?"

Leah nodded but did not answer. Instead, she unknotted the string securing the brown paper package on the bed and began to unwrap it. She lifted out a pair of boy's jeans. Why, they looked just like the ones his young son wore!

She looked up, but Thad was gone. She heard the front door click shut and the thump of his footsteps across the porch. Teddy took one look at his father's receding figure and bolted after him.

Leah straightened her spine, shook out the strange-looking American trousers and a long-sleeved red plaid shirt. Since she had stepped off the ship in San Francisco she had not seen one woman wearing clothes like these, not even here in Smoke River. She fingered the boy's shirt. At least it was red; in China, red was a lucky color.

With shaking fingers she slipped free the frog closures down the front of her beautiful scarlet wedding gown and let it drop to the floor. Her life as Mrs. Thaddeus MacAllister had begun.

Chapter Five

"Pa?"

Thad peered into the dusty gloom of the barn, where Teddy was hunched over on a mound of fresh hay. "Yes, son?"

"I don't like her, Pa. She wears funny clothes and she looks real diff'rent, and she doesn't talk to me."

Thad knelt to look into the boy's stiff face. "More like you're not talkin' to her, isn't it?"

"I don't got anything to say to a Chinese lady." His chin sank toward his shirtfront and Thad waited. Teddy usually took his time with more than one sentence.

Thad gazed about the musty smelling barn interior, idly searching for Hattie's sewing machine. Was that it, there in the far corner? That burlap-draped lump next to the hay rakes?

"Pa?" Teddy raised his head, then let it droop again. "Yeah?"

"How come you married her? Do you like her better'n me?"

The boy's muffled words cut into Thad's heart like a cleaver. He gathered his son into his arms and held him tight.

"Theodore Timothy MacAllister, there is no one—*no one* in this entire world—I like better than you. And there never will be. You're my son, and I love you more than…" His voice choked off.

He wanted to do what was best for Teddy. At the same time he wanted to ease Leah's way into their lives, to fill the hole left by Hattie when she'd died.

After a long silence, he heard Teddy's voice, the words mumbled against Thad's Sunday best shirt and fringed deerskin vest.

"Pa, d'you think maybe she'll cook supper for us?"

Thad chuckled. "I think maybe, yes. Now, how'd you like to help me find something in our barn?"

Teddy's voice rose an octave. "A horse?"

"Not a horse, son. A sewing machine. Your momma had one, but she never used it, so I stored it out here in the barn somewhere. You've got sharp eyes. Where do you think it might be?"

Teddy sat up straight and studied his surroundings, moving his eyes from the array of shovels and axes against one wall to the bridles and harnesses that hung on the opposite wall, to the two saddles draped over a sawhorse in the corner—one man-size, one slightly smaller, for a woman. That one had belonged to his mother.

Purposely he looked away, then pointed to a burlap-draped object in the opposite corner. "I bet that's it!"

"Might be," Thad said. He rose and pulled the covering aside. "Well, look at that—you're right. Come on, son, think we can lift it?"

"Nope."

"You want to give it a try?"

Teddy's lower lip jutted out. "Nope."

Thad shrugged and started to jockey the oblong sewing cabinet away from the wall. He remembered it, and seeing it again brought a funny pain in his chest. Before he could draw another breath, Teddy was puffing beside him. Together they hauled the machine across the hay-strewn barn floor until they reached the entrance.

Thad swung open the double doors, but when he looked back, Teddy had his head down on top of the once-shiny cabinet and was gasping for breath. Obviously the load was too heavy for the boy. Damned thing was solid oak. Must weigh at least a hundred pounds.

He strode to the back of the barn, grabbed up a large gunnysack and spread it on the floor in front of the sewing machine.

"What do we do now, Pa?"

"Now, we go to work again."

They rocked it back and forth until all four legs sat squarely on the sturdy hemp sack.

"Think we can pull it, Teddy? Slide it over the ground to the porch?"

The boy eyed the load with a frown. "Nope."

"Want to try at least?"

"Nope."

But when Thad stooped to grasp one corner of the sack, Teddy was at his shoulder, reaching for the other.

"Good lad," Thad murmured. "Let's go, then. One, two, three, pull!"

The sewing cabinet inched forward. They had to tilt-walk it over the barn door sill, but after that it bumped over the two-hundred-yard path to the cabin with only three stops along the way to let Teddy catch his breath.

Thad had to wonder at his son's sudden helpfulness. Had he decided Leah was not so bad after all? Or maybe Teddy just wanted to be close to his father? Thad guessed he'd been so wrapped up in mourning Hattie over the past year he'd pretty much ignored the boy.

His breath caught in a sudden rush of emotion. Had he really done the right thing? Would Teddy ever forgive him for marrying Leah, bringing a stranger, a *foreigner,* into his home? Turning his young son's life upside down?

"Pa?"

Thad straightened. They had reached the bottom step.

"How're we gonna get it up to the porch, Pa?"

Thad scratched his newly trimmed beard. "Well, let's see. I can heft one end, and you…"

Teddy's head drooped. "It's too heavy for me, Pa. I can't lift it."

"Right. Well, let's see if something else will work." Thad hoisted one end of the cabinet up onto the first shallow porch step, then switched ends and lifted it again. Teddy leaned his back against the oak case to keep it from slipping.

Just as Thad reversed his position again, the cabin

door banged open and a small jean-clad figure flew out. She looked so much like a boy Thad had to blink.

"Leah?"

"Yes," she said calmly. Without another word she positioned herself opposite Thad.

He stared at her slim figure. She'd rolled the sleeves of the red plaid shirt up to her elbows, revealing slender forearms, and the jeans hugged her rounded bottom in a way that made his mouth go dry. Her waist was nipped in with a narrow length of woven scarlet cord of some kind, and the upper part of the shirt swelled gently over her breasts.

He wondered suddenly why more farm women didn't dress that way. The garments were sturdy and practical. And on Leah—he swallowed—they were downright attractive.

He swallowed again as his brain churned out more images. What sort of undergarments did she have on? Did a Chinese woman wear a corset? A camisole? Bloomers? *What?*

He shook his head to clear his mind and focus on the task before him, drew in a deep breath and heaved the load up another step. Leah put her back against the opposite end and heaved, as well.

Teddy's mouth dropped open and Thad had to laugh. She'd just shoved a heavy cabinet up a step and she wasn't even breathing heavily. She must have worked hard in China all her life.

He gestured for his son to join Leah at her end. "Heave," he muttered. This time six hands gripped the heavy sewing machine and swung it up onto the next step, where it teetered for a moment, then settled with a thunk.

"One more step," Thad urged. When the cabinet finally rested on the porch, he surveyed his work crew with admiration. Teddy looked winded. Leah didn't appear the least bit tired. Her cheeks were flushed, but her gray-green eyes sparkled with triumph.

"Here's your sewing machine, Leah. Where do you want it?"

"Oh!" She dashed inside the small cabin interior, propping the door open with an empty apple crate, and stood studying the room. For the first time Thad noted that her feet were bare.

"Over there." She pointed to the far corner, where a cat-clawed brocade armchair rested.

Thad retrieved the gunnysack, and he and Teddy used it to slide the cabinet across the stained plank floor. When it stood where Leah had indicated, she stepped back and gazed at it with an assessing eye while the two males caught their breath and massaged their shoulders.

"No," she said at last. "All wrong. The light is not good." She pivoted in a slow circle to inspect each cabin wall in turn. "There," she said finally. "Under the window." She pointed to the opposite side of the room.

Thad and Teddy groaned in unison, but bent to the opposite corners of the gunnysack. "You're sure, now?" Thad asked drily.

Leah shot him a look. "Yes, quite sure."

Again Thad and his son traded glances. This time Thad rolled his eyes toward the ceiling and Teddy suppressed a giggle.

Leah crossed to stand opposite the two cabinet movers, and when Thad and Teddy started to slide their load across the floor, she laid her backside against the opposite end, lowered her head and shoved. The sewing machine scooted smoothly across the floor.

Leah spun around. "Yes," she breathed. "Perfect."

Thad's eyebrows went up. "You sure?"

Teddy clasped both arms over his chest and scowled at her.

Leah faced them both, her hands propped on her hips. "Of course I am sure! Did you think I would change my mind again?"

"Yep," Thad and Teddy replied in unison.

Leah looked from her new husband to his young son. Their expressions were identical—narrowed eyes, unsmiling lips and a tiny frown between their identical red-brown eyebrows. Teddy resembled his father, right down to his stance, with both hands jammed in his back pockets.

"I do not change my mind," she said quietly. "Once I decide what to do, I do not change."

Frowning, Teddy studied the floor. She shifted her gaze to Thad. A variety of emotions showed in his face, a combination of surprise, bemusement and apprehension. His expression puzzled her until she remembered she wore boy's clothing, her feet were bare and Teddy was not at all pleased that his father had married her.

She was in no position to insist on being accepted. Here in Smoke River she was safe and protected; she could endure a great deal of hardship and disapproval in the bargain. Still, a hard kernel of doubt niggled its way into her mind.

Thad and his son escaped to the barn, saying they had to care for the horse and do the milking. Tomorrow, Thad said, he would show Leah the chicken house and how to milk their temperamental cow.

As soon as the front door closed, she started to make the cabin habitable. Even the poorest hut in China had been better kept than this—neater and spotlessly clean. America was strange indeed.

She washed the sinkful of dirty dishes and pots in water she pumped and heated on the woodstove, then filled a tin bucket with more water, dumped in the last of her waning supply of powdered jasmine-scented soap and scrubbed the entire cabin floor on her hands and knees. When she rose at last, the floor squeaked under her bare toes.

Next she attacked the window over the sink and the one by the front door with a rag dipped in vinegar water, swept down the cobwebs drooping from the ceiling and dusted every surface she could find, from the oak headboard in the bedroom to the shelf of Teddy's schoolbooks, even the shiny black Singer sewing machine in its oak cabinet.

Then she climbed the built-in ladder to the loft, where she made up Teddy's disheveled bed and was straightening his jumbled collection of rocks when she spied a children's book lodged between the bureau and the wall. *East of the Sun, West of the Moon.* She had read it herself as a child. Suddenly she was glad her father had made her study so hard at his mission school.

Thad wanted an educated woman to care for and perhaps set an example for his son.

She dragged the woven rag rug that covered the loft
floor outside, tossed it over the clothesline and beat it
with the broom until the puffs of dust made her cough.

What next? She felt compelled to keep herself busy;
if she allowed herself to stand still for a moment she
would think about her marriage and the bed and the
coming night and Thad MacAllister, who was now her
husband.

What would it be like, lying close to him in the dark,
feeling his hands on her skin? Such thoughts made her
shiver.

She reswept the kitchen floor, rinsed out a camisole
and a pair of white silk drawers in the sink and hung
them on the clothesline next to the rug from Teddy's
loft. Now she must think about supper for the three
of them.

Chapter Six

The tiny pantry off the kitchen held a barrel of flour, sacks of sugar, rice, dried beans and potatoes, and a hanging slab of moldy-looking bacon. No carrots or peas or turnips or herbs. No fresh fruit, either—only a lone tin of peaches and a bushel basket half full of apples. What could she make out of such a conglomeration?

Hours later, footsteps boomed across the front porch and Thad walked in with Teddy at his heels. At the stove, Leah froze with her back to them.

"Somethin' sure smells funny, Pa."

"Looks different, too, son. Kinda…shiny."

Teddy clambered up the ladder to the loft and an instant later let out a squawk like an enraged rooster. "My bed's all diff'rent! And my rocks—somebody's been messing with my rocks!"

His head appeared over the railing. "*She* did it! I hate her!"

Thad ignored his son and gazed around the cabin.

Clean windows. Scrubbed floor. No dishes in the sink. Looked as if a cyclone had blown through the place. He began to frown before Teddy finished yelling. He liked what Leah had done. But for some reason deep inside he didn't *want* to like it. It seemed disloyal to Hattie.

But Hattie is gone. And Leah was here. He could hardly believe Leah was his wife now, and he had to admit his reaction to the state of his house had nothing to do with Hattie. He couldn't bear to think about it too closely.

The cyclone was standing at the stove. Apparently she was a fastidious housekeeper, and of course his son wouldn't appreciate that. Thad wondered why *he* didn't appreciate it.

The spit and polish this half-Chinese girl had shown in just a few hours reminded him not so much of Hattie as his Scots mother. She was long dead now, as was his father. That was one reason Thad had come to America—the Scots were starving. He had just passed his twelfth birthday and both his parents were gone.

Hattie, he recalled, had not been a particularly careful housekeeper, but she had been his lifelong companion. And because he had loved her, he had forgiven her any domestic shortcomings.

But seeing another woman in her place sent a blade through his gut. It wasn't that he regretted marrying Leah—just that he regretted losing Hattie.

Teddy clattered down the ladder and slouched toward the kitchen table. "I spose you want me to set out the plates," he grumbled.

Leah turned to look at him. "Yes, thank you, Teddy. That would be nice."

"Don't have enough chairs, Pa. Guess she'll have to sit on that old nail keg, huh?"

Thad met Leah's questioning eyes and to his relief saw that she was amused, not angry. She clapped her hand over her mouth to keep from laughing. Teddy's suggestion of the nail keg even brought a chuckle to his own throat.

"Well, son, you have two choices. Either you cobble up an extra chair or you eat your dinner standing up. Leah and I are sitting at the table."

"Aw, Pa."

"Don't 'Aw, Pa' me, Teddy. Take it or leave it. I'd tan your hide good if it wasn't our wedding day."

Teddy said nothing, but Thad noted that he dutifully laid three plates on the table and then disappeared.

"Hunting up a chair, I'd guess," he murmured at Leah's back. She'd found one of Hattie's aprons and tied it twice around her waist in an oversize, floppy bow. His heart gave an odd lurch at the sight. Dammit, he remembered that apron. Oh, God, he wished it was Hattie there at the stove.

But it wasn't Hattie, it was Leah. His new wife. Dammit, he could hardly bring himself to say the word. He focused on her slim figure and felt a flicker of warmth. He hadn't necessarily expected to *like* his mail-order bride and now the woman was his wife.

He didn't have to like her, he told himself; all he had to do was get along with her.

The front door banged open and in stomped Teddy,

dragging a dust-coated, straight-backed wooden chair. "Found it in the barn," he muttered.

Thad squeezed his thin shoulder. "Well done, Teddy."

"I hope it breaks when she sits on it!"

Thad bent and tipped his son's chin up with his forefinger. "No, you don't, Teddy. Things are plenty difficult for all of us right now, so you'll hold your tongue. From now on, if you want to say anything about my wife, you say it directly to Leah, understand?"

"Okay." Teddy sucked in a breath and sent a venomous look at her back. "I don't like you, Leah."

Thad grabbed the boy by his shirt collar, then heard Leah's calm voice offer a retort he could not have predicted with a crystal ball.

"I do not like you either, Teddy."

The boy's mouth dropped open. "Huh? How come?"

"Because," Leah said, turning to face him, "the things you say hurt my feelings."

Thad blinked, then caught Leah's steady gaze. He raised his eyebrows and gave his new wife as much of a smile as he could muster.

In an agony of unease, Leah watched Thad and Teddy seat themselves at the wooden kitchen table. She poured Teddy a glass of fresh milk from the pail Thad had brought in, then filled Thad's china cup with coffee that suddenly looked too black and too thick. Thad reached his spoon to the milk glass, dipped some out and dribbled it into the cup. Now it looked like water from a mud puddle.

Teddy poked his fork at his father's cup. "That sure looks awful."

Leah's face grew hot. "I have never made coffee before," she confessed. "In China we drink tea."

Hiding her face, she gathered up the three plates and whisked them over to the stove, where the skillet rested with her steaming dinner dish. There was no wok, so she had used the iron frying pan to cook in. She scooped a large dollop of the mixture onto each plate.

She placed Teddy's dinner before him. The boy wrinkled his nose. "What's that stuff?"

"That is called *chow fun*. It means 'vegetables with noodles.' In China, we make it with chicken."

"Eww," Teddy muttered.

Leah tried to see the dish through the eyes of a young American boy: a pile of thinly shaved potatoes covered with fried onions and topped with crumbled bacon. Of course, some ingredients were missing—not just chicken, but the noodles, crisp green peapods and a dribble of plum sauce. In China, the dish was special; here in Oregon it was obviously not.

Teddy dropped his fork and laid his forehead on the table next to his plate. "I can't eat it, Pa."

"Nobody's pushing you, son." Thad jammed his own fork into the mound on his plate and purposefully shoved a bite into his mouth. The apprehensive look on his face faded to surprise.

"Not bad," he said. "Pretty good, in fact." He gobbled another bite, then another. Leah ate quietly beside him, noting that he took only one tiny sip of the coffee she had made. Her throat tightened.

For dessert she had baked a traditional Chinese tart made of layered apple slices, but now she hesitated to present it. She would never understand American cooking. She feared she would never fit into American life no matter what she learned to cook. Finally she gathered up her courage, set the tart in front of Thad and handed him a knife to slice it into wedges.

The tart met with a broad grin from Thad and a glimmer of interest from Teddy. At least he tasted a bite. Then, without a word, he wolfed down his portion of the intricately assembled creation and held out his plate for another piece.

"Good!" Thad pronounced. Teddy said nothing, just sat staring at the empty tart pan. "Mama used that pan to flour the chicken before she fried it."

"Oh? What does 'flour the chicken' mean?"

Teddy smirked. "You don't know nuthin', do ya? You take a chicken leg and roll it around till it's all floury and then you fry it."

"Could you show me?"

"Uh, I guess so, if I—I have to," the boy stammered. "Maybe tomorrow."

"Tomorrow's Monday, son. Don't forget school."

Leah looked up. "I would like to walk to school with you tomorrow, Teddy."

"What for? You need to learn somethin'?"

"Oh, yes. There is much for me to learn about life in America. But that is not what I meant."

"Miz Johnson doesn't teach that stuff, 'cuz we already know it," Teddy snapped.

"Teddy," Thad said in a warning voice.

"I wish to meet your teacher, Teddy."

"Leah," Thad warned, "the schoolhouse is a three-mile walk."

"An' if it snows, Pa takes me on his horse. I bet you can't even ride a horse."

"No, I cannot. But I am used to walking. My father's school was two miles from our house, and I walked there every day, even in the snow."

"That was dumb," Teddy muttered.

Thad made a move toward his son, but Leah laid her hand on his arm.

"My father did not own a horse," she said. To avoid explaining, she cleared the table, poured Thad's coffee into the slop bucket and washed the dishes in water she'd left heating on the stove. Her anxiety mounted with every plate she dried. She knew he had not wanted to marry her; what would he expect of her? Would he want to sleep with her? And…perhaps more?

Thad seemed to be a reasonable, sensible man. And he'd had a wife before, so he knew…what to do in bed. But she most certainly did not.

A cup slipped from her shaking fingers and shattered against the floor. Before she could reach for the broom to sweep it up, Thad's hand closed over her shoulder.

"You're wondering about tonight," he observed in a low voice. He turned to snag the broom. "I'm wondering, too. We're husband and wife now."

"Yes," Leah murmured. "We are."

Thad cleared his throat. "But I don't really feel married, so maybe I should still sleep in the loft."

Leah met his steady gaze and her stomach flipped. He had offered marriage to give her a respectable way of escaping what was inevitable in San Francisco. He could never know how desperately she needed the safe haven he offered. If she had stayed in the city, Madam Tang would have quickly auctioned off her virginity to the highest bidder.

This was Thad's house. Thad's bedroom. She could not usurp it.

"I think perhaps we could share your bedroom."

He said nothing, just swept up the pieces of china and dumped them into the trash box next to the stove. Then he straightened to face her, and swallowed hard.

"You go on to bed, Leah. I'll be along in a while, after I have a talk with my son."

She lifted the broom out of his grasp. "Please do not. Have a talk, I mean. It will make him feel even more resentful. I will handle Teddy in my own way."

At that, Thad propped both hands on his hips and stared at her. "I keep being surprised by you, Leah. You're turning out to be some woman!"

"What does that mean, 'some woman'?"

To her astonishment, Thad's cheeks turned pink. "It means you are unusual. Not like other women."

She hesitated. "Is it…is it because I am Chinese?"

"Oh, hell no, Leah. That doesn't much matter to me." He reached out and gently squeezed her narrow shoulders while she stood before him, the broom still clutched in her fingers. Moisture burned at the back of her eyes.

"It will be all right, I swear." He lifted the broom out of her hands, turned her toward the bedroom and gave her a little nudge. "Go along to bed now."

She moved away quickly so he would not see her tears.

For more than an hour she lay in the big double bed and, despite the flutter in her stomach, her eyelids kept drifting closed. Thad did not come. The moon rose, sending a cold silvery light through the single bedroom window, and still Thad did not come.

Had he changed his mind and climbed up into the loft to sleep with his son? Or perhaps he was sleeping in the barn? Why did he not come to his own bed? Was it because *she* was there?

At last she heard the front door open, then close, and suddenly there he was at the foot of the bed. Bathed in moonlight, he looked to be coated in shiny armor. Like Ivanhoe, as she had imagined him when she was growing up. It had been her favorite book.

"You still awake?"

"Yes," Leah murmured. "I thought it polite to wait for you. I kept myself from falling asleep by thinking about…Ivanhoe."

A laugh burst from the tall shadow by the bed. "Ivanhoe!"

Thad began to unbutton his shirt. He fumbled with the buttonholes halfway down his broad chest, stalled, swore a Gaelic curse and abruptly yanked the garment off over his head. His wool undershirt followed.

"Ivanhoe wouldn't have to cope with buttons," he muttered.

"Ivanhoe," she heard herself say, "would have a squire to unbuckle his armor."

Thad's hands at that moment rested on the leather

belt at his waist. He stopped and sent her a challenging look. "You want to be my squire?" he joked.

"Oh, no," she cried. "I could never—"

He laughed softly. "Leah, you're gonna wash my clothes. You're gonna get so used to my trouser buttons you could undo them in your sleep."

She pulled the sheet up over her head. The next thing she knew the bed sagged under his weight and a long, very cold body stretched out next to her.

"Oh! You are frozen! Where have you been?"

He chuckled aloud. "I've been out talking to my wheat field. Do it every night, mostly to reassure my-self it's still there."

"Your wheat field? Why would it not be there? Is it growing?"

"Oh, aye. Little by little. But it's like waitin' for a kettle of water to boil."

Leah rose up on one elbow. "Do all American farm-ers talk to their crops?"

"Nope."

There was a long silence, and she wished she had not spoken out in such a bold manner.

"Dunno why I talk to the wheat, really. Well, that's not true—I do know. That crop means a lot to me for two reasons. One, it's a challenge. A gamble, really, but I like a challenge. Always have. And the other reason is this—when I was real young, about Teddy's age, back in Scotland, my da had a farm. One year there was an awful storm that killed all our crops except for the red winter wheat Da had sown. We lived on that wheat, and goat's milk, for a whole year. Nothing else survived.

Neither would we have, if not for that crop of wheat. Saved our lives, it did."

"That happens in China, too. If the rice crop fails, many people starve to death."

Thad grunted. "Guess that wheat field makes me feel, well, like no matter what happens, my boy and I will survive."

Leah gazed out the window. "Can you see your field from here?"

"Nope. Good thing, I guess," he said with a chuckle. "Otherwise I'd be mooning out the window half the time instead of milking the cow and feedin' the horses."

Silence.

"Leah, you're the only person I've told all this to. Townfolk think I'm a little crazy. Nobody grows wheat in Oregon. They're all getting a good laugh over my experiment, I guess. I'm in debt up to my ears for what's growing on those three acres, but I believe in a few years this whole territory will be growing wheat."

"Mr. MacAllister...Thad...?"

"Go to sleep, Leah. It's been a long day."

Go to sleep? "Are you not going to—?"

"Nope," he said. "We're married, but we don't hardly know each other. Let's give it some time."

Leah rolled onto her back and lay staring up at the ceiling. Thad MacAllister was a most unusual man.

Or perhaps he does not like me.

But then he laid his arm across her waist and gently nudged her closer. Her silk-clad shoulder and hip brushed against his skin and his warmth enveloped her like a fine wool robe.

"You sure feel warm," he murmured. "I've been kinda cold for a while."

Leah smiled into the dark. It was a good beginning.

Chapter Seven

Before dawn, Leah awoke and snuggled into the space where Thad had lain until a few moments ago. It was still warm and it smelled like him, a mixture of pine trees and sweat. She liked it. She liked *him*.

She thanked the gods of good fortune for finding this man, for allowing her to take this step—safe and protected—into a new life.

She glanced at the bedroom window where faint gray light was beginning to filter in. He must have left before dawn—to do what? She knew farm chores waited, scattering feed for the chickens and gathering eggs, feeding and watering the horses, milking the black-splotched cow she'd glimpsed in the pasture yesterday. It was the same in China, except that her mother had milked a nanny goat. What would Thad expect her to do?

Fix his breakfast! She scooted out of bed, hung the pink silk night robe on one of the hooks that marched across the wall beside the bedroom door, and pulled on the jeans and red shirt she had worn yesterday. The

stiff denim fabric scratched her inner thighs and the
pointy shirt collar jabbed her neck whenever she turned
her head.

How uncomfortable these American garments were!
She longed for the silky feel of her Chinese-style tunic
against her skin and the soft folds of the loose trousers.

The kitchen was as spotless as she had left it and, to
her surprise, a fire already crackled in the stove; Thad
must have uncovered the banked coals and added more
wood. He had even set the large tin teakettle on the
back burner. That must be a hint that he expected coffee with his breakfast.

But what to cook? The few American breakfasts she
had seen on board the ship from China consisted of
charred meat and a pan of something messy—eggs,
she guessed—mixed up into a dreadful-looking yellow
pile. She had eaten eggs in China, but they were boiled
in the shell and shiny as a full moon.

In the small pantry just off the kitchen, she found
the bag of coffee beans and a basket of fresh eggs. On
a shelf sat a pretty red-painted box with an iron handle and a tiny drawer that pulled out. That box had not
been there yesterday.

Oh! For the coffee beans! You were supposed to
grind them up before…

Hurriedly she gathered up four fresh eggs, covered
them with water pumped from the sink and set the pot
on the stove next to the teakettle.

"Aint'cha gonna make biscuits?" The querulous
voice came from the loft, where Teddy balanced on
the ladder, one elbow hooked around the railing.

"Biscuits?"

"You know, like little muffins, only they're not sweet." He surveyed her with disgust. "You don't know anything, do ya?"

Leah straightened. "I know a great many things, Teddy. However, I grew up in China and I did not learn to cook in the American way."

"Ya want me to mix up some biscuits? I know how 'cuz Marshal Johnson showed me once, but Pa won't let me do it." He clattered to the bottom rung of the ladder.

Leah grabbed a crockery mixing bowl and shoved it toward the boy. "Yes, please. Show me how it is done."

Teddy puffed out his chest, took the bowl and disappeared into the pantry. "This here's flour," he announced when he emerged. "And then ya add a pinch of saler'tus. Now you dump in a spoonful of bacon grease and a bit of milk, and then you squish it all together, like this." He plunged both hands into the bowl.

Leah nodded, committing the ingredients to memory while Teddy scooped up the mixture, dropped large lumps onto a tin baking sheet and shoved it into the oven.

"Don't tell Pa I made 'em, okay?"

"Okay. Do not tell your father that I did not know how." A conspiratorial look passed between them. Merciful heaven, perhaps the boy would grow to not hate her.

The back door thumped open and Thad tramped in, a milk pail in one hand and a basket of eggs in the other. He clunked both pail and basket in the pantry and strode into the kitchen.

"Mornin', Pa."

Thad ignored the boy. "Breakfast about ready?" His breath puffed white from the cold air outside. Carefully he avoided eye contact with Leah.

"Almost, yes." She opened her mouth to comment on his brusque manner toward his son, then changed her mind. Not in front of Teddy, she resolved. Any differences between her and her husband would not be aired within his son's hearing.

"I'll go wash up at the pump outside."

"Do you not wish to bathe in warm water? I can heat—"

"Bathe! I take a bath once a week, on Saturday."

"Me, too," Teddy added. "Pa, she's so dumb she doesn't even know how to make coffee."

Leah flinched. She'd been right the first time— Teddy did hate her. But Thad wasn't listening, and besides, this morning she had puzzled out the mysteries of the American brew and used the coffee grinder.

The back door slammed. Teddy fled up to his loft, leaving Leah, her teeth gritted, to set the table and check the biscuits.

Thad clunked back into the kitchen, his heavy boots slathered with mud, and plopped himself into one of the ladder-back chairs. Teddy slid onto the other, but Thad motioned him away. "That's for Leah."

Then he looked down at his breakfast. Two shiny white whole eggs stared up at him.

"What's this?"

"Eggs," Leah said quickly.

"And biscuits," Teddy piped. Leah set a napkin-covered bowl on the table.

"Try a biscuit, Pa."

"Soon as I figure out this egg thing on my plate." He sent a questioning look to Leah, who settled herself at the table and picked up her boiled egg. "In China, we do it like this." She lifted a spoon and gently tapped around the middle until a crack appeared, then adroitly split the egg into two parts and scooped out the inside with her spoon.

Teddy scowled down at his plate. "People in China are stupid."

"Eating an egg with a spoon like this is not stupid," Leah countered in a quiet voice. "It is merely *different*."

"And it's dumb, too," the boy retorted.

"Teddy," Thad warned. He noticed suddenly that his son's hair was uncombed and that Leah wore the jeans and shirt from the mercantile. Her feet were encased in the same satin slippers she'd worn yesterday. She'd need a pair of boots, too.

Absently he reached for a hot biscuit. "What size boot do you wear, son?"

Teddy kept his eyes fixed on Thad's hand breaking open the biscuit. "Dunno."

"We have any butter?"

"Not yet," Leah answered. "I have not collected enough cream to churn."

"How about jam? Some in the pantry, I think. Blackberry. Get it for her, would ya, Teddy?"

Teddy bolted from the table and, before Thad could draw breath, returned with a half-empty jar of last year's jam. "Here, Pa. Bet she doesn't know anything about makin' jam."

Thad bit into his biscuit. "Good," he pronounced. "Even without jam."

The boy's face lit up. "Have another one, Pa."

Thad moved his gaze from his son to Leah, who was studying the two intact eggs that still lay on his plate. He picked up his knife and whacked one in two, then attacked the other. The soft yolk spilled over his fingers, but it tasted okay, just like an egg. Sure was an odd way to serve them, though.

He glanced around the warm kitchen and felt something inside him catch. This was like it used to be when Hattie was alive—eating breakfast around the kitchen table. But it wasn't Hattie sitting across from him; it was a woman he scarcely knew.

Lord in Heaven, what had he done?

He'd changed his life, changed his son's life, in a way that could not be altered. Part of him didn't like it one bit. Another part of him, a part he kept hidden even from himself, did like it. It was like spring after a long, bleak winter.

He glanced at Teddy. He saw so much of Hattie in his son's eyes and cheekbones that it hurt every time he looked at him, as if a sharp stick was poking his heart. He knew he didn't give the boy as much attention as he should; it was just that he reminded him so much of her.

"You goin' to school today, son?"

"Yeah, I guess so."

Leah swallowed her last bite of egg. "I would like to go with you this morning, Teddy."

"What for? Miz Johnson don't teach any Chinese."

"Of course not," she said quietly. "As I said, I would like to meet your teacher."

"How come? You ain't my momma."

"No, I am not. But I am still interested in your education."

Leah shot a look at Thad, then grabbed his coffee mug and rose swiftly. She returned it brimming with a dark liquid that—he sniffed it—smelled like coffee! He slurped up a mouthful and swallowed.

"Better," he pronounced. Funny he'd not noticed before how beautiful her gray-green eyes were when she smiled.

After breakfast, Leah and Teddy started off for the schoolhouse. Frost sparkled on the grass and weeds along the road, and the air was so cold it burned Leah's nostrils when she drew breath. She wore her gray wool coat, buttoned up to her neck, and her only hat, a Chinese-style bonnet that did not cover her ears. Her feet, clad only in her satin slippers, were growing numb. Teddy had on a sheepskin jacket like his father's and a hand-knitted woolen cap that covered his ears; he did not seem to mind the biting air.

At first they walked side by side in silence, but when they reached the Thompson place, Teddy suddenly sped up. "I dowanna walk with you."

Leah kept pace with him, and he increased his stride. Again she kept up with him. When he realized he could not outwalk her, he broke into a run.

Leah laughed aloud. Teddy did not know how fast she could run. In their village in China, no one had been able to outrun Ming Sa's daughter; she won every race the merchants sponsored. She shrugged off her wool coat and started running.

By the time they passed Thompson's last fence post, she had caught up with him, and even though her hat flew off, she pushed on a dozen yards past him. When she looked back she had to laugh again.

Teddy stood in the middle of the road, his hands jammed into his jacket pockets, glowering at her. She retrieved her coat and silk hat and returned to his side. The boy was still panting; Leah was not even breathing heavily.

"How come you can run so fast?" he demanded.

"Because my legs are longer than yours." She did not tell him how many times she had been chased by the village bullies. They'd hated her because she was half White Devil. In their eyes, being half Chinese did not erase the shame of birth with a white man as her father.

She bent closer to Thad's son. "And a friend at my school taught me how to breathe properly and pace myself."

Teddy stuck out his lower lip. "That's not fair."

"Why not?"

"'Cuz you're older. And bigger."

Leah smiled at him. "That's only half of it, Teddy. Would you like me to teach you the other half?"

He kicked at a stone. "Naw. That's kid stuff."

Leah said nothing for fifty paces, then couldn't stand it any longer. "It is not 'kid stuff.' Listen to me, Teddy. Do you know how much money I won when I was your age and the candle merchant bet money on me? Seventy thousand yen!"

The boy's blue eyes widened. "Really? You mean you won money from gambling?"

"Well, *I* didn't gamble, exactly, but the merchants in our village did. Chinese people like to bet on things. They called me 'the White Devil's daughter,' but I won lots of yen for those shopkeepers."

Teddy frowned and pointed ahead to a small wood structure in a clearing, surrounded by maple trees. Gray smoke puffed out the chimney.

"There's the schoolhouse."

Inside the chinked log walls a dozen stone-faced children stared at her. They ranged in age from about six years to a gangly boy of perhaps fourteen. The schoolteacher, Mrs. Johnson, stepped from behind her desk and smiled.

"Good morning, Teddy. Is this your new—" the woman caught herself just in time "—your father's wife?"

"Yah. She's new, all right. She don't know nothin'." The boy fled to a seat in the back row, folded his arm on the desktop and buried his face in the crook of his elbow.

"I don't like her." His mumbled words drew a gasp from the students.

"She dresses funny," someone said. "She's wearing boy's clothes."

"She's a foreigner," another chimed. "She's a—"

"Children!" Mrs. Johnson silenced her pupils and

moved toward Leah with both hands extended. "Welcome, Mrs. MacAllister."

Leah's heart jumped. "Th-thank you, Mrs.—"

"Oh, call me Ellie, please. I hope we will be friends. I think you may need one here in Smoke River."

Leah knew she was staring, but she couldn't seem to stop looking at the tall woman. She had the bluest eyes she had ever seen, a darker blue than even Father's. And a smile so genuine it made Leah's eye sting.

"My name is Leah. C-could I speak to you in private?"

"Of course. Mary Lou, take over the class, please. Start with the spelling lesson." Then Mrs. Johnson—Ellie—opened the door and motioned Leah outside.

"I—" Leah's voice choked off. Ellie peered at her.

"Why, my dear, you're crying! Whatever is wrong?" She lifted Leah's cold hands in her warm ones. "Tell me."

"I— Oh, everything is wrong. I want to fit in, but I don't know how to do anything in the American way. Teddy hates me. And his father ignores both of us."

"Thad MacAllister ignores everyone these days. Ever since his wife died, Thad has been withdrawn."

"He is more than withdrawn. He…" No, she could not tell the schoolteacher the rest, about his lying next to her in bed but not touching her.

Ellie sent her a wry smile. "I know what it is like to be an outsider in this town. The women, especially, can be unkind." She stepped back and looked Leah up and down. "I am sure it will work out. You are quite pretty, even in boy's clothes."

"I do not know how to cook the American way, or what to wear, or what to say to Teddy. That is what I wanted to ask you about."

"Teddy has been lonely and lost for over a year now, but I think eventually he might come to appreciate your company."

"Do you…" Leah hesitated. "Do you think I should wear a dress, like the other women in town?"

"I think it might help," the schoolteacher said gently. "Thad will certainly notice you are a woman."

"A Chinese woman." Leah waited, holding her breath, for Ellie's response.

"Leah, people in small towns like Smoke River know the Chinese only from the railroad crews that have passed through. They were seen as 'different.' They drank tea, for one thing. And their clothing was most unusual."

Leah said nothing. She could do nothing to change her face, but perhaps she could do something else. "I must learn to be American," she confessed.

Ellie grasped her hand. "I have an idea. After school tomorrow, I want you to come with me to the dressmaker in town. Will you?"

Overcome, Leah could only nod. She squeezed Ellie's hand. "Yes," she managed to murmur.

"Three o'clock tomorrow, then. I'll drive Teddy home in my buggy and we can leave from your place."

Leah grasped both of Ellie's hands and squeezed them again. Luck seemed to be smiling on her; she wondered how long it would last.

The rest of the day passed in a blur. Leah skimmed

the thick cream off the milk pans and shook it in a glass jar until it thickened into droplets of butter. Next she baked bread—the kind they ate in China. She made it with flour and water, and it came out of the oven hard and flat, like a big rice cracker. Tomorrow she would use it to make toast for Thad's breakfast, and she would ask Ellie how to make those messy-looking eggs.

At noon Thad strode in, hung his jacket on the hook by the front door and rubbed his hands in anticipation of dinner.

Leah looked at him blankly. "Dinner? I thought dinner was in the evening. In China we eat only two meals a day, breakfast and…"

Thad noted her cheeks had flushed in embarrassment. For a moment she looked like a frightened young girl, but then her eyes snapped and she pursed her lips. He couldn't stop looking at her lips. They were the color of Hattie's roses.

"I made butter this morning," she announced. "And bread. Could you eat that?"

Hell, no, he couldn't eat that. A man working a ranch needed fuel, a substantial meal in the middle of the day. But, goodness, the hopeful look on her face made his insides jump.

"Sure," he said. He reached out to pat her shoulder, and she gave a choked cry and walked right into his arms.

Well, now! Her body trembled like a newborn calf, and he wrapped both arms around her. "Is it Teddy?"

She shook her head, her nose rubbing against his shirtfront.

"School?"

Again she shook her head.

Thad took a breath. "Is it…me?"

She started to nod, then shook her head so violently he had to grin.

"I know I'm gruff and preoccupied, Leah. I guess I've got too much on my mind."

She tipped her head back and gazed into his eyes. Lord, her eyes were beautiful. "What 'too much'?"

"Well, there's Teddy, for one thing. The boy needs to learn some manners."

Again Leah shook her head. "He knows how to behave, Thad. He does not want to be polite. He does not know what to do about…me."

Thad could sure understand that; he didn't know what to do about her, either. He liked holding her, feeling her soft, warm body pressed against his. He thought about kissing her, as he'd done at the church when they were married. He hadn't expected to soar up to the ceiling at the taste of her lips, and that had scared him.

He jerked his mind away from that kiss. "Then there's my field of winter wheat, the one I told you about last night. I worry about what the snow and the rain will do to my crop. Can hardly think about anything else."

Except her, he admitted to himself. He knew he wasn't paying much attention to her, but he sure as hell thought about her. How good her hair smelled, like some spicy rosewater with a hint of lemon. How small she was; how physically strong she was in spite of her delicate build. How surprisingly frank she could be.

She'd made him laugh more in one day than he had in the last month.

He'd like to take time to talk to her, tell her more about the wheat field he had so much riding on, but so far he couldn't bring himself to do it. He guessed he was afraid she wasn't going to like what he was trying to do. Or him.

But he'd married her, hadn't he? The pain of losing Hattie still sliced at him when he least expected it, but he was not sorry Leah had stumbled into his life. And he wasn't the least bit sorry he'd brought her to his home and into his son's life.

And his own. At the moment he felt both disloyal to Hattie and intrigued at the new prospect before him.

"I am a stupid man," he said against her temple. He let his hand rest on her hair for a brief moment. "Can't see what's right in front of me."

He'd seen her underwear hanging on the clothesline yesterday evening when he went to do the milking. The little scraps of fabric looked small and dainty—not like a farm wife's duds. For a moment he'd felt a stab of guilt at admiring them because they weren't Hattie's, but they were downright pretty, anyway. So pretty he couldn't take his eyes off them and he'd tripped over a gopher mound. Dammit, what was right in front of him was…Leah.

They ate in silence, punctuated by the snap of the cracker bread as Leah broke it into chunks. Thad stared at it, then at her. Leah thought the butter and the blackberry jam would help, but it did not seem to. Thad broke the chunks into tiny bits.

Heaven help her, she did not belong here. She did not belong anywhere. In China she was an outcast because of her white skin; here she was not accepted because she had straight black hair and tilted eyes. She hated not belonging, always being on the outside.

Being outside was a cold place. And it was so lonely she wondered if she would survive.

Chapter Eight

That afternoon Leah swept the floor, dusted the sewing cabinet, laid a fire in the fireplace and straightened the sparse shelf of books. She recognized all the titles; thanks to Father's supervision of her schooling, she had read every one.

But being well educated had not prepared her for life on an Oregon ranch. What should she cook for Thad's supper? Beans, perhaps. And more biscuits? She hoped she could remember how to make biscuits.

In the pantry she found the bag of potatoes and a braid of onions and one of garlic; she used both to flavor the beans. Finally she cut up a double handful of apples, loaded the slices into an iron skillet and sprinkled a mixture of flour, sugar and butter over the top.

Later Ellie stopped by to take Leah to the dressmaker in town. She had made a list of things she needed at the mercantile. Dried beans. Mustard and cinnamon. And green tea. But more than buying supplies, it was the visit to the dressmaker that made her uneasy.

The minute Leah climbed into the small black buggy, Ellie reached over and laid a book in her lap. *"Miss Beecher's Domestic Receipt-Book,"* she read aloud. "Recipes!" She opened the book at once.

Potato soup. Scalloped potatoes. Strawberry shortcake! "Oh, thank you, Ellie."

"My mother sent it from Boston," Ellie said drily as she flapped the horse's reins. "That is the third cookbook she's sent since Matt and I were married last summer. It's yours."

Leah devoured the book until the buggy pulled up in front of the seamstress's shop. The painted sign over the display window read *Verena Forester, Dressmaker.* Suddenly Leah's stomach knotted.

With the recipe book Ellie had given her she could learn to cook the American way. Now she must calm her jittery nerves and learn to dress herself like an American woman. With Western-style garments, she prayed she would fit in.

At the first tinkle of the bell mounted over the door, Leah felt a surge of hope.

Ellie approached the eagle-eyed woman behind the Butterick pattern stand. "Verena, this is Mrs. Thad MacAllister."

The woman's thin eyebrows rose. Her once-dark hair was gray-streaked, and her pinched face was white as flour paste.

"How-do," she said in a toneless voice.

Leah attempted a smile. "How do you do, Mrs. Forester?"

"It's *Miss* Forester, if you don't mind."

Leah covertly studied the woman while Ellie explained their mission.

"A skirt for Miz MacAllister?" Miss Forester barked. Her voice sounded tight as a Chinese drumhead.

"Yes," Leah said. "For me."

"Take off yer coat, then," Miss Forester snapped.

Leah slipped off the gray wool garment, revealing her boy's jeans and plaid shirt.

The older woman's small eyes narrowed. "Huh. Sure could use some advice." She pulled a tape measure from her pocket and flicked it around Leah's waist. "What didja have in mind?"

Leah looked to Ellie for help.

"A plain work skirt, Verena," the teacher said. "And a shirtwaist."

"Any lace?"

"Just a bit at the neck, I think. Mrs. MacAllister lives on a—"

"I know right enough where she lives," Verena declared. "Isn't like I never heard of Thad MacAllister. Isn't like I'd forget a man like him. Thad and I are old friends. Good friends."

Something in the woman's tone made Leah blanch, but Ellie ignored the dressmaker's pointed words. "Make the skirt of gray melton cloth, if you have it," she directed. "And the shirtwaist of…let's see…percale. Would you have a gray-and-white stripe?"

"Nope."

"Oh, could it be red-and-white?" Leah blurted. "Red is a very lucky color in China."

"Ain't in China now," Verena muttered. "I have a

red striped muslin that'll do for the likes of you, seein' as you're a—"

Ellie jerked her hand away from a bolt of black sateen. "Verena!"

"Ain't used to Celestials," Verena mumbled. "They talk funny. Look funny. Dress funny."

Leah stepped up to the counter. "I am sorry if it offends you, Miss Forester. If you were in China, I believe *you* would look and sound just as 'funny' to the people there."

Verena glared at her and snapped her jaw shut. Ellie coughed politely. "Could you have the garments ready by Friday?"

"Friday! Well, I dunno. I—"

"Mrs. MacAllister will pick them up on Friday, when she visits the mercantile," Ellie announced.

"Oh. In that case… I've always been happy to see Thad. He's always been…well, not exactly a stranger."

The schoolteacher frowned, took Leah's elbow and firmly steered her out the door. "Let's have some tea at the hotel, shall we? It may help take the sting out of Verena's sharp tongue."

Mute with fury and hurt feelings and questions about Verena Forester she could not articulate, Leah could only nod. They seated themselves at a small table in the hotel dining room and ordered tea.

"What did I do wrong, Ellie?"

"You did nothing wrong. That old maid was rude and insulting." An odd expression came over Ellie's face. "I have just realized something. Verena may be a trial, but I shall never again describe any woman as an 'old maid.' For more years than I wish to count, I was considered an old maid, too. It was an extremely unhappy time in my life, but it taught me something."

Leah folded her hands in her lap. "What did it teach you?"

The plump waitress brought a fat china teapot and two cups.

"Thank you, Rita." Ellie reached for the teapot. "I learned how people see other people. How unthinking folks can be."

Leah tried to smile. "What will being insulted by the dressmaker teach me?"

Ellie sipped her tea and set the flowered cup back on its saucer. "Verena is a fine seamstress. And perhaps she has what we call a chip on her shoulder. You see, Verena was close to Thad and Hattie. Perhaps what you learned today was how to pet a porcupine?"

Both women laughed. Even Rita, who was unobtrusively listening by the coffee stand, chuckled and twitched her apron. Verena Forester had sewed it, and the mean-tempered dressmaker had insulted her, as well. "It's good enough for a hired hotel waitress," she'd said. Rita had been too humiliated to respond.

Now the waitress rubbed her palms together. This new woman in town might prove interesting.

That night, following the instructions in Miss Beecher's recipe book, Leah dumped the entire pot of boiled beans into a baking dish and added some molasses and the mustard she had purchased at the mercantile.

Her reception by Mr. Ness, the proprietor, had been so unfriendly she'd forgotten all the other items on her list except for the mustard. Mr. Ness had insisted she buy the most expensive brand, "imported from France." Now she wondered if Thad would even notice.

Teddy noticed right away. "What's that awful smell?" he shouted from his loft.

"Boston baked beans," Leah answered.

"We don't live in Boston," he yelled back. "And I ain't eating' any of your stinky ol' beans."

Leah sighed and then studied the biscuit dough she had mixed. Let him protest all he wanted; she had found instructions for making biscuits on her own.

Half an hour later she spooned the baked beans onto three plates and arranged two hot, fresh biscuits alongside each serving. She didn't have to announce supper was ready; both Teddy and Thad beat her to the table. She noticed their hair was slicked down, their faces were clean and their hands were scarcely dry from washing up at the pump. She added another small log to the firebox and slid her sliced apple crumble into the oven to bake.

Thad downed a forkful of beans while Leah fervently prayed she had followed Miss Beecher's recipe correctly.

"What in tarnation…?" He scooped up another bite. "What didja put in these, anyway? No beans I ever ate before tasted like these."

Leah's heart tumbled down to her slippers. She rose, clenched her hands under her apron and faced him. "I added some mustard. Mr. Ness said it came from France."

"France, huh?" He gobbled down another bite while Teddy watched.

"Pretty good! Try some, Teddy."

Teddy picked up his fork but just sat there while his father ate.

"What else does Ness have that comes from France?"

Leah began to relax. "I do not know what else Mr. Ness stocks at his store. He—he made me feel so unwelcome that I did not look. I walked out."

"He did, did he?" Thad sent her a questioning glance and broke open one of Leah's biscuits. The two halves fell into his hands like fluffy white clouds.

"Did Teddy make these?"

"No, I didn't, Pa. Bet they're awful, huh?"

Thad shoved in a buttery bite and then closed his eyes. "What do you want to bet, son? This is the best darn biscuit I've tasted since—"

He stopped abruptly, opened his eyes and stared at Leah, who was sliding back onto her chair with an odd smile on her face. He couldn't stop gazing at her; she looked so pleased with herself her cheeks had flushed rose.

Teddy stabbed his fork into his beans and in the next five minutes cleaned his plate faster than Thad had ever witnessed.

"These here are Boston beans," the boy explained to Thad. "Kin I have seconds?"

Leah sat up straighter, an expression of disbelief in her eyes. Her chest swelled under the red plaid shirt until Thad thought she might pop off a button. He let himself look longer than he should have, then wrenched his attention back to his plate. What a surprise his new wife was turning out to be.

And then she plopped an oversize spoonful of something that smelled like apples and brown sugar into a bowl, and passed him the cream pitcher. At the first bite, the crispy topping on the dish melted on his tongue. Whatever it was called, it was even better than last night's tart. Maybe even better than one of Hattie's apple pies.

He closed his mouth with a snap. Nothing would ever be better than Hattie's apple pie. Nothing would ever be better than having Hattie in his kitchen, no matter what she cooked.

He finished eating in silence.

After the dishes were washed, Thad noticed Leah pacing from the wide-armed chair to the settle, then back to the chair, while a sullen Teddy dried the plates. She seemed kinda fidgety. She'd been fidgety last night, too, and all at once he thought he knew why.

Going to bed with him made her nervous. He would never force himself on her, but she didn't know that. He didn't want to explain his reticence; it had too much to do with Hattie.

It would take time until he could muster the courage to risk his heart again. Something inside him knotted tight at the thought of caring about Leah too much, but he knew he couldn't make love with her only for physical release.

Leah's soft, clear voice startled him out of his meanderings. "I looked over your bookshelf today. Perhaps I could read aloud?"

Thad grabbed at the offered distraction. "Sure. Choose any book you like."

"I dowanna listen to a dumb old story!" Teddy announced.

Leah sighed. What was it Lao-zu said about progress? Two steps forward, one step backward? With Teddy it seemed *all* the steps were backward.

She ignored the boy's outburst, sent Thad a half smile and settled his leather-bound copy of *Ivanhoe* in her lap. With a surreptitious glance at Teddy's hunched shoulders, she began to read.

"In that pleasant district of merry England," she began, "there extended in ancient times a large forest—"

"Aw, Pa, this is boring." Teddy stomped across to the loft ladder and started to climb.

"No, it isn't, son," Thad returned in a quiet voice. "Just listen."

Leah skipped some pages ahead. "They stood before the castle of Cedric, a low irregular building containing several courtyards and turreted and castellated towers."

Teddy plopped down on the bottom rung of the ladder. "What's 'cast'llated' mean?"

On the back of an old calendar, Thad quickly sketched a castle with square stone towers, surrounded by a moat. "This is where Cedric the Saxon lives. Looks a bit like Scotland," he commented.

Leah glanced up at him. "You have read this, have you not?"

"Yeah. When I was about Teddy's age. That copy belonged to my father."

"What's a Saxon?" Teddy blurted.

Leah explained about Saxons and Normans, and Thad sketched the Battle of Hastings and a Templar knight in full armor. Teddy pulled his face into a scowl but kept listening.

She continued reading until the boy's eyelids drooped. Finally, at his father's suggestion, he dragged his thin frame up the ladder, and Leah found herself alone with Thad.

She waited for him to say something. Instead, he stood up, stuffed his hands in his jean pockets and began to pace from the living room to the kitchen and back, studying the floor.

What was wrong? Why would he not meet her eyes? "Thad?"

He kept pacing.

"Thad, have I done something wrong?" Perhaps she should not have made the biscuits for supper? Or read from *Ivanhoe?* Goodness, there were so many things in America she did not know about. How was she ever going to live in this house with him and his angry, hurting son, in this unfamiliar town, without making mistakes?

"Thad, what have I done?"

He stopped abruptly and swung to face her, his expression shuttered. "Wrong? Leah, you've done nothing at all wrong. Except," he added with a fleeting smile, "maybe yesterday's coffee."

"Then why are you walking back and forth like that instead of—"

"Going to bed," he finished. "Damned if I know. Just worried, I guess."

"Is it about our marriage? About me?"

"Naw, not about you. Not exactly, anyway. I'll explain later."

Before she could think what to say, he was out the front door, his boot heels rapping down the porch steps. She choked off an involuntary cry.

Something *was* wrong. Something he would not tell her, which made it more disturbing. She could do nothing if she did not know what the problem was. She thought back over the evening. He had liked their supper, or at least she thought he had. And he did like *Ivanhoe,* otherwise he would not have drawn those pictures of the castle.

And then she remembered Verena Forester's words. *I'd never forget a man like Thad.*

It was frightening, this not knowing, like feeling eyes upon her, following her every move. She could not escape the fear, but she could not let it smother her.

She sucked in a breath, pushed the black, frightening thoughts to the back of her mind, and resolutely made her way down the short hallway to the bedroom.

Chapter Nine

Leah lay unmoving on the far edge of the double bed, her mind in turmoil. She knew Thad was not asleep; she could hear his measured breathing in and out, and she guessed that he lay staring up at the ceiling, as she did.

She could not begin to sort out her own feelings, let alone Thad's. Was he disappointed in her? She thought she had made some progress toward being a wife. With the help of Miss Beecher's book she was learning to cook the American way. She could learn to milk the cow and ride a horse. She could even learn to ignore the hurtful and unsettling comments from the dressmaker, Verena Forester, and Carl Ness at the mercantile in town.

She tightened her lips. Given enough time and luck, she might even befriend Thad's disgruntled son. Perhaps he would want to hear more about Ivanhoe. Perhaps she could learn to make cookies. American boys liked cookies, did they not?

No matter what, she was not going to give up.

But at this moment, lying here with Thad close enough to touch if either of them moved an elbow, she did not know what to do or say. Did he want to touch her? Did she *want* him to touch her?

He had returned to the house very late, undressed in the dark and climbed into bed without a word, his chilled skin smelling of pasture grass. She drew in a long, slow breath. She was not going to give up on Thad, either. After all, he had been her husband for only two days.

His low, rumbly voice washed over her roiling thoughts. "You're kinda quiet tonight, Leah. Anything troubling you?"

She thought for a moment. Should she be honest or evade the question? "I am trying hard to be a good wife and a good mother to Teddy, but—" she clenched her fists beneath the covers "—for each thing that goes right, something else goes wrong."

He chuckled softly. "Did you expect to learn everything in just one day?"

She turned her face toward him. "I do not know what to expect. You walked out of the house as if something was troubling you, as if you were not pleased with me."

"You're wrong, Leah. I am pleased with you."

"But are we not… I mean, did you intend our marriage to be in name only? Many Chinese have such an arrangement," she added quickly. "But I thought that here, in America, it would be different."

Thad released a soft groan. "Is that what you expected? A real marriage?" She reached out to touch his shoulder, and he covered her hand with his warm, callused palm. "Is it?"

"I do not know," she said. "I must be honest, Thad. I am a bit frightened of it." She waited, not breathing, for him to say something. Outside, a hen cackled, and she could hear the wind pick up, rustling the pine and maple trees near the house.

Very slowly Thad rolled toward her. He did not touch her, but the heat of his body spread over her skin like warm oil.

"Come here," he whispered. He laid one arm across her waist and pulled her close. "You know that I was married before. Hatt— My wife was killed in a train wreck a year ago. I guess I haven't gotten over it yet. In a way, I still feel married to her."

His voice dropped to a whisper. "I like you, Leah. That's one reason why I married you. In time, I hope it will be good."

Leah turned slightly, and her bottom brushed against his groin. She ignored his sharp intake of breath and the low sound that followed.

He pressed his lips to the back of her neck. "I like you a lot," he muttered.

A jagged line of fire rippled down her spine. Oh, yes! This was what she wanted.

As if he'd read her mind, he tightened his arm about her waist. "Good night, Leah."

She lay without moving, wondering at the pleasure his touch brought. Wondering why he did not want more. After a time his breathing evened out and she knew he slept.

* * *

On Friday, Thad was busy repairing the fence around his wheat field, so Leah went into town with school-teacher Ellie Johnson to pick up her new skirt and shirt-waist at the dressmaker's. Verena was her usual frosty, blunt-spoken self, but Leah stiffened her resolve and tried not to let the woman's obvious disapproval and her odd, veiled hints about Thad upset her.

"Don't look right," she said when Leah donned her new garments. "A fine skirt and a ruffled shirtwaist on a Celestial. Thad always said he liked a woman who looked like a woman. You know, English, or maybe Scottish."

Leah clamped her lips together and kept silent. The seamstress meant one that looked like a white woman. Leah knew Thad's wife had been friends with Verena, but was there something else, something since Hattie's death, that she did not know about?

It was worse at the mercantile. Inside it was warm and cozy; the air smelled pleasantly of wood smoke from the potbellied stove and coffee from the pot sitting on top. But the proprietor, skinny, sandy-haired Carl Ness, dogged her every step up and down the aisles, as if he expected her to steal something.

Finally she turned to confront him. "Mr. Ness, would you have any green tea?"

"*Green* tea?" He snorted. "Never heard of green tea. Only for Celestials, I s'pose. I sure wouldn't put it on *my* shelves."

Leah worked to keep her voice polite. "Do you have cinnamon, then?"

Ness peered at her with a frown across his angular brow. "Whatcha want with cinnamon, I'd like to know? Kinda fancy for a Celestial, ain't it?"

She put her tongue between her teeth and bit down. Tears stung her eyes, but she managed to speak in a civil tone. "That, Mr. Ness," she said evenly, "is none of your business. I will need a large tin of cinnamon. Powdered, if you please."

An even more hurtful encounter came later, when she and Ellie stopped for tea at the hotel dining room. Ellie spotted two friends seated in the far corner. "Darla and Lucy," she confided to Leah as they crossed the room to join them. "They were my bridesmaids when I married Matt last summer."

The two young women stopped their chatter when Leah and Ellie approached. "Darla, Lucy, this is Leah MacAllister."

Both women looked up but did not speak.

"Mrs. Thad MacAllister," Ellie added. "Leah, these are my friends, Darla Weatherby and Lu—"

Before Ellie could finish the introduction, Darla and Lucy plunked down their teacups, snatched up their shawls, and brushed past them without a word.

"Darla? Lucy?" Ellie called after them.

The one in a dark green wool skirt and matching jacket spun around. "Your eyesight must be suffering, Ellie. She's Chinese! A Celestial."

Pain lanced into Leah's chest, so sharp it shut off her breathing.

Ellie's blue eyes snapped. "It's *your* eyesight that is

failing, Darla. Mrs. MacAllister is an American, just like you and me."

"Oh, no, she's not," the one called Lucy hissed. "She will never be one of us. *Never.*"

Leah stepped back as if she had been struck, sank onto a chair and sat stone still with her eyes on the carpeted floor.

Ellie bent over her. "Oh, Leah, I do apologize for them."

Numb, Leah could say nothing. She started to rise, but Rita, the plump, red-haired waitress, appeared at her elbow with a cup of hot tea.

"I'll bring another cup for you, Miz Johnson, if you're stayin'."

"Thank you," Leah said, her voice not quite steady. "We are most certainly staying."

Rita grinned and hurried off toward the kitchen. Ellie sat down across from Leah, her lips twisted. Unexpectedly she reached across the table and took both Leah's hands in hers.

"There is an old saying in my family, Leah. 'The enemy of my friend is my enemy, too.'"

"Oh, Ellie, you must not—"

"Yes, I must. Don't argue, Leah. This is important. I think perhaps—" she lifted Leah's cup off the saucer and swallowed a gulp of tea "—this is going to be war!"

Rita came with a second mug of tea, and the two women raised their cups and chinked them together.

Rita moved off to one side and shook her head in sympathy. "If there's gonna be a war," she muttered, "I sure know which side *I'd* pick."

It was raining hard when the two women arrived back at the house. Leah scrambled out of the buggy, grabbed up her new skirt and raced toward the front porch, while Ellie drove off down the muddy road. On the first step, Leah turned to wave, and stopped short.

Across the rain-swept pasture strode a tall, long-legged figure wearing a water-soaked gray Stetson. Thad. She watched him for several seconds, wondering why he wore no jacket or rain poncho in the downpour. He marched through the stinging drops, apparently unaware of the rain pelting his chest or the rivulets of water streaming off his hat brim.

Without slowing down or even looking up, he moved steadily through the sopping grass, splashing through spreading ponds of rainwater without altering his pace. Then he raised his head for an instant and Leah caught her breath. The piercing gaze that usually missed nothing was focused on something in the far distance.

The set of his shoulders was so stiff it sent goose bumps up her arms, and he was so distracted he walked right into a low-growing coyote bush. Her heart began to hammer. Thad MacAllister was a courageous and kind man. A man she was beginning to care about. She cringed at the obvious distress in his face.

What could be wrong? Had Teddy done something without his approval? Had *she?*

She glanced down to where the wet hem of her new gray melton skirt poked out from under her coat, hiked it up and started across the yard toward him. In the next instant she found herself running.

"Thad! *Thad!*" Her voice did not carry over the

drumming rain. She was within three arm lengths of him when he stopped and raised his head. Leah stumbled to a stop in front of him.

His surprised voice rumbled deep inside his chest. "Well, now, what's all this?"

"Where is your jacket?" she said in a choked voice.

"In the barn. Wasn't raining when I started out." Awkwardly he reached out and ran his hand over her damp hair. "You're soaking wet, Leah. What are you doing out here?"

"I—I saw you from the porch, and I wanted—"

What? What did she want?

The answer came in a flash of understanding.

"I wanted to be close to you," she blurted. "I—I mean I wanted to come and meet you." She dropped her head in the submissive gesture she had learned from long years of training at her mother's hand, then slowly lifted it until their eyes met.

His face looked tired, his eyes worried. His gaze wandered, focusing on her forehead, then on her nose, her mouth, her hair. "You're wet, Leah," he said again.

"So are you, Thad. I saw you coming across the field and I… You looked worried about something."

"Lord in Heaven, I am worried about something. I'm half eaten-up inside with worry."

"Your wheat field?"

His eyes had an odd, haunted look, and he was trying hard to slow his breathing. "If this storm keeps up, all my new-sprouted seedlings are gonna wash away. And there's nothing—*nothing*—I can do to stop it. Dammit, I don't like feeling helpless."

Leah nodded, took hold of his arm and tugged him forward. "Come into the house, Thad. I…" Oh, what could she do to take his mind off his worries? "I—I planned to bake cookies for Teddy, and I might need some help."

She had no idea where that thought came from, but it did not matter. She could do little to comfort Thad outside in this driving rain; inside the house it would at least be warm and dry.

Thad took another step forward. She latched on to his hand and urged him up the porch steps and through the front door.

The house smelled of the bread she'd baked this morning. Not hard, brittle Chinese bread, but yeast bread, soft and fragrant with crisp, golden crusts. Leah slipped off her coat and started toward the kitchen. "I will make you some fresh coffee."

Behind her, Thad made a strangled sound. "What in the—? What happened to your regular clothes?"

"Ellie Johnson and I visited the dressmaker this afternoon. Verena Forester made this skirt for me, and the shirtwaist, too." Leah twirled in place and waited for him to say something.

His gaze slid over her, but almost at once he looked away. "Your hem is soaking wet, Leah. I'll light the fire." He bent to touch a match to the kindling and small logs she had laid in the fireplace.

Leah ran her forefinger over the wisp of lace at the collar of her new percale shirtwaist. "You do not like it?"

"Well, it's—uh, it's just that you look…different."

She knotted her fingers together so tightly they hurt. "I am trying to look different. I am trying to look like the other women in Smoke River."

"Yeah, I guess." His voice was flat. He turned away and strode into the kitchen. "I'll make the coffee." He hadn't even bothered to shed his rain-soaked garments.

She felt like screaming. Did he not like her dressed like other women? Or was it that underneath he did not like *her,* his misfit half-Chinese wife? In the next minute she heard the grating of the coffee mill in the pantry.

Thad kept grinding the beans until the receiving box overflowed, sprinkling aromatic grounds over the clean pantry floor. He should sweep up the mess he'd made, but damn! First he needed coffee.

He swallowed hard. He didn't want to look at Leah wearing a breast-hugging shirtwaist and a skirt that swirled gracefully over her hips. Her cheeks were flushed with pleasure, and suddenly he found it hard to breathe. Leah was more than attractive. She was downright beautiful.

Damnation, what did he do now?

Keep his mind off her, for one thing. Don't look at her. Don't get close enough to catch the spicy, lemony scent of her hair. And for heaven's sake, don't touch her! He already knew what her skin felt like, smooth and warm as fresh cream. But he was afraid if he let himself lay a single finger on her, he'd be lost.

He wasn't ready. He didn't want to risk loving any woman, ever again. Sometimes he wondered if he'd ever be ready.

He dumped the ground beans into the speckleware

coffeepot and shook his head. Sure felt as if something had clobbered him when he wasn't looking.

He'd never feared much of anything except hunger since he was a kid in knee pants, and now he was feeling uneasy over two uncontrollable things that had presented themselves in the last few days: a field of struggling wheat seedlings and an intriguing woman. It was enough to make a man wonder about himself.

He heard the bedroom door shut, and when he turned he saw that she'd left her wet skirt and a white ruffled petticoat draped over a chair close to the crackling fire. He couldn't stop staring at that petticoat. What else was she wearing underneath? Ruffled drawers? A camisole with a pink satin ribbon at the neck?

He grabbed the boiling coffeepot off the stove and splashed a mug full to the brim. It was too hot to drink, but he gulped a scalding mouthful down anyway and tried not to think about sleeping next to her tonight.

Chapter Ten

Thad mopped the cold raindrops off his face using a huck dish towel, but even the roaring fire in the fireplace couldn't shake the cold that ate at his vitals with sharp, clawlike teeth. It was more than the chill he'd taken tramping up and down the rows of tiny seedlings without his jacket. It was fear, and it cut bone deep.

He tried not to watch Leah's unconsciously arresting movements as she flitted about the kitchen, alternately dumping sugar and butter into a bowl and mashing up boiled potatoes in another. Suddenly he was so damn randy he felt like a fourteen-year-old.

Leah paused, flour sifter in hand, to peer at him. "Do you like cinnamon?"

"What? Oh, sure. Whatever you say."

She frowned thoughtfully. He hadn't heard a word she had said.

When the first batch of cookies was browned, she loaded some onto a plate and took them up to Teddy in the loft. The boy lay curled up on his bed, and she set the cookies next to him. He reached out a hand to poke one. "Eww! What are these things?"

"They are cookies, of course. Molasses crisps. I made them according to my new recipe book." Hesitantly she touched his shoulder, but the boy edged away.

"Teddy, what is wrong? You do not like cookies? Are you sick?"

"Naw, ain't sick or nuthin'." He rolled onto his side and listlessly poked the cookie once more. "It's Pa, I guess. He's hardly even looked at me all day. How come these molasses things look so funny?"

Leah studied her cookies. They did look funny. She had tried to pat each piece of dough into the shape of a horse, but during baking her horses had swelled into elephants.

"What's wrong with Pa?" the boy asked, his mouth full. "Did I do somethin' bad?"

Leah scooched down beside him on the bed. "You have done nothing bad, Teddy. Your father is distracted. And worried."

"How come?" Surreptitiously Teddy folded a cookie into his hand. Leah picked up one, as well, and nibbled off the horse's thick legs as she pondered how to answer Thad's son.

"With all this heavy rain, your father is concerned about his wheat field."

"Pa's never planted wheat before. Nobody around here's ever planted wheat. All the other ranchers say he's crazy." The boy bit off the head of his horse cookie. "Is Pa crazy?"

"No, your father is not crazy. He is…well, he is pre-occupied."

"What's 'procupied' mean?" Teddy swallowed his morsel of cinnamon-dusted cookie. "Pa doesn't hardly talk to me. Maybe he's mad at me? Or maybe he doesn't like me anymore."

Leah's teeth clenched. "Teddy, your father is not mad at you."

The boy said nothing.

Leah patted his bony shoulder. "Your father loves you very much," she said quietly. "But he is a man, and right now a man would be thinking about… He would have a lot on his mind."

"Like what? What's so important?"

"Well, Teddy, I wish I knew, exactly. But it does feel as if he is ignoring us, does it not?"

"Sure does. Feels awful." Teddy polished off the horse's hindquarters.

Leah's heart gave a little lurch. Yes, it did feel awful. It felt as if Thad didn't care about either his son or her. He was treating them both as if they did not matter. It made her feel hollow inside. Unwanted. It must feel even worse for Teddy.

She shook off an insistent thought, but it popped right back into her brain anyway. In one way, family life in America was much like life in China; fathers worried about food and shelter and ignored their children. And their wives. Perhaps men the world over were like that. Missionaries in China struggled to survive, just like their flocks. She was beginning to understand some of her mother's sadness when Father was worried.

"I bet Ivanhoe'd never forget about *his* son!"

Leah found her throat so tight she could not speak for a moment. "Would you…would you like me to read more about Ivanhoe?"

"Yeah, I guess so. You read pretty good, even if you are—" The boy grabbed the last cookie to hide his embarrassment.

She climbed down the ladder and found Thad sitting motionless in the armchair by the fire, staring into the flames, both hands curled around a mug of coffee. Deliberately she walked in front of him on her way to the kitchen, but he did not even look up.

A black finger of despair scratched at the edges of Leah's mind. Whatever he was struggling with, his actions were distancing himself from Teddy. And from her. If his unreachable moods continued, his son's feeling of well-being, and her own, would shrivel and die.

"Told ya you was loony to plant wheat, Thad." Carl Ness leaned over the mercantile counter and spit the words in Thad's face.

"What would you know about it, Carl? You've never farmed so much as a patch of mint."

The older man grunted. "I hear the talk around town. Seems like you've bit off something you can't chew." Carl's thin lips pulled back into what passed for a grin. "Two somethings, as a matter of fact."

"Yeah?" He'd had about enough of Carl Ness this morning. Something festering inside him felt as if it was going to explode any second.

The storekeeper took one look at Thad's face and checked whether the area behind where he stood was empty. He sure didn't need six feet of Thad MacAllister charging over the counter at him.

"Yeah," Carl blustered.

Thad took one step closer. "What's the second something, Carl?"

He edged backward. "That wife of yours. That Celestial. Ain't never gonna work out."

That did it. It was one thing to ride a man for his choice of crop to plant; it was another to insult a man's choice of a wife. Thad's hands tightened into fists.

"Why in hell are you so sure it isn't going to work out?"

The mercantile owner dropped his gaze and studied the smooth wood counter. "Well, just look at her. She don't fit in with Smoke River folks. Never will. The ladies are already declaring war on her."

"War?" Thad exploded. "Not on *my* wife, they're not. What's got into this town, anyway?"

Carl snorted. "One Celestial woman, that's what."

"Shut your mouth, Carl. Give me a bushel of apples and some coffee beans. And don't say another word."

The proprietor sneered. "Coffee, huh? I thought all them Celestials drank tea."

"Or whiskey," someone said from the back of the store.

"Whooee, I'd sure like to see that little Chinese gal three sheets to the wind, wouldn't you, boys?" This last gibe came from Whitey Poletti, the barber, who now lounged at Thad's elbow.

Without a word Thad spun toward the man and laid him out flat with a single punch. The next thing he knew someone had pinned his arms from behind and a voice was speaking in his ear.

"Don't do this, Thad. It'll only hurt your wife when she has to bail you out of jail."

Thad shook himself to clear the red haze from his vision. Marshal Matt Johnson released him, slapped him on the back and thrust the bushel basket of apples against his chest. Then he swung the ten-pound bag of coffee beans onto his own shoulder and steered Thad out the mercantile door.

At the hitching rail in front of the store, Matt lifted the apples out of Thad's grasp, waited until he'd mounted his horse and dropped the sack of coffee beans across his lap.

Thad eyed the marshal. "Thanks, Matt."

He grinned up at him as he grasped the horse's bridle. "Sure thing. And Thad, if it comes up again, remember Poletti has a mean left hook." He slapped the horse's rump. "Give my regards to Leah."

That evening at supper Thad appeared deaf to Leah's quiet inquiries about his trip to town, and he was again ignoring Teddy's chatter about his school day.

"And then Manette—she's only six, and she's French like her momma, an' she knows lots of foreign words—anyway Manette pushes old Harvey offa me an' calls him a name and kicks him in his privates. An' then… Pa? Pa! Are you listening?"

Leah's quick glance at Thad's face confirmed Teddy's fear; his father was not listening. Instead he was staring down at his boots, apparently focused on something inside himself.

A dart of anger bit into her chest. This could not continue. Not only was Teddy hurting, but she herself was wrestling with fury at Thad's indifference. Tonight, when they were alone in the bedroom, she would speak to him.

She studied her husband's drawn face. Something had happened in town today; a purple-blue blotch spread across the knuckles of his right hand, but he had refused to say a word about it.

Or about anything else—not the savory stew she'd labored over using bacon and potatoes; not the new ruffled apron she wore, which she had whipped up on the sewing machine that afternoon. Not even the pile of clean work shirts she had ironed today.

"Thad?"

"Mmm?"

"Do you not like stew?"

"What? No, no, it's fine. Just not hungry, I guess."

She didn't believe him for one second. Ever since he'd returned from town he'd worked hard shoring up the makeshift dam he'd constructed to keep his wheat field from flooding. Even if his mind was somewhere else, surely his belly must be clamoring for food?

"Shall I read more of *Ivanhoe* after supper? Teddy wants to know what happens to Isaac the Jew."

"Yeah, Pa," Teddy exclaimed. "I wanna see if they torture old Isaac."

"Thad?"

"What? Oh, sure. Sure."

Leah bit back a groan. Enough was enough. She could hardly wait until they were alone.

She lifted the book down from the shelf, seated herself in the chair by the fireplace, opened the volume and began to read.

"'Strip the Jew, slaves,' said Front-de-Boeuf. 'And chain him down upon the bars.'"

Teddy sucked in a breath. "How come they're so mean to Isaac? Is it because he's a Jew?"

"Not exactly," Leah said. "It is because Isaac is—" she almost choked on the word "—*different*. In those days people persecuted what was different. Many hated the Jews. Those people were prejudiced."

And, she acknowledged with a ripple of unease, it was much the same today.

"But not Ivanhoe, huh! An' nobody in Smoke River's prej'dist, huh?"

Leah made an involuntary sound. Over Teddy's head, her eyes locked with Thad's.

"Sure they are, son," Thad growled.

Leah marked her place in the leather-bound book with her forefinger. "Remember the mean things the students at school said about me that first morning? That I looked funny?"

"Sure, but you're not a Jew."

"No," Leah said with a sigh. "But here in America I am different because I am half Chinese."

"I bet Ivanhoe wouldn't care if you was Chinese."

Leah had to laugh. "Ivanhoe had never seen a Chinese person. Or talked to one or—"

Thad sent her a look that melted her insides. "Slept

with one," he interjected. Immediately he looked away, unfolded his long legs and stood up. When he stepped around Teddy he absentmindedly ruffled the boy's unruly brown hair. "Time for bed, son."

Leah glanced up at her husband, but once again his eyes were distant. Deliberately she closed the volume on her lap. She must speak to him. Now. Tonight.

Teddy scampered up the ladder to his loft. Leah sat still for a moment, staring into the dying fire, then roused herself and headed for the bedroom. She undressed quickly, sponged off in the basin of warm water she had heated earlier on the stove, and drew on her silk sleeping robe. It was one of her Chinese garments, but she liked it because it absorbed the heat of Thad's body when she lay next to him.

She liked sleeping with Thad. She liked being close to him, listening to his voice rumble near her ear, feeling his soft breathing fan the back of her neck.

Thad paced back and forth on the front porch, his hands jammed into his jean pockets. He hated winter. When he thought about the months between now and spring, his mind went cold and his thoughts became brutally clear. He could do nothing about his wheat seedlings except pray the winter storms would leave them undamaged. Right now, he knew he had to think about other things. His son, for one.

Maybe it was about time for Teddy to have a pony. Matt Johnson had a colt about old enough to ride; maybe by Christmas…

Hell's bells, he didn't want to think about Christmas. He'd hated it ever since Hattie died. He didn't want to think about Leah, either. Sure would be easier if they didn't sleep in the same bed.

It was getting harder to crawl in bed and lie next to her. Something about being close to her made him sweat, and when he tried to nail it down, whatever it was choked him with fear. It grew worse each night.

He walked twice more around the barn, then tramped back into the house, to find a light still glowing under the bedroom door. Quietly he twisted the brass knob and pushed it open. A kerosene lamp burned low on the bureau.

He kicked off his boots, dropped his trousers and shirt onto the rocking chair under the window and puffed out the lamp. He hesitated, then lifted the quilted coverlet and slid into bed.

She didn't move.

"Leah?"

"Thad, we need to talk about something."

Oh, damn, here it came. She was unhappy. She wanted more from him, and he wasn't ready. He hoped that the ache gnawing at his heart would fade in time, that he'd get over Hattie's death, but...

But what if he never healed? What if he kept backing away from Leah, protecting himself by not caring about her? Hell, if he kept avoiding her, he'd lose her, too. Either way he was damned. Maybe she wasn't tough enough for life out here on the frontier and she'd leave him, go back to the city.

He didn't want to talk about this. It hurt even to think about it. But Leah was his wife now, for better or worse, and she deserved honesty.

"What's on your mind, Leah?"

"Teddy."

Teddy! Thad closed his eyes in relief. "What about Teddy? Something wrong at school? Are the kids still riding him about his new moth—"

"Nothing is wrong at school," she said in a quiet voice. "Something is wrong at home."

He thought that over while he tried to get his heart-beat back to normal. Had he and Teddy argued about something? Nothing came to mind. In fact, he could not remember having much of any conversation with his son all week long. Oh, Lord, that was it. Had to be.

"Thad, Teddy needs you. He has lost his mother, but he should not have to lose his father, as well."

"He's not losing me."

"He is losing you. A son needs to be noticed by his father."

"I do notice him."

After a long silence she spoke again. "When my mother died, my father withdrew into himself, into a shell that excluded me. I was not a child, as Teddy is, but it was miserable for me. It was as if Papa had died, too, and left me alone in the world."

"But my son is not alone, Leah. He sees us both every day."

"But he *feels* that he is alone. His father is not here, really—he is always preoccupied. Thad, it feels as if you are somewhere else, somewhere Teddy cannot follow you. He needs you to pay attention to him."

Thad dragged in a breath. "Yeah. I see."

He kept silent for some minutes, mulling over her

words. Leah was right. Now that she'd laid it out before him, he could see the truth of it.

She touched his shoulder. "The happiest I have seen Teddy was the day he helped you move the sewing cabinet from the barn to the house."

"So?"

"Perhaps you could let Teddy help you with another task tomorrow?"

"Yeah? What about school?"

She gave a small laugh. "How do you say it…let him 'play the hook' tomorrow. Being with his father is more important than one day of school."

Thad raised himself on one elbow. "You mean 'play hookey?' Leah, you are a surprise in a dozen ways." Without thinking, he leaned over and kissed her.

Too late he realized it was a mistake. It started as a brief brush of his mouth over hers, but almost instantly it changed. She was soft and she smelled good, like soap and some kind of spicy scent. She tasted good. She felt good.

And, God forgive him, he was damn hungry for her.

Chapter Eleven

Her lips were hesitant, but after his first taste, Thad didn't care. The slight pressure of her mouth against his sent a bolt of pleasure down his backbone and into his groin. Her skin was as smooth as that silk gown she wore every night. Smoother, even. And warm under his hands. He ran his tongue over her bottom lip, and when he heard her sigh against his mouth, his brain exploded.

He kissed her until he was dizzy with shock and with wanting, until he feared he would hurt her with the pressure of his searching mouth. Her arms crept around his neck. Between kisses his breath came in ragged gasps. Oh, Lord, he was drowning. This was like nothing he'd ever experienced before, not even with Hattie.

Thad felt himself tumble into a bottomless chasm of sensation. His eyes burned; his tongue where it touched her mouth tasted honey-sweet. His mind floated up above himself somewhere. And dammit, his groin ached.

Hell's bells. Kissing Leah took him soaring to places

he had never been. Unexpected places. Unforgettable places.

He lifted his head, felt her soft breath against his lips and smiled into the darkness. Aye, she was bonnie, all right.

"Thad," she whispered. "Don't stop."

"Got to stop," he murmured. "I'm getting short of breath."

And short of caution. He knew it was too soon, that he would regret it in the morning, and he didn't want any regrets after their first time. He wanted it to be full of joy.

He would wait. He *had* to wait. Leah deserved a whole man, not one so torn up inside that his heart was split in two.

"Thad?" She touched his face with her fingers, moved them slowly over his mustache until they rested on his lips.

"Hmmm?"

"Why did you stop kissing me? Did you not like it? Or perhaps I did not do it right?"

He groaned deep in his throat. "Hell, yes, you're doing it right, Leah. More than right. The problem is me."

He should roll away, leave her alone.

"You do not want me," she said quietly.

"Leah…" Heavens above, how could he explain something he didn't understand himself? He wanted her, all right. Any man with half an eye and a beating heart would want this beautiful, unusual slip of a woman. The truth was he wasn't sure it was the right time.

He couldn't let himself take her just because he was a man and she was willing. It had to be more than just physical wanting. It had to be because he was fully committed to her, and, heaven help him, he couldn't do that yet.

"I think I understand," she said softly. "It is too soon after your first wife."

Thad let his breath out with a shaky sigh. "Only part of it is because of Hattie. The rest is because of you."

"Oh?"

She said nothing else and he smoothed his hand over her hair. "I don't know how to say this, Leah. I don't want to be unfair to you. I don't want to do anything that would hurt you."

She said nothing. He swallowed hard and went on. "And there's something else. I don't think I could stand getting my heart broken again. I can't risk it yet."

She was silent so long he wondered if she'd fallen asleep, until he heard her quiet, calm voice near his ear.

"You are a good man, Mr. MacAllister. A very special man. I like you very much."

Morning caught Thad by surprise. He'd slept past sunup, and while a part of him wanted to roust himself out of bed to check his wheat field and feed the stock, another part wanted nothing more than to lie here with Leah beside him.

He'd gone way too far last night. Too far and too fast. But she must have liked it, or she wouldn't be smiling at him that way, kind of shy and happy, with her cheeks all pink.

In the next moment she sat up, pulled on her work jeans and a shirt and disappeared out the bedroom door. Thad closed his eyes and thought about last night. Before he knew it, he'd drifted off again.

A thump from the kitchen brought him wide-awake. Hell, he'd never slept this late. What the devil was wrong with him?

He rolled out of bed, pulled on a pair of jeans and a clean shirt, and followed his nose into the kitchen. Damn, something smelled good.

He had to laugh at himself. *Everything* smelled good this morning.

"Morning." Dammit, his voice was unsteady.

"Good morning." Her voice was soft, almost hesitant.

"Leah—"

She placed one finger across his lips. "I have your breakfast ready," she said quickly. "You will be surprised."

Surprised? She hadn't stopped surprising him since he'd first laid eyes on her.

At the kitchen table he found a mountain of fluffy scrambled eggs on his plate, along with crisp bacon and some kind of crunchy toast Leah had dreamed up using day-old biscuit halves crisped in the oven.

Teddy banged down the loft steps. "Mornin', Pa."

"Isn't it a school day? You're going to be late."

"Today's Saturday, Pa."

"Ah, is it, now? Well, then." He shot a glance at Leah.

"How would you like to help me with an important project I've been putting off?"

Teddy gaped at his father. "You really mean it? What kinda project?"

Thad glanced again at Leah, bent over the oven where her biscuit toast was warming. "Today we're going to teach Leah to ride a horse."

She jerked upright and the baking sheet clattered onto the floor. *"What?"*

"It's time, Leah. Can't have you stuck out here with no way of getting to town without Ellie Johnson stopping by with her buggy."

Leah stared at him in disbelief. "Ride a horse?" she said in a thin voice.

Teddy eyed her over his glass of milk. "You ain't scared, are ya?"

She whirled away and snatched the baking sheet up off the floor. "Y-yes, I am scared. In China we did not have a horse."

"We'll help ya, won't we, Pa?"

Thad reached over and ruffled Teddy's uncombed hair. Leah's heart skipped at the sight, then dropped like a stone into her stomach at the thought of climbing up onto a horse.

"I—I will try." But a horse was so…big. Tall as a hay wagon, and those huge yellow teeth could bite, and it could kick hard enough to break her leg. Oh, heavens. She wondered how she would survive today.

The horse looked even bigger up close. Thad had saddled the animal in the barn, and now led it out into the upper pasture, where Leah waited. Her breath choked off.

Teddy jigged up and down with excitement. She suspected part of the boy's excitement was the anticipation of seeing her fail. Taking another step backward, she sighed. Perhaps Thad's son would never accept her; it was too much to hope he would come to *like* her.

It was a beautiful animal, a glossy dark brown, with slim legs and a steady gait. But it was still a horse. A big, muscular horse.

Thad walked the mare over to a thick pine stump. "Her name's Lady. She's real gentle, Leah. You're gonna like riding her."

Oh, no, she would not. She gazed up at the big black eye the animal fixed on her and shuddered.

"C'mon, Leah." Teddy was off to the stump like a shot. She followed slowly, her palms damp.

Thad positioned her in front of the mare. "Most important thing is for you to let the horse get to know you." He placed her hand on the animal's nose. The skin rippled under her fingers, and she jerked away.

"Let her smell you all over."

Smell her! Leah stood rigid with fear while the horse snuffled at the neck of her shirt.

"Ya must smell good," Teddy chirped. "She likes you!"

"Now," Thad instructed. "You watch me take off her bit and bridle, see how it's done, and then I want you to put them back on."

She watched his hands, committing his every move

to memory. Then he thrust the jumble of paraphernalia at her and stepped aside.

"Your turn."

Her hands shaking, Leah repeated his motions in reverse order and finished by looping the reins around the saddle horn.

Thad sent her an encouraging grin. "Good. Now, the saddle."

She stared at the bulky leather contraption on the mare's back. To her horror, Thad loosened the wide, beltlike thing under the animal's belly and hefted the saddle, stirrups and all, off the horse. He plopped it onto the tree stump, where Teddy perched.

"Now you do it," Thad instructed.

Leah stopped breathing. She could never lift that heavy thing. Never. Despite the pleasure his kiss had brought last night, at this moment she hated Thad MacAllister.

He removed the saddle blanket, shook it out and handed it to her. "Put this on first. Then set the saddle on top."

"But I cannot possibly lift it! It must weigh forty pounds."

"This is a lady's saddle," he said in a patient tone. "It only weighs about thirty-five pounds."

She lifted her chin. "I weigh just one hundred pounds, Thad. I cannot—"

"Sure you can. One thing I've learned about you, Leah, is that you're stronger than you look. C'mon, give it a try."

One thing he had *not* learned about her was that she

was really, really afraid of this huge horse. She did not want to do this.

But she had to acknowledge that now she was a woman living on a ranch, not a village in China. An American woman would do this every day of her life.

Clenching her teeth, Leah approached the stump, gripped the saddle, front and back, and pulled it toward her. She could do that much. But could she hoist the heavy thing up onto the horse's back? Never in a thousand years.

Oh, goodness gracious. She did want to please Thad. Even if she didn't think she could, she knew he would make her try.

And there was another matter, as well. She wanted to prove something to herself. She wasn't sure exactly what, but the knowledge straightened her spine.

She refolded the saddle blanket and spread it on Lady's back, then studied the waiting saddle with dwindling courage.

"Whatcha waitin' for, Leah?" Teddy yelled. "Ain't chicken, are ya?"

"I am thinking," she replied. She decided what she had to do, and prayed she had figured out a way to do it. She rolled up the sleeves of her plaid flannel shirt, stepped forward and gripped the leather contraption.

She tensed her muscles, sucked in a gulp of air and heaved the saddle up off the stump. Turning her body, she began to whirl in a circle, clutching the heavy object and picking up speed as she rotated. With a final burst of energy she aimed the saddle at the horse's back and let go.

To her amazement, the heavy leather thing sailed up and settled onto the folded saddle blanket. She could scarcely believe it. If Teddy and Thad were not shouting and applauding, she would think it was a dream.

Triumphant but out of breath, Leah faced her cheering section. "I did it!"

"You did," Thad confirmed. "Very clever."

But her pride in her accomplishment didn't ease her trembling muscles. "Could I please learn the rest tomorrow?"

"Coward!" Teddy chortled.

Thad just snorted and shook his head. "Adjust the stirrups and tighten the cinch."

She did as he directed, wondering at every motion where she got the strength.

"Now," he directed, "climb up on the stump, then maneuver the horse close and stick your left toe in the stirrup."

She sent him a desperate look, but he was leaning over, talking to Teddy, and did not see. Suddenly she regretted suggesting that Thad and Teddy undertake a task together. Now it was not Teddy who felt left out, but she herself. Something began to simmer deep inside her.

She clamped her teeth together and clambered onto the stump.

"Grab the saddle horn and swing your right leg over the horse's rump," Thad instructed.

Over the horse's rump? Impossible. She wished with all her heart that Thad MacAllister would *shut his mouth!*

But she knew she must learn to ride sooner or later.

She stepped into the stirrup and willed her body upward, over the horse's hind quarters.

Before she knew what was happening, she flew completely over the saddle and smacked down onto the ground on the animal's other side. "Ow! Ow, ow!" She sat up and spit the dust out of her mouth.

She could hear Teddy's laughter and she shut her eyes against tears of embarrassment and pain. Then Thad was bending over her.

"You all right?" His voice sounded pinched.

"N-no."

Instantly he knelt beside her and laid his hand on her shoulder. "Are you hurt? *Teddy, shut up!*"

Leah could not speak. All she wanted to do was hit this man over the head with something and then throw herself into his arms and sob.

"Come on, lass." He helped her up. Keeping his arm around her shoulders, he walked her around the mare and back to the stump.

Oh, no. He wanted her to try again? Every muscle below her waist rebelled.

But all her life she had hated giving up. For one thing, she hated hearing Teddy laugh at her. They had laughed at her in her village in China, too. And for another, Thad was right. She did need to know how to ride. In fact, she and Ellie had planned to meet at the dressmaker's on Monday. She could not ask Thad to come in from his fields every time she needed to get to town.

She hauled her aching body to the stump and climbed up onto the flat surface once more. Her legs were shaky, but she had learned something. She did not have to take a flying leap into the saddle; she merely had to plant her rear end on the hard leather seat.

Again she stepped into the stirrup, gripped the saddle horn with her left hand and heaved herself upward. Her stiff body settled neatly in the saddle.

The mare stood quietly for a moment and then bolted.

The reins! Leah had forgotten to grab the reins! In a desperate attempt to stay seated, she bent forward, plunged her fingers into Lady's coarse mane and hung on.

The animal circled and whinnied and finally bumped to a stop, so abruptly Leah tumbled sideways off the mare's back. She hit the ground on one hip, but this time landed harder, driving her teeth into her lower lip.

Blood filled her mouth. She spat out the viscous stuff and spat again until her saliva was clear.

This time, Teddy did not laugh. Thad had stood close to his son, gripping his shoulder, but when Lady bolted, he'd let go and sworn. When Leah hit the ground, he sprinted toward her.

She sat with her legs bent, her face pressed against her knees.

"Leah, are you hurt?"

She shook her head but didn't lift it.

"Leah?" Thad dropped beside her and folded her slim form into his arms.

"Don't try to talk," he murmured. "Just breathe slow and easy. When you think you can walk, I'll help you into the house."

She shook her head.

"You don't want me to help you?"

Another negative shake.

"You don't think you can walk? I can carry—"

"No." She let out a whimpery cry.

Thad rolled his eyes at the blue sky overhead. Women were puzzling creatures. She was hurt, but he didn't know how badly or where. Didn't know whether she could walk, or if she even wanted his help. He rested on his haunches with her trembling body in his arms and felt like a complete fool.

She disengaged herself, wobbled to her feet on her own and started forward. The look on her sweaty, dusty face was so determined it sent a shimmer of alarm into his gut.

"Leah, what are you doing?"

"Trying again," she muttered through blood-smeared lips.

Thad blinked. "Oh, no, you're not. You've had enough for one day."

She didn't answer. Instead, she stalked deliberately back toward the mounting stump.

Thad stepped in front of her, blocking her path. "No," he said.

"Yes," she hissed. She marched around him. "Bring the horse."

Teddy clung to Thad's leg. "She's awful stubborn, ain't she, Pa? Don't let her do it."

Hell, yes, she was stubborn. And brave. Against his better judgment, he strode off to lead Lady back into position, and then watched the slim, dirt-smeared figure in blue jeans and a shirt and a pair of Teddy's old boots scramble again onto the stump. She turned to look at him with fire in her eyes.

Lord, she was beautiful.

Teddy clung to his thigh. "I'm not gonna watch."

Thad ignored him and the boy's hands fell to his sides.

This time Leah wound the reins twice about her left wrist, then propelled herself up onto the mare. Thad let out an unsteady breath. At least by now she should know how to control the animal.

Or did she? She sat motionless in the saddle, as if unsure what to do next.

"Lift the reins," he called. His voice was hoarse.

She raised her hands, and after a hesitation, the mare moved a step forward.

"Kick her!" Teddy yelled.

"No!" Thad thundered. "Just touch your heels to—"

Too late. The horse stepped daintily forward, slowly at first, then broke into a canter. Lord in heaven, the mare would run away with her!

Teddy grabbed Thad's belt and jerked it. "Pa?"

"Leah! Pull back on the reins. Pull back!"

But she did not. Instead, with a defiant little shake of her head, she rode the mare to the pasture fence, managed to turn the animal in a big, sloppy circle, and then headed back toward them at a fast trot.

Thad swallowed over a lump the size of a pinecone. She had to be completely unnerved. Either that or she'd gone completely loco. Maybe it was the Chinese in her. Whatever it was, it scared him to death.

But, he admitted, he sure admired it.

She pulled back on the reins, slowed the horse to a jerky walk and then brought it back to the stump.

Pop-eyed, Teddy turned his face up to Thad's. "Man, oh, man, Leah is somethin', huh, Pa?"

Thad's throat was so full he could not answer. Lady halted at the mounting stump and Leah started to dismount. With one foot in the stirrup, she searched blindly with the other for the top of the block.

Thad shot forward and caught her about the waist. "Leah," he murmured. "You can let go of the reins now."

Finger by finger, she released her grip on the leather lines, and he lifted her off the horse. "Kick your boots free of the stirrup," he instructed. When she managed it, he set her on her feet.

"Pa?" Teddy danced at his side. "Kin I have a horse?"

Thad caught his wife's gaze and a look passed between them. He shook his head. Leah, however, gave him a shaky smile and nodded.

Maybe she was right—his son needed his own horse. A pony. But right now it was the last thing he wanted to think about.

He turned away from Teddy and concentrated on guiding Leah toward the house. She took a single hesitant step, but in the next moment a gray pallor washed over her face and she crumpled to her knees.

Thad scooped her into his arms and started for the house with Teddy scampering at his heels. They were halfway to the porch when she regained consciousness. She lifted her head, then snuggled her face against Thad's shoulder, reached her arms around his neck and clung to him.

That took him by surprise! She needed him!

He stopped short. Jumpin' jennies. He hadn't had a single thought about Hattie all morning. He sucked in a lungful of crisp, cold air, shook his head and tramped up the porch steps and into the house.

She needed him. What a feeling!

Chapter Twelve

Thad thrust open the front door and set Leah down as gently as he could. Her legs buckled, but she managed to grab on to his arm and hold tight. With his help, she staggered across the living room and collapsed into the wide-armed chair by the fireplace. Thad's chair. She hadn't the strength to move to the settle.

Teddy stomped through the door. "I could do that easy, Pa, honest I could. I could ride a horse as good as Leah. She did it, and she's not near as smart as me."

Thad ruffled his son's hair and then turned away. "I'll go tend to the horse."

Teddy darted after him. "Please, please, Pa. When do I gets to have a horse?"

Leah was too tired to correct the boy's grammar. She listened as Teddy followed his dad all the way to the barn, begging for a horse of his own, but she could hear nothing from Thad. Grateful to be left alone, she leaned her head back against the damask-covered chair and closed her eyes.

Riding a horse was not impossible, she reasoned. It was the before and after that took their toll. Swinging that heavy leather saddle into place took more strength than she had—or thought she had. But when she realized she had managed to do it anyway, she felt a warm rush of pride.

An hour later, Thad scrubbed his hands and face at the water pump in the yard and waited while Teddy did the same. Together, they had fed Lady, and then Thad had left Teddy to put fresh hay in her stall while he tramped out of the barn and walked the perimeter of his wheat field. *Damn, the seedlings look bedraggled, but there was no sense mooning over it now.*

When he entered the house, his first glimpse of Leah by the fireplace brought him up short. She was curled up in his chair, sound asleep, her arms wrapped across her dirt-smeared shirt. He had to chuckle. Their noon meal was definitely not going to be on time, but somehow he didn't mind. She was worn-out, so he let her sleep.

He managed to chop up kindling and lay it in the fireplace and get a blaze going without waking her up. Then he rattled around in the kitchen, slicing up a loaf of Leah's bread for bacon-and-butter sandwiches.

"Oh, boy," Teddy chortled. "My favorite." He chomped a huge bite and chewed noisily. "Leah's never gonna be ready to ride to town on her own, is she, Pa? I bet I could learn how real quick!"

"Don't talk with your mouth full, son."

Teddy snapped his jaws shut and swallowed. "Well, she's not, is she?"

Thad flicked a glance at his wife, still asleep in the

chair by the fire. Was she ready? Maybe, maybe not. But he knew enough about Leah to know she would consider herself ready, and the first chance she got she'd be halfway to town before he could blink. He had to admire her spirit.

Leah might look small and delicate, but he was learning that on the inside she could be as tough as tanned leather and determined as a bull. He'd known strapping farm wives who hadn't near the grit his Leah showed. Hattie, he recalled with a stab of regret, hadn't even come close. He remembered the morning she'd wept over a rosebud he'd accidentally snapped off.

He cobbled together an extra-thick bacon sandwich, laid it on a saucer and settled it on Leah's lap. She didn't move a muscle.

"She's not dead, is she, Pa?"

"No, son. She is very much alive." More alive than he expected, in fact. The rush of respect and pride that flooded his heart was even more unexpected.

"Come on out to the corral with me, Teddy. Think you could help me fix the gate?"

"Sure, Pa. I kin do all kinds of stuff. Something I think you forget."

Leah woke at dusk, gobbled the sandwich she found on the saucer in her lap and gulped down the cup of now-cold coffee Thad had left on the side table. Bless the man. But she must rouse herself to cook their supper. Thad would want more than sandwiches for his evening meal.

She tried to propel herself up from the chair, but her

stiff, aching body and trembling legs would not obey. Lord, she was all but crippled! Finally she managed to push herself onto her feet. Every muscle in her back rebelled, especially across her bottom, but she managed to inch her way into the kitchen. Her legs felt like soft cheese. It hurt even to sit down on a dining chair to rest.

Doggedly, she consulted Miss Beecher's recipe book, then limped from the stove to the pantry, gathering up potatoes and carrots for stew with something called "dumplings."

When the big iron pot was bubbling away on the stove, she heated a kettle of water, manhandled it into the bedroom and returned for a small enamel basin. Grateful to be alone, she stripped off her dirt-covered jeans and sweaty shirt.

The water was soothing on her face and arms, but what she really wanted was to plop her bottom right down in the basin and soak in the warm water. She decided not to risk it; she might not manage to get to her feet again.

She dried off, eyed her new gray skirt and the red striped shirtwaist, and groaned. The prospect of donning the petticoat and the lacy camisole Ellie had talked her into buying was not the least appealing. Instead, she pulled on her blue Chinese-style trousers and the soft, loose overtunic.

The silk slid comfortingly over her bruised limbs and posterior, and she sighed with relief. Instead of wrestling with starched petticoats, ladies' scratchy lace shirtwaists and long, cumbersome work skirts, perhaps she would sew more soft silk Chinese garments.

She jolted upright at the thought. No! Not one single Chinese garment! She might be more comfortable when she wore them, but she would look different from other women. If wearing the constricting Western-style clothes would help her to fit in with Smoke River townspeople, then that was exactly what she would do.

Tomorrow, she resolved, she would saddle up the mare—*heaven help her, could she really manage that again?*—and ride to the mercantile in town. And—she bit her lip—purchase lengths of stiff blue American denim and scratchy wool for American lady clothes.

Thad and Teddy returned to the house after finishing up the evening chores to find Leah in the kitchen, hobbling from the stove to the table. Her motions were so stiff Thad winced each time she took a step.

Teddy sniffed the air. "Pa, what smells so funny?"

Leah turned toward him, an iron pot of something in her hands, and tried to smile. Thad jerked forward to take the heavy container from her and set it in the center of the table. He noted that she'd already put out plates and bowls. Her hip and leg muscles must be screaming.

Teddy wrinkled his nose. "That's our supper? What're those fuzzy white things on top?"

Leah supported herself against the table with one hand. "Those are dumplings. I found the recipe in Miss Beecher's book."

"Ewww. They look like moldy mushrooms."

"Nothing I cook will ever please you, will it, Teddy? I might as well give up."

Thad sent her a pained look, then laid his hand on

his son's thin shoulder. "You don't have to eat them if you don't want to, Teddy."

"Okay, 'cuz I sure don't wanna get poisoned. I told you she don't like me."

Thad ignored him. "Leah, you need to sit down." He pulled out a chair for her and she edged carefully onto the wooden seat. One glance at her pinched mouth told him she was in real pain. "I've got some liniment that might help later," he murmured. "For now, what else do you need on the table?"

"Just milk for Teddy," she answered in a tired voice.

He strode into the pantry, returned with a crockery pitcher and poured his son's glass full. Then he seated himself and began ladling the rich-looking stew and a fluffy dumpling into each bowl.

Teddy made a show of pushing his single dumpling around and around without taking even a taste.

"Stop playing with your food, son, or you'll be the one needing the liniment."

"Aw, Pa."

Thad silenced him with a look. "Hush up and eat."

The boy gobbled down everything except the dumpling, then scrunched up his face and spooned a tiny bite into his mouth. He chewed slowly, his eyes widening.

"Feels kinda mushy, but tastes good."

Thad polished off two bowls of stew, but Leah could eat only a single bite before she laid her spoon on the plate and stretched her back.

"Go on to bed, Leah. I'll—" He checked himself as he noted his son's crestfallen look. "Teddy and I can wash up and then I'll get the liniment from the barn."

She struggled to her feet and shuffled across the floor to the bedroom. Shaking with fatigue, she shed her tunic and trousers, then donned her silk sleeping robe. The skin on her backside burned as if seared with a hot iron, and the slightest touch was agony. She folded back the quilt, the wool blankets and the top sheet, then very carefully crawled onto the bed on her hands and knees.

She had been foolish. To earn the admiration of her husband, she had overridden her good sense and her instinct for self-preservation. Her mother would have called her a goose!

It wasn't admiration she needed from Thad, it was acceptance, and she had that. She had had his acceptance from the beginning. What more did she want?

More than acceptance, she admitted. She wanted him to look at her the way he looked at his son when no one was watching. With a half sob she sank down onto her side and closed her eyes.

Thad stepped quietly through the bedroom door with a square bottle of brown liquid in his hand. "This oughta fix you up. Roll over on your belly."

She gave an involuntary gasp and opened her mouth to protest, but every inch of her body ached. Without a word, she did as he directed, shifting onto her stomach with a groan. The muscles of her abdomen contracted in bands of discomfort; she must have strained them, as well.

Thad edged onto the bed beside her. "Now, then." His warm fingers hesitantly skimmed the knee-length, pink silk robe up to her waist and she froze. She didn't want him to see her naked. She must look awful, all scratched and swollen.

"Honey, you've got bruises like I've never seen before. Must hurt like hell."

Curiosity battled with her modesty. "What does it look like?"

There was a long, long pause, during which she heard his breathing catch and roughen. At last he began to slosh the brown bottle up and down. "Looks like a war zone. You've got great big patches that are turning purple and black, and some that are green around the edges."

Leah cringed in embarrassment.

"And some yellow splotches," he added. "And some red, raw places, too. I'm surprised you can walk."

She stifled a cry. "I can't really. To cook supper I dragged a chair halfway between the stove and the pantry and sat down on it a lot to rest."

His low chuckle made her catch her breath. "You're one brave lass, Leah. Hold still, now."

He uncorked the bottle and she knew he was dribbling some liniment into his palm. Then she felt his broad, warm hand rest on the small of her back and slowly begin to move. She sucked in air.

"Hurt?"

Oh, yes. It felt like fire to be touched. But gradually the skin under his fingers began to grow warm, and a penetrating heat bloomed. Waves of comforting warmth washed up her spine. Thad moved his hand lower, toward the curve of her hips.

"Feel good?" he muttered. Dammit, his voice was

hoarse. Sure felt good to *him*. Just touching her smooth skin made his heart beat like the hooves of wild horses on the run.

"Yes," she murmured against the sheet. "That feels wonderful. Do some more."

He bit back a chortle. She liked it, did she? Well, God save him, he liked it, too. He liked it very, very much.

Too much.

Hell, what was happening to him?

Dammit, he knew what was happening. His groin swelled into an insistent ache. He wanted her. He'd reasoned it all out the night before—how it wasn't the right time yet—but, darn it, he was still a man, and he wanted her.

He swallowed again and kept moving his hand around in lazy circles on her body.

Leah began to make soft little moans, whether of pleasure or pain he couldn't tell. Tentatively, he pushed the pink silk higher, exposing more of her backbone, and waited for an objection. Nothing came out of her mouth but more gentle little sighs.

He poured more liniment into his palm and smoothed it up and down her spine, moving slowly from the little nub of her tailbone to her hairline at the back of her neck. He sure hoped this was doing her some good; it was stirring up nothing but trouble for him.

"Leah?"

"Hmmm?"

"Think you've had enough? Liniment, I mean?"

"No," she said, her voice drowsy. "Not enough."

His heart somersaulted and the bulge in his jeans

hardened into a shaft of granite. Heavens above, he couldn't take much more of this.

Maybe he'd sleep in the barn tonight.

For another quarter hour he rubbed and sweated and tried to keep his mind off her warm, silky skin and on her sore muscles.

"Thad?"

His hand stilled on the curve of her hip. "Yeah?"

"I should sleep on my stomach tonight."

"Sure." His throat was so thick he found that single word hard to articulate.

She wriggled her shoulders. "Would you pull my night robe down again?"

He closed his eyes. "Sure. Whatever you want."

It was the last thing he wanted to do, but he managed to work the silky garment down to cover her hips. His hands shook more than aspen leaves in a stiff wind.

Yeah, he acknowledged with more than a twinge of regret. Definitely the barn.

Chapter Thirteen

The next morning Leah was so stiff and sore she could not leave her bed. Thad brought her a boiled egg and some toast for breakfast, and for supper a bowl of beans and two of Teddy's odd-shaped biscuits.

Thad confessed he'd spent the night in the barn and hadn't slept much.

"You do not need to sleep in the barn," she had protested.

"I do. I...well, I don't want to disturb you when you're hurting."

She could tell by his voice there was something he was not telling her, but she kept quiet. She thanked God for this steady, caring man; he seemed to like her well enough. She had thought he even liked kissing her, but perhaps she was wrong?

The memory of his mouth moving over hers brought an odd ache below her belly. She wanted him back, lying next to her at night.

Around noon, Teddy poked his head into the bedroom. "Pa 'n' me are goin' fishing. Kin I dig up some worms in your garden?"

"Pa and I," Leah said gently. "Yes, there are lots of worms in the garden. Take a tin can."

The two were gone all afternoon, and when they returned Teddy showed off his string of five brown trout. "Betcha don't know how to clean the innards out of a fish, huh, Leah?"

But I do know, she thought. She refrained from challenging the boy; it was progress enough for him to ask politely for the worms.

That evening, Thad rubbed more liniment on her sore back and legs, and in spite of her resolve to stay awake, she drifted off to sleep, smiling into the pillow.

Thad MacAllister was a good man.

That night Thad again decided he couldn't disturb her. Hell, he *wanted* to disturb her. He wanted to do more than just lie quietly beside her, but he didn't feel right about it. Once again, he tramped out to the barn and rolled himself up in worn, musty-smelling blankets.

But he couldn't sleep for the thoughts roiling in his brain. Physically, it felt right to claim her. But, God help him, emotionally, he felt himself holding back.

He appreciated Leah's efforts to learn to cook. She kept the house neat and she cared for Teddy. Some days Thad could scarcely believe his good fortune. It didn't matter to him one whit that she was half Chinese or if she was not as tough and work-hardened as other farm wives. Thad liked Leah for herself alone.

He would try like hell to be worthy of her, to wait until he could commit his whole self to her with no twinge of regret or guilt about Hattie. His conscience would not allow him to make love to Leah and think of Hattie; it wasn't fair to Leah. He knew in his gut it wouldn't be right.

In the morning, Teddy plopped down beside him on a hay bale. "Is Leah gonna be okay, Pa?"

Thad jerked. "What? Oh, sure she is."

The boy's head drooped. "You weren't even listening."

"You're right, I wasn't." Thad touched his son's shoulder. "Think it's about time you learned to rope a horse, don't you?"

The boy bolted to his feet. "Yeah, Pa! You won't forget, will ya? Like last time? I guess you musta got mad at me or somethin'."

Thad winced. "No, son. I won't forget. And I'm not mad at you, I'm just, well… I've got things on my mind."

"'Bout Leah, I bet, huh?

He didn't answer.

Teddy shot him a look of disgust and busied himself with his shoelaces.

The next morning Leah rose at dawn with renewed determination to carve out a place for herself in Smoke River. All her life she had yearned to belong somewhere, really belong. Growing up in China she had never felt accepted by the villagers where she had been taunted and excluded because she was *"yang guizi,"* a foreign devil. She had never been accepted as the daughter of Franklin Cameron and Ming Sa.

Here in Thad's world, on the Oregon frontier, she longed to feel welcome. She hungered to belong, not just as Thad MacAllister's wife, but as herself. As Leah MacAllister.

After breakfast, a preoccupied Thad tramped off, then reversed direction and came back for Teddy.

"Gosh, Pa, I thought you forgot me, again."

Thad ruffled the boy's hair and together they went to inspect the fields.

Leah knew the alfalfa and wheat seedlings were struggling through the winter storms, and that the wheat especially worried him. There was so much to do on a farm besides grow things—caring for the horses and the milk cow, now heavy with a calf; rebuilding damaged fences; repairing the chicken house, where the wind had torn off slats. Thad had even found time to turn over the soil for the kitchen garden she planned for spring.

Last night, as he was rubbing liniment on her sore muscles, he had talked about his wheat. She knew he had borrowed money on the ranch to finance the experimental venture. It meant everything to him, and she was beginning to understand why. Not just because it was a challenge and a far-seeing experiment, but because it was something concrete Thad felt he could control in an uncertain world. A world where a runaway train could kill a man's wife.

He told her again about watching his Scottish family struggle against starvation when he was a boy. Thad had been scarred by that. He tried to hide it, even from himself, but his fear still lived deep inside him. Whole days went by when he stared into the fire and ignored both her and Teddy.

She tried not to let his withdrawal bother her, but her heart ached for Teddy. Thad's young son could not understand his father's bone-deep concern for something as simple as a field of sprouting wheat. At times she wondered if Thad himself understood it completely.

Whether or not he did, she had her own challenges to face. She could not bother Thad when he was working long, long hours in the fields; today, she resolved, she must saddle up Lady on her own and ride into town to visit the mercantile.

The minute she'd made the decision she suppressed a shudder. Could she really do it? Could she once again haul the heavy saddle up on top of that huge animal?

Very carefully, Leah drew rein near the hitching rail in front of the mercantile and let out a breath of relief. She had done it! Saddled the mare and ridden all the way into town on her own without falling off.

The barber, Whitey Poletti, was sweeping the board walkway in front of his shop. Last week Ellie had told her about the daily sweeping contest between Whitey and Carl Ness, the mercantile owner. It had continued for years, and this morning it seemed the barber was beating Carl in the race to finish first.

She bunched up the long gray melton skirt she wore, kicked her foot free of the stirrups and dismounted. Before leaving the barn this morning, she had practiced it four times, but she still had to think out every move.

Mr. Poletti planted his broom in front of her and leaned one white-coated arm against it.

Leah nodded at him. "Good morning, Mr. Poletti."

"No, t'aint," he snapped. "Yer standin' right where I was sweepin'."

"I am sor—"

"Nah, you ain't. Don't know our customs, can't talk our language, ner nuthin'," he muttered under his breath. "Damned foreigners."

"—rry," Leah finished. The broom bristles poked at her boots.

She drew her frame up as straight as she could. "You will notice, Mr. Poletti, that I speak perfect English." She struggled to keep her voice even. "My father was an American. A teacher."

"Move!" he ordered. "Yer in my way."

"Oh, I had not noticed." She enunciated each syllable with extra care. "I beg your pardon." She turned toward the mercantile entry.

"Huh!" the barber snorted at her back. "Damned Celest—"

The bell over the mercantile door covered the barber's last word. Carl Ness glanced up from the newspaper spread on his counter; without the faintest glimmer of a smile or even a nod of recognition, he immediately looked down again.

"Good morning, Mr. Ness."

The store owner kept on reading. Leah shifted from one foot to the other. Twice. Still he did not speak; he did not even look at her. Instead he kept his sharp, narrow face bent so low she could see the bald spot under the wisps of sandy hair on his head.

"Mr. Ness?"

The shopkeeper slammed the flat of his hand onto the newspaper. "What do you want?"

All at once she remembered her first visit to the mercantile. Carl Ness hated Celestials. The scowl on his face said it all. He hated her because she looked Chinese.

"Mr. Ness," she persisted, pitching her voice loud enough to be heard throughout the store. "I came to purchase some fabric. For a skirt I intend to sew."

"So?"

"You carry bolts of fabric, do you not?"

"Yep."

Leah gritted her teeth. "May I see some?"

The mercantile owner glared at her without speaking, and her pulse began to throb at her temple. The man was being deliberately rude. Well, she could be just as deliberate.

"Never mind, Mr. Ness." She swept her gaze over the empty aisles. "I can see how busy you are this morning. I will find the bolts myself."

She pivoted away from the counter and marched up and down the aisles of shovels and skillets and lanterns until she found what she wanted. Bolts of wool, blue denim, and a variety of calico prints were stacked high on one shelf. Denim, she decided. And the red calico for a shirtwaist.

She muscled the heavy bolts off the shelf, returned to the counter, where Mr. Ness was still bent over his newspaper, and dumped the load next to the black iron cash register.

"Five yards of the denim, please. And three of the calico."

Ness shuffled a few feet to his left, lifted a large pair of scissors tied to the counter with a grimy string, and measured out the fabric along a yardstick nailed to the counter edge. With a vicious twist of his bony arms he ripped off the measured yardage. The sound jarred her nerves almost to the breaking point.

"That'll be seventy-five cents."

"Please add it to the MacAllister account."

"Thad MacAllister don't have an account here," Ness stated.

Stunned, Leah stared at him. "Why, of course he has an—"

"Not anymore, he doesn't." The mercantile owner shuffled back to his newspaper.

Leah slapped her palm down on the counter so hard it stung, but she got his attention. "My husband *does* have an account at the mercantile, Mr. Ness. And you will please add this purchase to it."

She reached out, spun the wheel of brown wrapping paper next to the cash register, tore off a length and neatly bundled up her fabric. Ness stared at her, but she swept past him to the entrance.

The jangle of bells on the door mocked the words echoing in her brain. Her father's words. *Turn the other cheek.*

No! This time she could not follow Father's teaching. This time she was here in Smoke River where she was fighting to belong, and this time she would fight back!

* * *

Furiously Leah pumped the sewing machine treadle up and down with her foot and struggled to tamp down her anger. When the blue denim gradually turned into a four-gore Western-style work skirt, her frown began to lift. By the time she cut out pieces for the red calico shirtwaist, using her old one as a pattern, she had calmed down enough to unclench her jaw and let herself cry it out. She basted and wept for an entire hour.

At dusk Thad tramped in, followed by Teddy, who had been out clearing weeds from her kitchen garden. Thad took one look at her reddened nose and swollen eyes and swore aloud.

"Carl Ness, is it?"

Leah nodded. "How did you know?"

"Heard about it from Whitey Poletti next door." Thad laid his hand briefly on her hunched shoulder. "I let Carl know he won't get away with insulting you." He chuckled deep in his throat. "One was all it took."

She blinked. "One what?"

Thad looked up at the ceiling, down at the plank floor, anywhere but at her. When he spoke she had to strain to hear him.

"One, um, punch. Straight to his gut."

"Oh, Thad, you shouldn't—"

"Yes, I should, Leah. I had to." He chuckled again. "Sure felt good."

By Christmas, Leah's life had settled into a work schedule for cleaning the house, doing the farm chores that fell to her and helping Teddy with his homework. On Mondays she hauled the tin washtub into the side yard, built a fire in the pit Thad had dug and filled with bricks, and boiled the mud and grime out of their jeans and shirts and smallclothes and her own work skirts and aprons.

Tuesdays she heated the two sadirons on the stove and ironed everything except for her pink silk night robe. That she smoothed by hand and hung by the fireplace. Wednesdays she mended Teddy's jean pockets and frayed knees and Thad's split shoulder seams, and cut and sewed new striped-ticking skirts and lawn shirtwaists for the warm weather she prayed would come soon. The cold, dreary winter months were eating away at her spirits.

Thursday was baking day. By noon, eight fragrant loaves of bread crowded the kitchen table, and by evening at least one apple pie or dried-peach cobbler was bubbling in the oven. On Fridays, Leah sewed and later sat hemming her new garments in the armchair by the fire. She was also knitting a muffler for Thad. Red, for good luck.

Each week was a repeat of the one before. She cooked and scrubbed floors and swept the kitchen and the porch, made up the beds with clean sheets, dusted and straightened Teddy's loft, and put out clean towels.

She liked the work. She liked the house. And she especially liked her new family. Teddy was still resentful to the point of being rude, but every so often she caught him gazing at her with a puzzled look in his eyes. Perhaps he was inching toward accepting her.

She genuinely liked Thad's young son. He was bright and curious, and deep down, she suspected he could be as kind and caring as his father. At least the boy's gibes at her were now spread over days instead of hours.

Each chilly morning Thad tramped out to the barn before dawn to milk the cow and feed the horses, and Teddy dragged himself off to school. All day Thad worked in the fields and did not return until after dark. Leah sat by the fireplace, waiting for the sound of her husband's boots on the porch steps and thinking about her life, and about Thad—how his voice lapsed into a Scots burr when he was angry. How soft his mustache felt against her bare neck at night, and how his warm breath caressed her skin into shivers when they lay like two spoons, her back to his chest.

She bent forward to bite off a thread. Lately she had begun to want more at night than his arm casually draped across her waist and his soft breathing near her ear. The fantasies she conjured while sewing by the fire made her blush.

But each night she lay in the big double bed beside a man who was not just tired but silent. Distant. She wished he would touch her as he had the nights he had rubbed her back with liniment. Or kiss her, as he had done months ago. Weeks went by but he never did.

Now she heard a step on the porch and her heart sped up. Quickly she laid aside the skirt she was hemming and raced to the door. But when she swung it open, it was not Thad who lurched into the room; it was Teddy.

Blood dribbled out of both nostrils, down his shirt and onto his jacket front. One eye was swollen and turning purple, and he was trying hard to choke back sobs.

"Teddy! What happened?" She pulled him across to the fireplace and started to unbutton his jacket.

"Got into a fight," he muttered.

"Are you hurt?" She pressed her scrunched-up apron to his bloody nose. "Let me see your eye."

The boy tipped his face up and Leah gasped. It was worse than she'd thought; one side of his face and forehead, including his eye socket, was shadowed by a dark, spreading bruise.

She untied her apron and stuffed it into his scraped hands. "Hold this tight against your nose." From the kitchen she brought a huck towel dipped in cold water, then pushed him down into the big armchair and laid the compress on his face.

"How did this happen?"

Teddy drew in a shaky breath. "I punched Harvey Poletti an' he punched me back. Lots of times."

"You mean you two had a fight?"

His thin shoulders slumped. "Dunno how to fight. I just kept hitting back. I hit Edith Ness, too."

"Edith? But Edith is only six. And she is a girl. Teddy, you should never hit a girl." Leah lifted the folded towel from his swollen face, swung it in the air to cool it and gently replaced it.

"Pa's gonna lay me out somethin' awful."

"Was the fight your fault?"

"Well, guess I kinda started it when I punched Harvey."

"Teddy, why did you hit him?"

The boy tried to look away with his one good eye. "'Cuz he said somethin'."

"Said what? What did Harvey Poletti say?"

"I can't tell you."

In the silence that followed Leah heard the hiss and pop of the log fire, the lid rattling on her simmering kettle of soup and the ragged breathing of the battered boy in front of her.

What should she say?

Torn between concern for Teddy and fear of what Thad might do to the boy, she worried her fingers into a knot. She wasn't Teddy's mother; she wasn't even a real wife yet. Most of all she knew she should not come between a father and his son.

"Are you hurt anywhere else?"

The boy groaned. "My shoulder's kinda sore, an' Edith kicked me in the shin real hard."

"Oh, my. Let me see."

He pulled up his pant leg so Leah could check the angry red mark on his shin and the dried blood on the reddened scrape. She had just started into the kitchen for another towel when she heard Thad's boots on the porch.

The instant the door opened, Teddy leaped out of the armchair and threw himself against his father's legs.

"What's this, now?"

"He's hurt," Leah called from the sink. "He had a fight at school."

Thad bent over his son. "That right?" The boy wrapped his arms around Thad's neck and his father clasped his thin body.

"Ow! My shoulder hurts."

"You want to tell me about it, son?"

"No. But I guess I got to, huh?"

Leah flitted distractedly about the kitchen while Teddy sobbed out the whole story. She noticed that he left out whatever it was the Poletti boy had said that had started off the tussle.

Thad did not press him to explain, and after a while the two of them disappeared. Oh, no! Thad would not whip him, would he?

She heard their raised voices on the porch and, after a while, Thad's low chuckle. When they came inside for supper, Teddy was grinning.

"Guess what, Leah? Pa's gonna teach me how to fight."

She nodded and caught Thad's gaze. "Turn the other cheek" apparently did not always work out here in this rough country. At that moment she made a decision of her own. She would teach Teddy the tricks she had learned to protect herself from the village bullies back in China. She would not tell Thad what she was doing— she would just do it.

As soon as the dishes were washed and put away, she crawled into bed and lay planning what maneuvers to show Teddy, and sorting out her mixed feelings about her marriage.

She liked Thad more than she had ever liked a man before, but he did puzzle her. She thought he liked her, but after that one night when he had kissed her, he had never approached her the way a husband would approach his wife.

Why? Was it only his preoccupation with the wheat

field? With each passing day the question grew more insistent.

Now she could hear thumping sounds coming from the living room, and Thad's voice, then more bumps that sounded like something hitting the floor. Then Teddy groaned, and Leah didn't relax until she heard his bubbling laughter and Thad's low voice saying something.

She curled up into a ball and closed her eyes. She had no right to fault Thad for anything. Even if he thought marrying her had been a mistake, he had saved her from a life of bondage, rescued her from a fate she could scarcely imagine, and given her not only his name, but a home and a purpose.

The man was an overworked, worried rancher with a growing son. She had no right to feel lonely; she was simply not included in Thad's careworn life. Perhaps all American wives were treated the same.

Hours later she felt Thad's weight beside her. She rolled toward him, seeking his warmth. "Is Teddy all right?"

"Sure he is."

"Are *you* all right?" She held her breath, but he did not answer her question.

"Know what I think?" he said after a moment.

"No. What?"

"I think you have a champion knight, like Ivanhoe."

"What? I do not understand."

Thad laid his hand on the back of her neck, swept aside her hair and pressed his lips just below her earlobe. "Teddy's fight was about you."

"Oh." She knew that much; she had not expected

Teddy to tell Thad. "But Teddy does not like me. He resents my presence."

Thad gave a short laugh. "Could be that when you read about Ivanhoe you're teaching him something about chivalry. Seems the Poletti boy said something insulting about you, and Teddy smacked him in the mouth so hard he's got tooth scrapes on his knuckles."

Leah twisted toward him. "You are *proud* of him!"

"I am that."

"Oh, no. Thad, we cannot allow him—"

"Aye, we can, lass. 'Tis what all red-blooded Scotsmen would do—protect their women."

Thad propped himself up on one elbow so he could see Leah's face. Something was different tonight. He couldn't put his finger on it, just…something about her seemed…well, softer. More vulnerable.

Hell and damnation, you randy fool! She'd been waiting since their wedding night a month ago to be a wife in more than name.

He pulled her close and then his breathing stopped.

Deep down he wasn't sure she still wanted him, at least not the way he wanted her. Worse, he wasn't sure what he would let himself do about it, even if she did want him.

Chapter Fourteen

Some nights, like tonight, Thad got hard just touching Leah's skin. He wanted to hold her against his body and kiss her until his brain shut out all those thoughts about being sensible. About being fair to her.

This was sure as hell one of those nights, because he could scarcely keep from rolling her over into his arms. He so wanted to make her his.

He couldn't let himself think about it. But with a groan of frustration he realized he couldn't *not* think about it. About her—this woman who had moved into his house and into his life.

He had to admit Leah was moving into his heart, and he was beginning to be terrified in a way he only half understood.

He had loved Hattie. When she died his life had stopped, but now he was starting to feel alive again. He felt something for Leah—in fact, he felt a great deal for her. And deep down it scared him. If he let himself love Leah and then lost her, he would never recover.

But.

He could hear her breathing softly beside him. "Leah?" he whispered. His voice came out harsher than he'd planned.

She brought her small, capable hand to his bare chest. "Yes, Thad?"

Desire flooded him, made him ache. "Leah, I want—I want to make love to you."

She laughed softly. "Yes, I want it, too." Then she pressed her lips to his shoulder.

He lifted her chin and caught her mouth under his. Kissing her was like tasting something cool and soft and finding a blaze beneath the surface. He hadn't expected it to feel this different; was it because *he* was different?

She parted her lips and he slid his tongue between them. A little moan escaped her, but he couldn't stop tasting her. She was so sweet and hot he suddenly wanted to weep.

A voice in the back of his mind yammered for him to stop, but he couldn't. Not now. There was only Leah and him, and he wanted all of her. Now. His hunger and his need were making him crazy, and when she moved in his arms he knew he was lost.

"Tell me to stop if you don't want this," he said, his voice gravelly.

"I do want this," she murmured. "I have wanted this for a long time, Thad. I have waited for it." She brushed her lips against his throat. "I am glad it is happening now."

His groan was muffled in the lemony scent of her hair. He skimmed one hand up under her silk night robe and found her breast, small and firm as a melon. Gently he ran his fingers over the nipple, stroking the soft flesh until it hardened into a peak.

Then, slowly and deliberately, he moved his hand below her waist into the soft hair between her thighs. He parted her legs and stroked his finger over her entrance. She was wet and hot. Oh, heavens above, he couldn't stop. He would explode if he didn't take her.

Gently, he pressed one finger into her soft, moist heat. She sucked air in between her teeth and he heard her voice.

"Yes," she murmured. *"Yes."*

He withdrew, then touched her again, deeper. And then he went still deeper, until he met a slight resistance.

She made a small moan of pleasure and arched to meet his hand. Oh, he knew he'd long since passed the point of stopping.

She murmured his name against his lips and smoothed her small hands over his skin, caressing him all the way down to his engorged member. His body decided for him; he couldn't go back now.

Willing himself to go slowly, he rose above her, positioned himself and entered her as gently as he could. She gasped when he pushed past her maidenhead, and then she was moving with him, murmuring his name. Her breathing grew erratic and soon she was panting, as he was.

"Am I hurting you?" he whispered.

"No. *No.* It is wonderful. *Beautiful.*" She tightened her arms around him with a strength that surprised him.

All at once she cried out and he felt her inner muscles pulse around him. With a shout he came to his own climax.

He clung to her through spasms that bore him up to heaven and held him in a net of stars. The unexpected feeling that flooded him was so intense, so rich, so… humbling, it scarcely seemed real.

Nothing, *nothing* in his entire life, had ever been like this.

He waited until their breathing calmed, then rolled onto his side, taking her with him. May God forgive him, he would never forget this night.

"Thad?" Her voice trembled. "Is it always like this?"

He opened his mouth, but was unable to speak for a good half minute. "No. It's never been like this."

"I am glad," she whispered. She nuzzled her head into the crook of his shoulder. Thad lay still, holding her until her breathing evened out and he knew she was asleep.

His eyes stung, then filled with moisture. God had given him an irreplaceable gift.

And, dammit, it scared the stuffing out of him.

Thad dabbed his biscuit into the remaining egg yolk on his breakfast plate. "Forgot to tell you something last night."

At the stove frying eggs for Teddy's breakfast, Leah stilled. A warm blush swept up her neck. Thad had said everything last night, but it hadn't been in words. Her heart still had not stopped its hiccuping rhythm.

"What did you forget to tell me?"

"About the barn dance next Saturday. I stopped in

at Verena's shop yesterday when I was in town. She reminded me."

"Verena?"

"Verena Forester. You know, the dressmaker."

Oh, yes, Leah knew Verena Forester. The woman was noticeably cool every time Leah stopped in for a pattern or a bit of lace. The dressmaker always asked about Thad—how was he? What was he planting this year? She made it very plain that Thad claimed a special place in her heart.

Last week, Leah's friend Ellie had taken her to tea and told her why. Verena had wanted to marry Thad after his wife died, and that explained at least some of the dressmaker's rude treatment of her. The rest of it, she knew, was because of her Chinese heritage.

She slid a plate of fried eggs and biscuits in front of Teddy and joined them at the breakfast table. Thad reached over and snagged one of the biscuits from Teddy's plate.

"The dance will be out at the Jensen place. We'll take the wagon."

Teddy hung his head over his plate. "Pa, do I hafta dance with a girl?"

"Sure you do, son. Girls are nice." He sent Leah a secret look, and then jerked upright. Girls *were* nice! And Leah…well, Leah was more than nice. All at once he couldn't breathe.

"Aw, Pa, I don't like girls. At school they all tease me. All 'cept Manette Nicolet, and she's only five."

"Tease you about what?"

Teddy studied his half-buttered biscuit. "About, um, about Leah."

Two forks clattered onto china plates. Leah stared at the boy. "What do they say?" Thad demanded. His voice was barely under control.

Teddy's gaze moved back and forth from the flour-sack tablecloth to the butter dish. "They say all kinds of stuff, Pa. About how Leah don't belong here, an' she's too pretty to be…to be… They say she's prob'ly a—"

"Teddy!" Thad raised his hand.

Leah knew what he was about to say. "They say I must be a bad woman because I am Chinese," she finished.

Teddy's head drooped even lower. "'Cept they don't say 'Chinese.' They say 'filthy Chink.'"

Ice water flooded Leah's veins. Thad's fist smacked the table so hard the sugar bowl jumped. "Do they, now?" he roared.

"Yeah. I punched Edith Ness on the nose, an' Miz Johnson whaled us both good. My rear end was sore for a whole day."

"And?" his father asked, his voice suddenly quiet.

"And now Edith an' her sister Noralee won't speak to me."

Leah sat rooted to her chair, torn between anger on Teddy's behalf and humiliation at being called a— Well, she need not think of that. The cruel slur cut deep. She wanted to cry, but at the same time a small part of her wanted to laugh over Teddy's girl problem.

Thad's russet eyebrows lowered. "Will Edith Ness be at the dance?"

"I s'pose so, Pa. Mr. Ness is gonna supply the apples for bobbing."

Leah laid her hand on Thad's forearm. "Do not make an issue of it. I have been called names before."

Frown lines creased his forehead. "I won't have it," he said heavily. "Not as long as you're my wife."

Leah's cheeks grew hot and she looked down into her lap. Oh, no. Already she could see him bloodied and battered after some fight on her behalf.

She stood up abruptly. "I—I am going out to feed the chickens."

"Again?" Thad gave her an odd look. "You fed them once already this morning. Don't you remember?"

Oh, yes, she remembered. She had purposely crawled out of bed before the sun was up, tossed a handful of grain into the yard for the hens and then clambered back under the covers next to Thad. What had happened after that she would never forget.

She could not help smiling. But she noticed Thad was staring intently out the window. And not smiling.

Teddy hung around all that day while Leah baked bread and made apple pies and scoured out the butter churn. For a while she thought the boy was hoping for a sweet snack, but he refused the bread and strawberry jam she offered, and he even turned up his nose at a slice of fresh apple pie.

Something was wrong. Finally, late in the afternoon, he sidled up to her while she was rolling out another piecrust.

"Leah? Kin I ask you somethin'?"

"You can ask me anything, Teddy. What is it?"

"Remember when you showed me how to run fast? Like you learned in China? Well, I was wonderin'… Do you know anything about, well, about fighting?"

"Isn't your father teaching you how to box?"

"Yeah, but he keeps talkin' about playing fair and not hittin' below the—you know."

Leah propped her floury hands on her hips. "And you want some tricks, is that it?"

"Yep." His grin told her everything.

"And you think I know about these tricks, do you?"

"Yep. You told me about the bullies chasin' you back in China. I bet you were good at gettin' away from 'em, huh?"

Leah had to laugh. She had been very good at defending herself, she acknowledged. The proof was that she was alive, she was here and she was whole in body and spirit.

"Yes, I could defend myself, Teddy. An old shopkeeper in our town took me aside one day and taught me some things."

"Show me," the boy said. Then he quickly added, "Please."

Very well, she would show him some of the tricks old Chen had taught her. "Ways young miss can fight," he had said.

Right there in the kitchen she demonstrated how to step in close to an opponent, slip her foot around behind his legs and tip him over backward.

"Wow, that's real smart!" Teddy crowed. "Show me some more."

"Well, there's a way to let someone try to punch you, and use momentum to pull him off balance."

"What's momtum?"

"Force. You use the force of the blow that is aimed at you to your advantage. That way, you can pull someone to the ground without getting hit. Like this." She demonstrated with a feigned punch at Teddy, and when he punched back, she caught his arm and tugged him over.

"Hey, that's pretty keen!" He practiced a few "pulls" on his own and then turned to Leah. "D'ya know any more tricks?"

"The most important thing about fighting is not a trick, Teddy. Shall I tell you?"

"Yeah, tell me!"

She knelt before him and looked straight into his clear blue eyes. "The most important thing to remember is—" *What am I doing? Teaching Thad's son to cheat? Yes, I most certainly am.*

"Well, as I was saying, the most important thing is this—don't ever let them know you're scared."

Moonlight flooded the road to the Jensen place. The night air was crisp and so clear Leah could see the lights from town. Thad pulled up close to the entrance, and she and Teddy scrambled off the bench and waited while he drove off to park the wagon and see to the horse.

The barn was lit up with Indian lanterns—candles stuck in punched-out tin cans filled with wet sand. By the time they reached the double plank door, Leah's hands were icy and the inside of her nose burned when she drew breath.

Thad caught up to them, slapping his leather gloves together. "Let's go on in. It's cold out here."

Teddy hung back. "Pa, do I hafta?" With each syllable, white vapor puffed out of his mouth.

"No, you don't have to, son. But it's the manly thing to do. Besides, it's warm inside and out here it's colder than a witch's—uh, colder than snow. It's your choice."

The boy shivered, then resolutely marched into the barn after his father.

Music rose from one corner, where an old man with a long, curly beard sawed away on a fiddle tucked under his scrawny chin. Two younger men strummed banjos, accompanied by a thumping washtub bass; the town barber, Whitey Poletti, plucked the strings as if he were snipping off hanks of hair.

Leah listened to the din with astonishment. Such noise! Worse than the riotous New Year festivals in China, with belching dragons and firecrackers and cymbals. The screechy fiddle reminded her of squawking chickens. She clapped her hands over her ears.

Thad bent toward her. "Kinda loud, I guess."

She nodded in agreement; her voice would never be heard over the two twanging banjos. Thad led her to a wooden bench set against one wall, gestured to Teddy to stay with her, and strode off toward the refreshment table.

Couples whirled and circled on the polished plank floor; watchers ringed the sidelines. Leah's gaze fastened on the booted and slippered feet milling before her. She could see no pattern in the couples' steps; why did they not bump into each other?

Teddy scooted closer. "I bet you don't know how to dance, huh, Leah?"

"Not like this, no. In China my father taught me a dance he called a Virginia reel and another called a Highland fling."

"Sure are funny names."

"I will tell you a secret, Teddy." She tipped her head down and spoke close to his ear. "The Chinese in our village thought Father's dances were funny, as well. No one had ever seen such wild antics as Scottish dancing. They all laughed when Father tried to teach them, and after that I learned Chinese dances to try to fit in."

"I bet dumb old Chinese dances have stamping and yelling, too."

Leah bit her lip. "Oh, no. A Chinese dance is very slow and graceful and—" She broke off when Thad returned with a cup of lemonade for Teddy and two small glasses of amber liquid. Whatever it was, it smelled like varnish.

"In a Chinese dance," she continued, "a lady uses her fan for expression."

"Huh! Bet I wouldn't like it. I don't like any kinda dancing."

Leah sought Thad's gaze, and his eyes met hers over his glass. He saluted her with it and swallowed the contents in one gulp.

She would do the same, she decided. After last night, she felt like toasting her husband. She brought her lips to the rim, tried not to breathe in the fumes, and then tossed all the liquid down as Thad had done.

Fire exploded in her mouth, burning all the way

down to her stomach. She struggled to draw in air, but found her throat paralyzed. And scorching hot.

She tried to speak but could not utter a sound. Thad set his glass on the bench and began to pound her back with the flat of his hand. Finally, she dragged in a lungful of air and tried to form a word. What came out was an odd wheezing sound. Her eyes watered. The inside of her mouth felt raw, and her lips were numb.

"Guess I should have brought you a glass of lemonade instead of whiskey."

She nodded her head so hard her neck hurt. "Never tasted whiskey before," she rasped.

"Pa, kin I taste some?"

"Nope. But you can quick bring some lemonade for Leah."

Teddy raced off to the refreshment table and Thad slid his arm around her shoulders. "I sure am sorry, Leah. Whiskey is strong stuff. Guess it was a bad idea."

"No," she said hoarsely. "It was a good idea." Even with the burning in her throat, she felt like celebrating the closeness she and Thad had shared last night. It would be a precious memory to carry in her heart all the rest of her life.

Teddy returned with the lemonade glass clutched in both hands to avoid spilling, and Thad rescued it from his grasp.

"Isn't that Edith Ness over there, son?"

Teddy wrinkled up his face. "Dunno. She and Noralee are twins. They look 'xactly the same."

"You going to ask her to dance?" Thad inquired, his voice casual.

The boy's shoulders twitched. "Who, me? Why would I wanna do that?"

"It's called mending fences, Teddy. Patching up a quarrel."

"I didn't quarrel with her, Pa. I bashed her on the nose."

Without a word Thad set off across the floor, threading his way among the whirling couples to where Edith Ness sat on the sidelines with her parents and twin sister.

Teddy gaped after his father. "Pa must be goin' crazy."

"Perhaps," Leah agreed. She watched Thad's tall figure stride across the noisy room and bend to speak to the young girl in dark braids. The woman sitting beside her, with the same color braids wound in a coil at the base of her neck, must be the girl's mother. Beside her, sitting stiffly upright, was Verena Forester, an expectant look on her face.

Thad spoke to Mrs. Ness and then offered his hand to the girl.

"Golly," Teddy whispered. "Why would Pa wanna dance with Edith?"

Leah had a good idea, but she kept it to herself. Unaware of Verena's unspoken invitation, Thad escorted the girl out onto the floor, and the other couples made room. He positioned Edith's hands as far up on his arms as she could reach and rested his hands lightly at her waist. They did not dance, exactly, just moved one step in one direction and another step in the opposite direction, rocking back and forth in time to the music.

Leah watched, astounded, as her husband and Edith appeared to be conversing. The girl's lips were moving, and after a few minutes she tipped her small, pale face up and Thad leaned down and said something.

Instantly Edith looked stricken and she dropped her gaze to her buttoned-up shoes. Thad kept talking, and the two of them kept moving back and forth to the music. Edith's cheeks reddened and her lips pressed together, and then he bent down again and said something else. This time she nodded and laughed.

Teddy poked Leah's arm. "What's Pa talkin' to her for? She doesn't know *anything*. She's just a dumb girl."

The fiddle music stopped. Thad escorted Edith back to her mother and started across the floor toward Leah and Teddy again. He was smiling.

Leah touched Teddy's hunched shoulder. "I suspect that your father has smoothed some ruffled feathers."

"Huh?"

"Never mind. Here he comes." She rose to meet him.

"Leah, would you take my whiskey glass over to the bar and see if you can get whoever's there to refill it? I need to speak to Teddy."

The bar Thad referred to consisted of two wide planks propped on sawhorses, crammed with all shapes and sizes of bottles, some with labels, some without. Leah wove her way through the crowd and at last reached the short, chunky man posted behind it as bartender. Seth Ruben, she recalled. Darla Weatherby's brother-in-law. Leah had been introduced to him at the mercantile week before last.

She produced the empty glass and held it out. "Mr. Ruben, could you refill this, please?"

The man's eyes widened, then narrowed, and a scowl twisted his face. "I could, but I'm not goin' to. Don't serve Celestials at this bar."

Chapter Fifteen

The bartender stared at Leah so long she wondered if a fly was crawling across her nose. Then he drew himself up, puffed his chest out and shook his head.

Perhaps she had not heard him correctly over the music. "Mr. Ruben? Please, would—"

"Nope."

"Oh, it's not for me, it's for my husband."

"I said no. 'No' means not a chance in hell."

Leah blinked. "But—"

"Bar's closed," he snapped. "At least to Celestials. Now, git!"

She gaped at the rotund little man. "That is unfair," she said in a quiet voice. She could not tell if he had heard her, but he avoided meeting her eyes. Squashing down the stab of pain in her chest, she turned her back on him and recrossed the floor.

Thad took one look at her face and the empty glass in her hand and jerked to his feet, fists clenched.

"Don't, Thad. Don't make a scene and spoil the Jensens' party."

"I damn well *will* make a—"

She grabbed at his shirtsleeve. "Do not," she murmured.

Teddy tugged on his father's pants leg. "You sure look mad, Pa. What'cha gonna do?"

Leah waited, watching the muscles in Thad's jaw flex as he ground his teeth.

"Pa?"

She leaned down to the boy. "Do not ask him anything right now, Teddy. Your father is…thinking."

"Thinkin' 'bout what?"

"Oh, about…some more fences that might need mending."

"We don't have no broken fences! I know, 'cuz I check 'em out with Pa every spring."

Thad was paying no attention to their exchange, but Leah could tell something was on his mind. His mouth had firmed into a flat, unsmiling line.

"I'll be right back, Leah." Deliberately he moved off toward the refreshment table.

"Gosh," Teddy grumbled. "Pa's been real funny ever since Ma died."

Leah's chest tightened. "That must have been a hard time for you both."

"Ever'body tried to help. That sewing lady, she brought pies and things most every day."

"You mean Verena Forester? The seamstress?"

"Yeah, that's the one. I didn't like her one bit."

"But," Leah murmured, "your father apparently did."

"He never said nuthin'," Teddy mumbled. "And anyway, when Pa asked if I liked her, I told him no, 'cuz that was the truth. After that, she stopped comin'."

Leah clenched her hands in her lap. That explained more than Teddy could ever know about her marriage to Thad.

In the next moment a small blonde girl in a ruffled yellow gingham pinafore marched up to Teddy.

"M-Manette," he spluttered. "What're you doing here?"

"I came with *Maman* and Papa and Uncle Rooney."

"I thought Mr. Rooney was yer grandpa."

"*Oui,* he is, but he likes me to call him Uncle Rooney, anyway. Do you want to dance with me?"

"Can't," Teddy said quickly. "Don't know how."

For a long minute Manette's blue eyes assessed him in silence, then she reached out and grasped both his hands. "Come with me. I will teach you."

Manette half dragged him onto the dance floor. At the edge of the circling couples, she demonstrated a very simple pattern of dance steps—two forward and two back. He tried it out a few times, but before he could fit it to the music, a male voice rose over the din.

"Choose yer partners for Star of the Sea." People began to scramble about the floor, forming squares of four couples each.

"One couple needed over here," the caller yelled. Thad reappeared and grabbed Leah's hand. Apparently he had dealt with the bartender a bit roughly— his knuckles were scraped. Without a word, he pulled her halfway across the floor to fill out the square.

Leah glanced at the couple across from them and

went cold all over. Carl Ness stood with his wife, Linda-Lou, who immediately narrowed her eyes. On her left, a scowling Seth Ruben, with a telltale bruise forming on one cheek, slouched next to his frail-looking silver-haired partner; she pursed her thin lips and averted her gaze.

And, oh heavens, to *her* right was a hard-eyed Whitey Poletti, partnered with Verena Forester. The dressmaker stared at Leah as if she had red spots all over her face, then shifted her gaze to Thad and smiled.

But then, to Leah's horror, each of the three other couples in the set turned their backs and stalked away, leaving Leah and Thad standing alone on the dance floor. As she passed, Verena slowed her steps to mutter, "You're not good enough for him. You don't belong here."

Stunned, Leah could think of nothing to say. Thad protectively circled his arm about her waist and swept her off the floor past the whispering crowd. "Looks like things are coming to a head," he murmured.

"At least," Leah said in a tear-clogged voice, "they are not throwing melon rinds and rotten eggs at me as they did in my village in China. But tonight I think I would prefer melon rinds and rotten—"

"Yeah," Thad agreed. "At least it's more honest."

Neither of them spoke on the drive back to the ranch. Even Teddy seemed subdued. Leah relived the deliberate rudeness of the townspeople over and over in her mind. Part of her could not believe people could be so blatant about their dislike of her. Another part saw the insults for what they were—fear of anyone who looked different. Even so, that knowledge did not ease the lancelike wound in her heart.

When they reached the ranch, Thad strode off to the barn without a word of explanation. Leah clamped her jaw tight.

Could he not see her distress? He was acting more like a Chinese husband—remote and preoccupied—than an American one. Perhaps it was true that all men were the same: when confronted with a threat, they stormed off to fight whatever it was.

Leah sighed over the sharp rock lodged in her throat. Her mother always said reasoning with people was more effective than using fists, but she was learning that reasoning was much harder.

She choked back tears, tumbled into bed and curled up into a ball. After what felt like hours waiting for Thad, she fell asleep.

Thursday was Leah's weekly baking day. Thad tramped out to the barn to doctor a lame foot on his horse, and a glowering Teddy had gone off to school, so she was alone. She had just set four loaves of bread to rise when a gentle tap sounded on the front door.

Oh, no, not Teddy with another bloody nose. Cautiously she swung the door open to find an attractive, sun-browned woman in a blue wool skirt and knitted shawl. Leah recognized her at once—she was the woman who had stood up with her at the wedding.

"*Bonjour,* madame. I have come for a *tête-à-tête.*"

"A what? I do not understand."

The woman smiled. "A 'lady visit.' That is what we say in France."

Leah resisted the sudden impulse to hug the woman and eagerly motioned her inside. Her guest stepped into the living room and glanced around approvingly.

"You remember me, I hope? I am Jeanne Halliday. Jeanne Nicolet before I marry my husband, Colonel Halliday. Your son's friend, Manette Nicolet, is my daughter."

"Oh, of course. Please sit down. Would you like some tea?"

"*Oui, merci.* Now I will tell you why I come. My husband and I attended Monsieur Jensen's dance in the barn last Saturday night. We saw what happened, and I came to speak with you."

Leah could only stare at her.

"I think you are very strong not to scream at Monsieur Ruben and those rude ladies who walked away from your dancing square. Square dance," she amended.

At the sink, Leah pumped water into the teakettle. "I did want to scream. But there are already enough people in Smoke River who dislike me. I did not want to add more."

"*Alors,* I understand. It is because you—and I—we are considered 'different.' When I first came to Smoke River, no one at all would speak to me."

Leah set the kettle on the stove while Jeanne settled herself at the kitchen table. "I am glad you came, Mrs. Halliday."

"*Bon!* To friends, I am Jeanne. We shall be good friends, *n'est-ce pas?*"

"Oh, yes, I hope so! I...I—" She gulped, afraid she would cry and disgrace herself. She blinked away the tears that stung her eyelids. "I feel so alone in Smoke River. I want so much to fit in, but the only woman who is friendly is Ellie Johnson, the schoolteacher."

"Of course. Madame Johnson is from the city of Boston. She knows something of the world beyond Smoke River. As I do."

Leah set a cup of tea before her guest and Jeanne stirred in two spoonfuls of sugar. "Now we talk about the men, eh? Your husband and my husband, they are much alike. Independent, am I correct?"

"And stubborn," Leah added with a smile.

Jeanne laughed. "And, how do you say, one-minded."

"Single-minded. Exactly."

"Let us be frank. Men in Oregon are not like men in other places. And our husbands—"

A laugh burbled out of Leah's mouth. "Our husbands are definitely Oregon men."

"Vraiment!"

"We are trapped."

"Ah, *non*." Jeanne gave her an assessing look. "Say instead that we are happy."

"Happy? Oh, Mrs.—Jeanne, I wish that were true. I am finding life here in the West very...well, difficult."

"Ah, je comprends. But our men—my husband, Wash, and your husband—they love us. Many women are not so fortunate. Do you know Mrs. Sorensen?"

Leah shook her head.

"No? Ah, well. I say we are not trapped. We are understood and we are respected by the people who matter most—our *bons hommes*. Our good men."

Leah fervently wished that would be true of Teddy, as well. Perhaps that would come in time, but she was losing hope. At times she sensed a hesitant warmth in the boy's eyes, but mostly, winning his approval felt like a long climb uphill.

Jeanne finished her tea, studied the half-knitted muffler on the settee and folded her hands on the table. "I wish to invite you to join the Ladies' Knitting Circle. We meet at the dressmaker's shop, upstairs in her apartment, on Saturday afternoon."

"You mean Verena Forester's shop? Oh, I do not think… You see, Verena does not like me."

"That is possible, yes." Jeanne took a careful sip. "But more likely she is merely jealous."

Leah's cup clattered onto the saucer. "Jealous? I thought she just didn't like me. Why would—?"

Jeanne cleared her throat. "She is jealous because you have Monsieur MacAllister, and she does not."

Leah sat without speaking for a full minute while Jeanne poured them both more tea.

"Jeanne, are you sure my husband is the reason?"

"*Oui,* I am sure. It is simple. Verena wants what you have, but because of you, she cannot have him."

And then the Frenchwoman said something that made Leah's breath catch. "Mademoiselle Forester has always wanted Thad. Even when he was married to Hattie."

Leah suddenly found herself smiling at her guest.

"I think the Ladies' Knitting Circle sounds very nice. I will come."

Jeanne touched the rim of her teacup to Leah's. "*Bon.* My husband would say you have the grit."

Grit? Leah rolled the word around in her head. Did she really? Did she have enough of "the grit" to carve out a place for herself in Smoke River? A place where she belonged? Where she fit in?

She was used to being an outsider—it had been the same in China. Because of her parents' mixed marriage, she was not accepted as either Chinese or as white. Instead, she'd been shunned. Leah Cameron was the White Devil's daughter.

Jeanne took her leave an hour later. Leah punched down her bowls of rising bread with extra vigor, then sat by the fireplace to think. Saturday night's exclusion at the barn dance had hurt.

In Luzhai the villagers had called her *Juk Sing*— Miss Nobody. What did the Smoke River townspeople call her behind her back?

Then again, perhaps she did not want to know.

She'd thought it would be different here in America. Did not the Americans have their Bill of Rights? And did not their Declaration of Independence say that all men are created equal?

Her mind buzzing, she automatically washed and dried the tea things and shoved the carefully shaped loaves into the hot oven. By the time the crusty bread was baked and set in the pantry to cool, Leah had steadied her unease and felt a surge of hope.

She also had the beginnings of a plan.

* * *

Thad tramped around the perimeter of the three acres of winter wheat he'd watched struggle to life, breathing in air that smelled of green grass. For weeks the field had looked like a huge square of fuzzy green carpet, but over the last few days of early spring sunshine, the seedlings had burst into life and now began stretching tentatively toward the sky.

He leaned one hip on the split-rail fence to admire it. When the light hit it just right, it looked like a luminous patch of golden mist hovering over a still, yellow-green lake. He'd never seen anything more beautiful. Or more promising. Looking at it brought deep-down pleasure. And, he acknowledged, maybe a feeling of invincibility. Might be irrational, but there it was.

It grew harder and harder for him to stay away from this field. Each day it looked different—taller—as the tiny fingers of wheat reached toward the sun. The stalks looked frail, vulnerable, but his gut told him he was doing the right thing. Farmers in Washington Territory to the north were getting rich shipping wheat all over the country. Why not here in Oregon?

He turned away toward the pasture gate and the hard knot of apprehension in his belly returned. He had to admit it wasn't just about the wheat; it was about Leah.

Hell and damn. He was blundering through the days like a lovesick boy, falling more in love with her with each passing hour. At the same time, his fear of once again having something snatched away from him ate at his gut.

The realization shook him to his bones. He had no

idea how to protect himself from loving a woman. If he ever lost Leah, as he had lost Hattie… Heaven help him.

His throat tightened. Somehow he knew he had to keep Leah at a distance.

He tramped up to the front door and into the small house she had transformed from four gloomy, gray walls into a sunlit haven of peace. Every time he walked inside, that fear bit into his gut. All of this—his wife, his wheat field—could be wiped out in a single second.

The house seemed unnaturally quiet, and then he re-membered Leah was visiting Ellie Johnson, the school-teacher. He had thought about taking Teddy fishing for trout in Swine Creek, but the boy had already made plans with Harvey Poletti, the lad who'd bloodied his nose a month ago. He knew he should spend more time with Teddy, but maybe it was better for his son to make friends.

Restless, Thad roamed through the kitchen, the living room and finally, against his better judgment, ended up in the bedroom. The quilt, the pillows, even the striped yellow window curtains smelled like Leah, a lemony scent with a hint of soap. Hell, he loved ev-erything about her.

He stalked out onto the front porch and strained his eyes in the direction of the road. He needed to do some-thing to keep his mind off Leah; maybe he'd ride over to the Halliday place and ask about Matt's new colt. Teddy's birthday was coming in April. It didn't take a genius to figure out his boy wanted a horse of his own.

Teddy's eighth birthday fell on a dry, warm day in mid-April. Matt Johnson had brought the roan colt over on a lead the night before, and Thad had hid it in the barn. He could hardly wait until morning.

At breakfast, Leah poured him a second mug of coffee and he leaned forward in his chair to fold his hands around it.

"Teddy, could you help me out this morning?"

The boy's face brightened. "Sure, Pa."

"Go on out to the barn and, um, check Lady over before Leah rides into town today."

The boy gobbled down the rest of his pancake and streaked out to the door to the barn. He returned in under a minute and threw himself into Thad's arms, knocking the mug of fresh coffee all over the breakfast table.

Leah did not care. She laughed while she mopped up the spill and exchanged looks with Thad. Hidden behind a hay bale in the new colt's stall was a brand-new boy-size leather saddle.

Teddy was so excited he could not stop talking. "Pa, he's just the most beautifulest horse in the whole world and I'm gonna call him Red and please kin I ride him today?"

Thad sent Leah a grin. In that moment she realized how long it had been since she had seen him smile. He had been so preoccupied lately both she and Teddy were feeling more than a bit neglected. At least, she thought with resignation, they had each other, and Teddy's insults weren't as barbed. Yesterday he'd said her hair looked like "rotted corn silk," but he'd set her hairbrush to dry in the sun, as she'd asked.

The spring weather grew warm, and then hot as the sun beat down on the fields. Thad spent a good deal of time watching his wheat grow taller, and while it made him feel good, at the same time an uneasiness fluttered in his belly; it felt like a flock of chickens with a fox in the yard. Somehow he figured that if he could maintain control over his wheat field, that meant he could control other uncertainties. That he would not be destroyed by some catastrophe that might snatch Leah away from him, as it had Hattie.

The only thing he could do to protect himself was not care so much about her. He was trying to distance himself from Leah, but it sure wasn't easy. At night he ached to touch her, to envelop her strong little hands in his, to twine his fingers into the shiny black hair spilling over her shoulders.

His fear of losing her was so gut-deep he wondered if he could ever shake it. He couldn't talk about it; mostly, he guessed, because he didn't really understand it himself. Every evening he managed to roll away from her and try to sleep while she lay breathing quietly, expectantly, in the dark.

All he knew for sure was that he didn't know how much longer he could keep this up.

Chapter Sixteen

When the ruts in the town road dried into a naviga-
ble washboard, Leah decided one warm Saturday afternoon to brave the Ladies' Knitting Circle. Would
she be accepted by the group? What should she wear?
What should she say?

Stuffing down her anxiety, she resolutely saddled
up Lady and slowly rode the mare to Verena Forester's
shop in town, wearing her best long skirt and ruffled
calico shirtwaist, and a tentative smile. After tying the
horse to the hitching rail in front of the barbershop, she
hesitantly climbed the stairs to the dressmaker's sec-
ond-floor apartment.

"Leah!" Ellie Johnson rose at once and embraced
her. "I'm so glad you are joining us."

Jeanne Halliday smiled a welcome from her chair
across the room and gestured to the empty place beside her. Verena gave her a cold-fish stare and Darla
Weatherby, seated next to Ellie, refused to speak or to
meet Leah's eyes.

Last in the circle was eight-year-old Noralee Ness,

daughter of the mercantile owner, who sent her a shy nod. Surprisingly, the girl had come without her mother or her twin sister.

Leah smiled at her. "Hello, Noralee. I did not know you could knit."

"Yes, ma'am, I can. Mama taught me last Christmas when I was in bed with the chicken pox."

Her spine rigid, Verena perched on a ladder-back chair near the refreshment table. "Tea, ladies?" When the dressmaker had poured tea into all the delicately flowered cups, Ellie rummaged in her knitting bag and produced a tin of sugar cookies, which she passed around.

The women talked about patterns and yarn colors and trim, their conversation peppered with a good bit of gossip. Darla reported that her mother had traveled to Saint Louis to visit her ailing sister and had brought back scandalous postcards, some with pictures of the new opera house. Ellie reported on her students' interest in holding a spelling bee.

Noralee chattered on and on about school, dropped a number of stitches and finally lapsed into silence. Verena inspected the girl's progress at the end of every finished row and corrected her errors none too kindly. Leah pressed her lips closed and held her tongue.

After the first hour, talk turned to Smoke River and the townspeople. Jeanne Halliday announced that two new foals had been born at the Double H ranch, which she and Colonel Halliday owned. Ellie hesitantly asked about Thad's wheat crop and what he hoped to harvest come summer. Her husband, Matt, was thinking about planting a wheat field next year, but he was waiting to see how Thad's crop fared this year.

Darla Weatherby spread the lacy black shawl she was working on across her knees and inspected Leah's half-finished scarlet muffler with undisguised disapproval.

"Red is so…bright, don't you think?" Darla said.

Leah looked up. "It's for Thad. So I can see him easily when he comes in from the fields at night."

"From his *wheat* field?" Darla sneered. "You know what they're calling it, don't you? 'MacAllister's Disaster.'"

"I heard it was 'Thad's Madness,'" Verena interjected.

Leah straightened. "No, I had not heard what they are calling it. For Thad's sake I hope it will soon be 'MacAllister's Triumph.'"

"Hah!" Verena snorted. "Everyone knows wheat doesn't do well this far south. Thad's brain is addled, has been ever since Hattie—"

"Hush, Verena." Ellie cut her off.

"Well, it's true," the dressmaker persisted. "Just look what he did last December, marrying again scarcely a year after—"

"Verena! Do hush up!"

"And now he's planted wheat," Verena sniped. "The man's addled, I tell you."

Addled! Under her knitting Leah twisted her hands. Thad was anything but addled. Troubled, perhaps, but not addled.

A thick silence fell. "More cookies?" Ellie offered quickly. The schoolteacher rose and passed around the

tin box; Noralee took three and sent Leah a sympa-
thetic look.

Her heart pounding with hurt and fury, Leah folded
the half-finished red muffler on her lap. "I am sorry that
some of you—" she looked directly at Verena and then
at Darla "—that some of you feel my husband has been
foolish. However, I do not believe he has. Throughout
history, all innovations have come from someone who
was willing to try something new."

Five sets of eyes were riveted on her. Drawing in a
shaky breath, she plunged on. "And about Thad's re-
marriage. Thad is a good man. He loved his wife and
it is unfortunate that she died, but I am his wife now,
and I am a good wife to him."

She lifted her chin. "Besides, who are you to judge
the private lives of other people?"

Verena sent Leah a look full of daggers. Darla gulped
and stared down at her lacy shawl. Ellie and Jeanne
nodded at Leah in approval and even young Noralee
Ness sent her a furtive smile.

Leah stood up. She could not leave Verena's apartment fast enough, but she managed not to race for
the door. She swept down the wooden stairs and out
onto the plank walkway where she had tied Lady. She
jammed her knitting into the saddlebag and yanked the
lead rope free. Lord in heaven, she needed a swallow
of whatever it was Thad drank at night.

She had her boot halfway into the stirrup when she
glanced over the mare's broad back and caught sight
of something that made her breath stop and her jaw
go slack.

"Third Uncle? *Third Uncle!* Is that really you? What are you doing here in Smoke River?"

The approaching little, rounded figure stopped short. He wore an impeccable Western-style suit and overcoat of dark gabardine, a white shirt and a bow tie of crimson silk. On his arm swung a jaunty red umbrella.

"Ming Lei? Niece Leah? I not recognize."

Leah gulped. "Third Uncle, how did you get here? And why have you come?"

The man's rolling gait took him around the horse to where she stood. "I come on train."

"From Portland? From San Francisco? *All the way from China?*"

"Yes! From Canton on ship. From San Francisco in train. Long trip with much smoke in cars."

Leah reached out and touched the man's shoulder. She had never particularly liked her mother's youngest brother; he had opposed her mother's marriage to Father, and afterward he had treated his older sister like a fallen woman.

"Third Uncle, Ming Cha, how did you find me?"

The black eyes twinkled. "Chinese Presbyterian Mission in city. Not hard to trace."

"But why?" she persisted. "Why have you come?"

"Times not good in China," he explained. "I sell shop in Luzhai. Start business here in Land of Gold."

Dumbfounded, Leah stared at the man. "Uncle, you cannot sell ground dragon horn and cherry ginseng elixir here in the West."

"Do not want to," he said with a grin. "I start baking business. You know, cake, cookie, even pie. I go to apprentice school in San Francisco and learn how."

"But Third Uncle, how could you leave China? It was your home!"

Her relative's round face sobered. "My family all gone since your mother, Ming Sa, die. You only family I have left."

Leah's senses began to spin. She reached for Lady's bridle, closed her eyes and hung on. This was too much to absorb; perhaps it was only a dream.

"I must offer you hospitality," she began.

"No need. I stay in hotel, like real Western shopkeeper," he said happily. "Tomorrow I look for place to open bakery."

She did not know whether to laugh or cry. Now there would be not one but two Chinese people in town. She suppressed a groan. She could just see the expression on Carl Ness's face.

She struggled not to smile. God forgive her, she hoped she would be there to watch when the mercantile owner met jolly, stubborn Third Uncle.

She rode home in a daze. At supper she explained to Thad and Teddy about her uncle's arrival, and sat dumbfounded on the dining chair while Teddy peppered her with questions.

"Is he a real Chinaman? From China, like you?" The boy could hardly wait to see him. "Does he wear funny clothes? Does he talk Chinese talk?"

A week passed. The weather grew hot and then hotter still. The sun seared everything. Leah irrigated her kitchen garden with buckets of used wash water, and spent the stifling afternoons sewing muslin shirts for Teddy and Thad and light seersucker skirts and lawn shirtwaists for herself.

And no matter how oppressive the weather, or how unsettled her nerves, each Saturday she saddled Lady, rode into Smoke River to visit the Ladies' Knitting Circle, and purposefully drank tea while the ladies gossiped. Once she made a plan, she stuck to it.

Her mother always said "A drip of water wears away the hardest stone." Perhaps that was how she had endured years of being called the White Devil's woman. Leah resolved she would not stop her own efforts until the "stone" wore away.

Today, instead of having to defend Thad's wheat-growing venture, she had to answer pointed questions about Third Uncle and his bakery.

"Yes," she acknowledged in as calm a voice as she could manage, "my uncle has come from China." And yes, he was planning to open a store—a bakery.

Over violent objections from Whitey Poletti and Carl Ness, Third Uncle—or Uncle Charlie, as he now wished to be called—had managed to rent the space next to Verena Forester's dressmaking shop. And the mercantile was now becoming the focus for what Leah recognized as growing unease on the part of Smoke River townspeople.

Uncle Charlie was undeterred. Blithely he set to work building shelves and storage bins, apparently unconcerned about whether he was accepted or not. Independent to a fault, in Leah's opinion, Uncle Charlie would accept no help or advice from her or from Thad; but each Saturday, Leah brought him a basket of vegetables from her now-thriving kitchen garden, or some squares of cornbread.

At first, Uncle Charlie could not find a boarding-house that would accept a Chinese man, and Rooney Cloudman was the only man who would stand next to him at the bar in the Golden Partridge Saloon. But with what Leah came to recognize as his typical persistence, Uncle Charlie moved into the tiny room at the back of his bakery and began collecting discarded pieces of furniture.

Slowly the bakery began to take shape. Leah helped Charlie paint the interior walls of the bakery a buttery-yellow, and she spent one entire Saturday washing the tall windows in front with hot water and vinegar. A handsome new Windsor stove came by Wells Fargo wagon from Portland, and then two glass-fronted display cases were shipped by rail all the way from San Francisco.

Both items met with glowering disapproval from the townspeople, but Uncle Charlie ignored them. However, Leah saw young boys lobbing stones at the windows one afternoon, and when she flew out of the store to stop them, their mothers met her with stony, unrepentant faces.

To Leah's relief, no matter what verbal abuse the barber and the mercantile owner heaped on Charlie, the sunny little man paid no attention.

The dry summer heat increased, and along with it came sharper and more angry objections to Uncle Charlie's presence. Leah began to see that what had started as the townspeople's unease over the bakery venture was escalating into outrage, exacerbated by the growing realization that the farming community was experiencing a severe drought.

Carl Ness resented Uncle's presence not only on the main street but anywhere in the community, and he was unpleasantly vocal about it. "Go back to China where you belong," the mercantile owner muttered. "No damned Celestial's gonna bake *my* cakes."

At the following Saturday knitting circle, Verena Forester plunked her teacup on its saucer and remarked in a piercing, acid-laced voice, "You let one foreigner in and when you're not looking, you've got all their relatives, too."

The remarks stung Leah, but they did not daunt Uncle Charlie. Sometimes Leah wondered if her uncle was deaf.

She, however, was most certainly not deaf. And as the hot, searing weeks of summer progressed, tempers and frustrations mounted. Every single gathering of the Ladies' Knitting Circle ended in an uproar.

Verena always started it. "That man has no business coming here to Smoke River. There isn't another Chinaman within a hundred miles, except for the railroad crew over in the next county, and they'll be gone come winter."

Each time the seamstress lashed out, Leah remembered what Teddy had told her about the pies Verena had brought when Hattie had died. And what Verena had apparently meant to Thad before his marriage to Teddy's mother.

"Charlie came because the last of his family is here," Leah replied quietly. "Charlie is my uncle. My mother's youngest brother."

"Well, then, why don't you both go back to China where you belong?" Darla snapped out the question and the others—except for Ellie and Jeanne, and even Noralee Ness—nodded their heads in agreement.

Leah decided at that moment that she would not be polite and refuse to respond, but that she would not back down, either. "I would not be welcome back because my father was not Chinese. Besides, my father did not want me to stay in China all my life. He wanted me to come to America."

"One wonders why, since you are obviously Chinese," Verena spit.

Leah paused to calm herself. "I am only half Chinese. The other half is American. My father was an American missionary."

It went on and on until tempers wore thin and hurtful words began to fly. Leah finally excused herself and escaped down the stairs, but all the way to the boardwalk she could hear the rising voices, like a hive of angry bees.

Some days, like today, she wondered whether her mother had really believed in the power of water dropping onto stone. Part of Leah wanted to give up and hide herself away in Thad's house for the rest of her life. But another part deep inside made her grit her teeth and come into town the next Saturday, and the next, and the one after that.

No matter what, she would keep moving forward with her plan to become part of Smoke River.

Chapter Seventeen

Summer turned so hot and dusty Leah dispensed with the tight corset Ellie had talked her into wearing. Being laced up into the whalebone garment felt like being imprisoned; she could not bend or reach or even breathe on the hottest days. True, she looked more like the other women in town, more American, but Thad did not even notice.

In fact, Leah reflected, these days she might be dressed in feathers and oilcloth and Thad would not notice. The thought nagged at her, and as the days progressed, she felt more and more rejected.

On this Saturday afternoon she rode into town beside Teddy on his new colt, which he had named Red. The scorching air was so suffocating that once they reached the main street it took her some minutes to recognize the enticing scent of something floating from the bakery.

Teddy sniffed the air. "Man, somethin' sure smells good, don't it?"

"Doesn't," Leah gently corrected.

The boy reined his colt up close to her mare. "Leah?"

"Yes, Teddy? What is it?"

"There's, uh, somethin' I wanna ask you, but I don't rightly know how."

Leah studied her eight-year-old stepson's tanned face under the brim of his boy-size Stetson. "Yes? You may ask me anything, Teddy. Except," she added with a grin, "how to learn to ride a horse."

"Well, then, here goes. What's eatin' at Pa? I never seen him so, well, disgrunted. That's a new word I learned in school."

"Disgruntled, you mean?"

"Yeah, that. What's wrong with him? Is he mad at us?"

Leah sighed. If she knew, she would do anything to fix it. Teddy was right; lately Thad had been growing more moody. Just this morning at breakfast he had seemed so distracted he'd left his toast unbuttered on his plate, and he forgot to drink his second cup of coffee. Then he'd agreed to go fishing with Teddy, but forgotten to dig any worms for bait.

This afternoon she had left him silent and frowning, pacing back and forth on the front porch. Something was definitely wrong.

"I think your father is preoccupied, maybe because of the drought we're having this summer. He worries about his wheat crop."

"Gosh, it's only one little field. He's got corn and alfalfa and—"

"Teddy, try to understand. To your father, his wheat

field is more than just a field. Like Red, here. To you, he's more than just a horse, is he not?"

"Gosh, yeah. Red's my bestest friend."

Teddy's vigorous nod did not allay her uneasy feelings about Thad. His wheat field *was* more than just a field to him, but *what* more? Thad was as impenetrable as the thick honeysuckle vine that was almost smothering the privy.

Did he regret marrying her? Did he wish he had married someone else—Verena Forester, perhaps? Or one of the other townswomen?

Or was it something else? Something about her?

Each night when he came to bed he briefly touched her shoulder, kissed her cheek and rolled away from her. Night after night her heart shriveled a bit, and she fell asleep aching for him. Now, as she and Teddy walked their horses down Smoke River's main street to the bakery, she tried not to think about it.

Uncle Charlie, wrapped in his white baker's apron, stood in the open doorway waving an oversize Chinese fan.

"Uncle, whatever are you doing?"

"Ah, Niece Leah. I send good cookie smell out to customers," he announced happily. "Also to dressmaking ladies upstairs. Teddy, you sweep floor and I pay you four cookies, okay?"

Teddy scrambled off his colt and Leah tied both horses to the hitching rail. "How is business, Uncle?"

"Some good. Sell big cake to Missus Rose at boardinghouse. Some bad. Mercantile boss make threat."

Leah's heart clenched. "What kind of threat?"

"He say 'Go away from town or something bad happen.'"

"He would not dare! This is a free country."

A rare frown crossed Uncle Charlie's round face. "Country itself not free, Niece Leah. Country is just land. 'Free' depend on people *in* country."

Disheartened, she climbed the stairs to Verena's apartment, thinking over Uncle Charlie's words. If it was people that made a country free, was that not true here in Smoke River?

"Leah!" Ellie Johnson rose from her chair and grasped her hands. "You are wearing a new shirtwaist!"

"Yes, I—"

"Saints preserve us," Verena screeched. "It's bright red! Ladies never wear red."

Leah slid onto the chair next to Ellie. "Why not wear red? Red is a very lucky color."

"Lucky for who?" Verena pressed. "For a Celestial, maybe. Not for an American."

"But I am an—"

"Don't be a goose, Leah," Darla injected. "It's not just that it's red. That style is just plain old-fashioned. For one thing, the sleeves are too full."

Verena smirked. "And the ruffle at the neck is all wrong."

"I like it," Noralee Ness whispered, just loud enough for Leah to hear over the clatter of the tea tray Verena set down. "I think red is pretty."

"Red," Darla interjected, "is in very bad taste."

Heat crawled up Leah's neck. She opened her mouth

to reply, then thought better of it. There were more important issues in Smoke River than the color of her new shirtwaist.

The mouthwatering scent of freshly baked cookies drifted on the warm air. "Mmm," Darla hummed. "Verena, your cookies smell enticing."

Verena's long, narrow face flushed. "I didn't bake today. I was up late working on Cleora Rose's wedding dress."

"Wedding dress! But Cleora is…well, she is twenty-nine!"

"So what if she is?" Ellie challenged. "I was the same age when I married Matt. At twenty-nine a woman can still be young and alive."

Noralee lifted her nose and sniffed. "What smells so good?"

"Cookies," Leah announced. "From the bakery downstairs."

She watched Verena's expression tighten.

"You mean that Chinaman is baking cookies?"

"Of course." Leah folded her hands in her lap. "It *is* a bakery, after all."

Verena grimaced. "Chinese cookies," she snapped. "What next?"

"Oh, no," Leah corrected. "Brown sugar cookies, I think. With raisins."

The dressmaker's eyes narrowed. "We don't want any Chinese cookies, or Chinese anything else, in Smoke River. Do we, ladies?"

"No!" Darla declared.

"We won't stand for it," Verena said, her lips thinning. Something in the tone of her voice sent a chill up Leah's spine.

Ellie, Jeanne Halliday and Leah sat frozen, without making a sound.

"I don't care if they *are* Chinese cookies," Noralee ventured in a small voice. "They smell good!"

"They are not 'Chinese' cookies, Noralee. Chinese cookies are very small and thin. These cookies are big." Leah held up her thumb and forefinger, rounded into an arc.

"That," Verena snapped, "is not the point."

Jeanne abruptly folded up the knitting in her lap. "*Alors,* what *is* your point, Verena?"

"The point, Mrs. Halliday, is that we do not want any foreigners in our town."

"But," Jeanne pointed out with a half smile, "I come from France. Does that not make *me* a foreigner?"

Verena swallowed, clamped her teeth together and began splashing tea into the flowered china cups.

Darla rose to carry the tray. "Your skin is as white as mine, Jeanne. But Charlie What's-his-name at the bakery definitely isn't white." Defiantly she stared at Leah.

Leah took a shaky breath. She was not afraid. What she felt was bone-deep fury. She had never known such anger, not even when the village boys in Luzhai had called her names and pelted her with fruit rinds.

It was not fair. Not fair to her Chinese uncle. Not fair to the Negro blacksmith at the livery stable or the Nez Perce hired man at the Hallidays' ranch. Not fair to anyone who was different.

"Oh, I see," she said into the sudden quiet. "Being an American means having white skin, is that it?"

"Yes!" Darla exclaimed.

"No," Leah said, her voice quiet. "I am an American, and my skin is not white." In fact, after a month of the summer sun, her usual creamy-golden skin had darkened in color. Now she was so sun-browned she looked more Indian than Chinese.

"Skin color, it makes the difference, does it?" Jeanne inquired, her eyebrows rising.

"That's not what we learned in school," Noralee said. "Is it, Miz Johnson?"

While Ellie responded to the girl's question, Leah slipped out the door, down the stairs and into Uncle Charlie's bakery.

"I would like some cookies, Uncle. A dozen of the ones you just baked and a dozen of the chewy kind with raisins."

Upstairs in Verena's apartment, Ellie was still talking when Leah stepped back inside and edged around to the tea tray. Hurriedly she arranged the cookies on a plate and passed it around the circle with unsteady hands.

She was shaking so hard she did not notice when Teddy barreled through the door.

"Leah." He yanked hard on her sleeve. "Pa wants you. Hurry."

Thad lay spread-eagled on the board sidewalk, and Leah bent over him, trying to control her racing heartbeat. Uncle Charlie sprawled beside him.

"Thad, what happened? What have you done?"

"He didn't do nothin'," Teddy volunteered. "Mr. Ness and the barber jumped on him and then that big guy, Ike somethin', he joined in."

Thad groaned and twisted his pounding head to look up at her. "That's pretty much it."

Her face tightened. "What started it?"

Thad drew in an uneven breath. "Ness was jawing at me about the drought, about what a fool I was to plant wheat in Oregon instead of barley or oats."

There was more, about Leah and Uncle Charlie being "dirty Chinks," but Thad wasn't going to repeat it. Carl Ness sure rubbed him the wrong way. All summer long, every single time Thad entered the mercantile to select things on Leah's shopping list, the mercantile owner gave him some cockamamie excuse for being fresh out of the items.

"The next thing I knew, Ness was trying to wrestle me out the front door, and Poletti, the barber next door, barrels out of his shop to help him. Oh, I almost forgot about Ike Bruhn, big strapping fella with a punch like a—"

"Sledgehammer," Leah interjected through tight lips. "I can tell from the condition of your face. Oh, Thad…"

He spit a mouthful of blood onto the walkway. "Uncle Charlie tried to help by leaping onto Ike's back, but Ike sent a right to his jaw that laid him out flat."

Uncle Charlie still lay unmoving an arm's length from Thad. Teddy bent over him, brushing his hand along the Chinese man's rounded shoulder. "He's breathin' okay," the boy reported.

Leah mopped at the blood pouring from Thad's scalp

with her petticoat hem, then felt him all over. "Does it hurt here?" She pressed on his rib cage. "Here?"

He jerked when she touched his collarbone. "Hell, Leah, stop poking at me. I hurt everywhere." But it sure felt good when she patted her small hand over his body.

She scooted to Uncle Charlie's prone figure and spoke near his ear. "Uncle, can you hear me? Are you hurt?"

"Hear fine," he replied in a trembly tenor voice. "Hurt maybe on head."

Leah inspected a puffy-looking lump on Charlie's forehead. "This looks like you ran into the bakery door."

"He didn't, neither!" Teddy yelled. "Uncle Charlie jumped on that big man's back while he was hittin' Pa. He was real brave!"

Thad forced his bruised body into a sitting position and focused on Leah. He didn't like the fiery look that came into her eyes. He half expected her to march into the mercantile and lay Carl Ness out behind his counter.

"Leah," he croaked. She twisted back to him and he got his right hand up high enough to lay it in her lap. "Can you get me home?"

Charlie sat up, then got to his feet and walked unsteadily back toward his bakery. "Uncle?" Leah called. "Do you need help?"

"I fine, Niece Leah. I eat cookies, then feel better." The snapping black eyes studied Thad. "You take care of husband. Very brave man."

"Teddy, can you tie your father's horse to yours and lead it home? Your father can ride double with me."

Teddy gave her a tentative smile. "Sure I can, Leah. I'm almost growed up."

Thad started to chuckle but caught at his chest instead. The question was, he thought with that clarity that always came when he was hurt, could he even mount a horse? Maybe she should bring the farm wagon?

Naw. That would take too long, and heaven help him, he wanted to be home in his own house so he could nurse his hurts in private. He'd mount the damn horse if it killed him.

Somehow Leah jockeyed him into the saddle, then hiked up her skirt, climbed up behind him and clasped her arms around his waist.

"Honey, honey, not so tight."

"I don't want you to fall off. Hold on to the reins, Thad."

Teddy was waiting on the porch by the time Lady and her double load stumbled to a stop next to the bottom step. Thad tipped himself out of the saddle, but his knees buckled and he hit the ground and rolled. Dammit, his ribs hurt! His back muscles were screaming, and his tongue was beginning to feel mushy.

With Teddy's help, he crawled up the steps. "Son, you remember that liniment I used when Leah hurt her back?"

"Yeah. It's in the barn."

"Get it."

His son raced for the barn. Teddy was a good kid. Guess he should tell him that more often.

And Leah… Hell, he'd tried hard to keep his mind——

and his hands—off her. It scared him spitless to even think about losing her.

He closed his eyes with a half-swallowed groan. Sometimes he wondered when she'd become so important to him. It had started long before they'd made love the first—and last—time. And now...

Dammit to hell, he loved her. Leah was stubborn, courageous, sensible, funny and devoted to him and his son. The joy that had flooded him when he'd made love to her that night was just...frosting.

Half supporting him, Leah maneuvered him into the bedroom. With her free hand she flipped back the quilt on the bed and he settled his bashed-up body on the cool, smooth sheet.

Teddy tramped in, the bottle of dark liniment clutched in his hand. "I put some water to boil, 'n case you wanna, uh, clean him up some."

Leah expelled a long breath. "Thad, do you have any spirits hidden away somewhere?"

"Yeah. In the pantry, behind the sack of sugar."

Teddy raced to get the bottle, and while Leah got a basin of hot water ready to wash him, his son helped him pour out and swallow two good slugs of whiskey. Hell, Thad thought, he'd better make it three, and he gulped down another.

Leah shooed Teddy out to tend the horses, then dropped a soft towel into the basin and began to remove Thad's blood-streaked clothes.

Oh, may the Lord have mercy on his soul. He was hard before she got to his belt buckle, and when she slid his drawers down over his naked backside, he was swollen and aching. As long as he stayed facedown on the bed, his manhood hidden, he might be able to handle it.

But with her every soft swipe at his bare skin, his control wavered. Finally she picked up the liniment bottle Teddy had brought.

"Dr. Neal's horse liniment!" she yelped. "*This* is what you used on me? *Horse* liniment?"

His mind warm and mellow after three shots of whiskey, Thad chuckled, then sucked in his breath at the pain it brought. "Worked, didn't it?"

Leah laughed softly. "Oh, my, yes."

"Well?"

"I am not sure this medicine will be effective on a man such as you."

"What's that mean? Leah, don't josh me now. I'm not up to it."

To his surprise, she planted a light kiss on his bruised shoulder. "I am not teasing you, Thad." She brushed her lips across the base of his neck.

He groaned. "Oh, no?"

"No," she said in a matter-of-fact voice. "I am seducing you."

With a gasp he came straight up off the bed. "Like hell you are."

"Lie down," she said quietly. "And hush up."

Chapter Eighteen

"Leah." Thad caught at the small hand rubbing his shoulder. "Leah, stop." Even with him belly-down on the bedsheet, his engorged member had ideas of its own. "I can't…"

She went on rubbing another palmful of the sagey smelling liquid across his neck. "You cannot what?"

"Well…" he rumbled against the sheet. "It's like this."

"Yes?"

"I like being with you, Leah. I like it a lot. Maybe too much."

Her hand stilled. "I like being with you, too, Thad. I do not believe there can be 'too much.'"

He trapped her wrist and lifted it away from his rib cage. "When you touch me…oh, man alive, Leah, I want you. But dammit, right now I can hardly move."

"Yes," she breathed. "I know."

Thad struggled to think clearly. "Liking you is not so much outside as it is…"

"Inside," she finished, her voice calm. "Yes, I know that, too."

She disengaged her wrist from his grasp and went on smoothing the aromatic lotion over his skin. Goodness, it felt wonderful. The liniment warmed his muscles and soothed away the pain. Hell's bells, everything Leah did, or said, or cooked or sewed or read aloud in the evenings was wonderful. He was in love with her up to his eyeballs.

His manhood was alive and eager, but his body hurt like blazes. Must have taken more of a beating from Ike than he'd thought. At any rate, he couldn't even think about…

Huh! He couldn't *not* think about it. He hoped Leah understood.

Her hands reached his lower back. "Leah." Her name came out of his mouth in a hoarse plea.

Her soothing fingers ceased their work on his bruised muscles and then she leaned over him and whispered something into his ear. It sounded like… Heavens, her voice was as ragged as his. And if that didn't tie him up in knots, he was made of iron.

The word she had whispered was *tomorrow.*

"Tomorrow, what?"

"Tomorrow perhaps you will be able to move without hurting."

His mouth went dry. Tomorrow he might be able to walk around with only a twinge or two; it was the day *after* tomorrow that scared him. Or rather, the *night* after. By that time he would be well and strong and half out of his mind with hunger for her.

There was no doubting it; he was in trouble. Focusing on his wheat field had worked up to a point, but it no longer stopped him from thinking about Leah. Wanting her. Sometimes, like right now, he felt he might go crazy.

Hell and damn, he was a coward. He kept edging away from her, protecting himself from another broken heart. At the same time a question nagged at him deep down inside, something he couldn't even put into words.

Was he losing more than he was gaining?

He twisted his head so he could not see her. He had to think about something other than Leah or his brain would explode.

"Every rancher in Polk County said wheat was risky," he muttered. "Maybe they were right. With no rain since December, the wheat will be scorched to a crisp before I can harvest it."

Leah said nothing, just sat quietly on the bed beside him and listened.

"You know I've gambled the ranch on that crop. If it fails, next year we might be broke. And hungry."

"We will not be hungry, Thad."

"Oh, God, Leah, what I'm trying to tell you is…" He waited until he regained control of his breathing. "I've got to keep my mind on the wheat right now. Not on you."

Leah's hands stilled. "Even at night?"

Thad made an odd sound in his throat. "Mostly at night. Can you understand that?"

"No, I don't," she said quietly. "I think that is an

excuse for something else, something you are not telling me."

Leah recorked the bottle of liniment with slow, deliberate motions and spent a long minute composing her thoughts. "There are many things about you I do not understand, Thad."

He made a sound in his throat, but when he said nothing, she went on. "You are building a barrier between us. And often you still ignore Teddy, who needs you very much."

He did not speak, just looked at her. The pain in his eyes made her tighten her resolve. It was time to get some things out in the open. With every single visit to town, she grew further from acceptance in Smoke River. She was beginning to understand why. Verena Forester.

Heaven help her, Leah had come to love this man. If he could not love her back, she would wither up inside and die. She eyed the half-empty bottle of whiskey on the night table.

"Leah, stop."

"Stop what?" Surely she had not spoken aloud?

"Stop rubbing my back," he said in a low growl. "And stop talking. I can't take any more."

Hot tears of fury rose in her eyes. "I cannot take any more, either." She snapped the sheet up over his body.

"What are you talking about?"

Leah took a deep breath and kept her focus on the whiskey bottle. "Things are not right between us, Thad."

He closed his hands into fists. "Yeah, I guess not."

"Is it Verena?" The words just slipped out, but when she heard them hanging in the silence she wasn't sorry.

"Huh? What's Verena got to do with it?"

"I thought…" Leah worked to control the trembling in her voice. "I think perhaps it was Verena you wanted. Not me."

He rolled over and tried to sit up. "Are you crazy?" Inexplicably he gave a harsh laugh. "It's you I married, Leah. It's you I want. And it's you who's driving me crazy."

"I do not believe you."

Thad stared at her, the astounded expression in his blue eyes slowly shifting into anger. "Well, gosh darn it." He reached out to touch her shoulder, but she pulled back.

He closed his eyes. "This'd be funny if it wasn't so damn…so damn gut-wrenching."

"I will not mention it again, Thad. But I am not sorry I spoke to you about it."

Without a word he rolled off the bed and stalked to the bedroom door. Then, remembering he hadn't a stitch on, he backtracked, threw on jeans and a shirt, pulled on his boots, and tramped out. Leah heard his steps pound across the porch and then fade into the yard.

Numb, she curled up into the warm spot his body had left, stuffed her fist against her mouth and choked down her sobs.

In the morning she went through the motions of cooking breakfast, sweeping the house and feeding the chickens, but her mind was on Thad. What could she do if he did not care for her as she cared for him?

That afternoon she could not face the Ladies' Knitting Circle. Instead, she rambled listlessly about the ranch, letting her feet carry her across meadows and pastures that were brown and parched from the relentless sun. She ended up at the fence bordering Thad's precious wheat field.

The spindly stalks looked half-dead already. The top growth was stunted, and the drooping wheat heads were beginning to dry up. *Dear God, his wheat venture is going to fail!* Her eyes stung.

If he would only let her be close to him, she might ease his anguish. But their conversation last night had resulted in a cool stiffness at breakfast that had never been there before. In a way she wished she could take all her words back.

But if she did, the barrier between them would never be resolved.

She mopped her eyes with the hem of her apron and tried to face things as they were. Thad's battered body had healed, but he was still preoccupied, and now she knew why. Verena Forester.

Thad was withdrawing from her more each day and Leah knew that at some point it could cease to matter. She gave a strangled laugh. Her mother would say she had married a pigheaded man.

A pigheaded man who wanted someone else.

That night she made Thad's favorite chicken and dumplings. After supper he passed her in the kitchen on his way toward the back door and patted her shoulder. She turned toward him, but he stepped away. He gave her a long look, then cleared his throat.

"I'll sleep in the barn tonight."

"The *barn!*" He was burying his head in the sand, and her heart along with it.

She went to bed alone and wept until her pillow was soggy. She could not stand being set aside much longer.

The week dragged by. Each day the merciless sun beat down, scorching her roses and the struggling vegetables in her kitchen garden. The freshly washed shirts and jeans and drawers she laundered were dry as soon as she clipped them on the clothesline.

The knitting circle was to meet again at Verena's on Saturday. Leah swallowed her distress and decided that yes, she must join them; she needed the companionship and the distraction of the ladies' talk—at least as much of it as she could stomach.

And the plan she had adopted called for her not only to remain strong, but if at all possible, to keep a serene face.

Besides, she needed a packet of needles and another bottle of Thad's whiskey from the mercantile. Her breath hitched in at the thought of dealing with Carl Ness, especially after he and Thad had come to blows, but she could not avoid it. Her throat ached as if she had swallowed a lumpy rock, but she vowed to go into town, do what she had to do and smile no matter what.

On Saturday the air hung hot and heavy in the small bedroom, so stifling it was hard to breathe. She stood in her muslin camisole and pantalets, staring down at the long flounced skirt and petticoat and high-necked red calico shirtwaist laid out on the bed. Any breeze on this oppressively warm afternoon would never reach her skin through all those buttoned-up layers; it was simply too hot and sticky to be wrapped up like a Chinese steamed bun.

Her Chinese silk tunic beckoned from the armoire. That and the loose trousers would let the air circulate and cool her skin. Why, she wondered, did not every woman in Smoke River wear similar comfortable garments during the hot summer days?

When she was dressed, she saddled up Lady and slowly rode into town, keeping her fears under control by focusing her tear-blurred eyes on the horse beneath her. The afternoon sun beat down on her wide-brimmed straw hat, and by the time she'd finished her business at the mercantile, calmed her nerves after Carl Ness's rudeness and climbed the rickety wooden stairs to the dressmaker's shop, her temples were pounding.

A familiar voice stopped her halfway up the stairs.

"Leah!" Ellie called from the landing. "My goodness, you're wearing Chinese—" Her friend broke off as Leah panted up the last few steps.

"Leah, are you all right? You look pale and your eyes—" Again she broke off.

She knew what her eyes looked like; they were swollen and puffy from crying. She could not explain, because Ellie, so in love with her devoted husband, would never understand.

"Come in, Leah. Verena has made lemonade. It will help you feel better."

At the doorway, Leah hesitated, pinched her cheeks to bring some color to her face and marched into the lion's den.

Everyone was present, even young Noralee Ness, whose lap robe for her mother was half-finished. Jeanne Halliday patted the chair next to her, and Leah sank onto it. How she wished she had brought Uncle Charlie's Chinese fan! Instead, she snatched off her sun hat and waved it back and forth in front of her face.

"How come you're wearing those Chinese clothes?" Noralee inquired with typical directness.

Leah took a deep breath. "Because they are cooler in hot weather." She looked at the flushed faces in the circle. "If I might suggest," she began with trepidation, "these loose-fitting garments are simple to make. I will donate an old tunic you could use for a patt—"

"Never!" Verena spit the word in Leah's face. "What an outrageous suggestion. Thad would never—"

Leah stopped her fanning. Outrageous, was it? What was outrageous were Verena's constant veiled hints about Thad.

"What an insane idea!" Darla blurted. "Are you suffering from sunstroke?"

Ellie shoved a tall glass of lemonade into Darla's hand and followed with a plate of cookies. Chewy ones, with raisins, Leah noted. They must have come from Uncle Charlie's bakery, and she wondered who had brought them.

"Didja all hear 'bout the town meeting tonight?" Noralee asked excitedly. "My father is organizing it."

Leah's spine stiffened. "Town meeting? No, I had not heard. What is the meeting about?"

A silence descended in the stifling room, so thick

Leah could hear the beating of her own heart. At last, Jeanne raised her head and cleared her throat.

"*Alors,* the meeting was called by Monsieur Ness and Monsieur Poletti, the barber. It is about the new bakery in town. Uncle Charlie's bakery."

"*My* Uncle Charlie?"

Verena gave an undignified half laugh, half snort. "Well, Leah, no one else in Smoke River has a Chinese uncle, now, do they? The town meeting is to decide what to do about it."

Ice water pooled in the center of her belly. "What do you mean, 'do about it'?"

Verena looked away. After an awkward moment, Darla spoke up. "It means deciding whether the people of Smoke River are going to stand for a Celestial moving into our town and starting his own business."

Ellie caught Leah's eye and leaned sideways toward her. "Leah," she said in an undertone, "you must come to the meeting. You must. The whole town is taking sides."

"Meeting!" Thad shouted at supper that night. "More likely a tar-and-feather party. Carl Ness ought to be behind bars."

"Who's gonna get tar and feathers, Pa?"

"They're gunning for Uncle Charlie, son."

Teddy's brow wrinkled. "What's he done?"

"Nothing," Leah and Thad said in unison. "Eat your supper, Teddy."

"But I wanna know about the meeting."

"So do we, son." Thad pushed his chair back from the table and stood up. "I'm going on into town early, Leah."

"But Thad…"

"I've got to go," he said, his voice quiet. "You know that sometimes people can get some crazy notions." He touched her shoulder. "I've got to keep Charlie safe."

She met her husband's steady gaze; the determined look on his face sent a shiver of fear up her backbone.

"Be careful."

He reached for her, pulled her out of the dining chair and folded her into his arms. "You are one sensible woman, Leah."

She struggled to steady her breathing. "I am a sensible woman who cares about you."

To her surprise, he kissed her thoroughly. His firm lips, and the scratch of his afternoon whiskers, warmed a hollow ache below her belly. When he lifted his head, he looked at her so long she wondered if she had flour on her nose.

In the next moment he was out the front door, and she heard his boots thud down the porch steps.

"Wish Pa'd taken me with him. We were s'posed to go fishin', but I guess he forgot."

"He could not take you with him, Teddy. Your father wants you to be safe tonight. With me," she added.

"Oh. Okay. I guess it's not so bad, bein' with you, Leah."

Not so bad? Was that acceptance she heard in the boy's words? Even approval?

Before dark fell, Leah washed up the dishes and Teddy dried them; then they walked out to the barn and he helped her saddle Lady. When she had mounted, Teddy scrambled up in front of her. She did not want Thad's son more than an arm's length away from her at the town meeting tonight.

"Golly, Leah. I've never seen tar 'n' feathers on anybody."

"Hush, Teddy. You do not want to see such a thing."

In the hour it took to reach town she thought about the look on Thad's face after he'd kissed her. Oh, how she hungered for more of Thad. Much, much more.

She also thought about the ugly situation that awaited them. Her husband was courageous, even gallant, to volunteer to keep Uncle Charlie safe. She knew that Thad had stood up for her in the past, and that it had cost him bloody knuckles and bruised ribs.

She could not help thinking that Verena Forester would never need such protection. No doubt Verena had never, ever felt she was an outsider.

A confrontation at the town meeting would drive Thad even further away from her. Was she costing Thad more than he was willing to pay?

She bit her lip until she tasted blood.

Chapter Nineteen

The town meeting was held in the large room in back of the barber shop. When Leah and Teddy walked inside, the noise was so deafening Teddy clapped both hands over his ears.

Screaming children raced around the perimeter until they were corralled by their parents. Townspeople stood nose to nose, shaking fingers in each other's angry red faces, until finally Carl Ness divided the crowd into two opposing groups facing each other on opposite sides of the room.

People found seats on whatever they could seize— extra chairs from the barbershop, empty barrels, wooden fruit crates with colorful labels pasted on one end, even cushions tossed down on the plank floor.

Leah shared a splintery apple crate with Teddy. "Golly, the whole town's here," he whispered. "Must be a hund'erd people."

Across the room, people were packed so tight they could scarcely move. Only a few drifted to the side where Leah sat with Teddy—Ellie and Matt Johnson; Jeanne and Colonel Halliday and their daughter, Manette. And—Leah's eyes widened—hulking, overweight Ike Bruhn.

Ike Bruhn? What was he doing on their side? She thought he hated the Chinese. Thad was just now recuperating from the beating Ike and Whitey Poletti had inflicted last week.

Near Ike sat Sarah Rose, owner of the white clapboard boardinghouse at the edge of town, and Rooney Cloudman, her boarder, along with Harvey Pritchard and his wife, from the Lazy J ranch five miles out of town. And old Mrs. Hinksley, a retired schoolteacher from Portland who boarded with Mrs. Rose with her sister, Iris DuPont. Ike's fiancée, Cleora Rose, sat across the room among the Nesses and the Polettis and everyone else opposed to Leah's Chinese uncle's presence and his bakery.

Leah counted only thirteen people on her side, and that included children. She lost count of the number on the opposite side.

"Where's Pa?" Teddy whispered. Leah scanned the gathering, but Thad's tall, lean form was nowhere to be seen.

"I do not know. He left the house early to find a safe place for Uncle Charlie in case..." She could not bear to finish the thought.

Carl Ness began banging a makeshift gavel on the small table before him. "Order," he yelled. "Come to order."

Carl's wife, Linda-Lou, sat on his right. To his left

perched their twins, Edith and Noralee. Leah noticed that Noralee was staring fixedly at her shoes.

Whitey Poletti sprawled behind Carl in an old barbershop chair, his white-blond hair slicked back with hair tonic. Sitting slump-shouldered as he was, the paunchy Italian resembled an oversize rag doll.

Carl stood up, hooked his thumbs in his front pockets and puffed out his bony chest. "I called this here meeting 'cuz of something important that's come up in Smoke River. Something that affects all of us."

A murmur of discontent circled the room. Undeterred, the mercantile owner continued. "Up till a couple of months ago, our town's been a pretty nice place to live. Now we've got us a problem."

Harvey Pritchard stood up at the back of the room and stuck both thumbs in his bib overalls. "Vat iss this problem?"

"The problem," Carl retorted, "is Charlie's Bakery. You'd know that if you and the missus came into town and visited the mercantile more often."

"Yah? Who iss Charlie?"

A ripple of anticipation followed the farmer's query. "He's a damn Celestial," Carl said, his voice tight. "You know, a Chinaman!"

Pritchard restraightened his bib overalls. "And vat has he done?"

Whitey Poletti shot to his feet. "Clean out yer ears, Pritchard. The Chinaman's opened a bakery, right next to my barbershop!"

"Ah, iss good idea, yah? Get shave and haircut and bring home cake."

The crowd laughed. Poletti grew red in the face. "But this here Charlie is a Celestial!" he shouted. "An immigrant! His real name is Ming Chow or somethin'."

"So vat? I and my wife, ve are immigrants, too. Ve are Dutch. My wrangler, he is full-blooded Nez Perce, and my cook, Maria, she comes from Mexico."

Whitey snorted. "Ya know, Pritchard, you live so far outta town you don't keep up with things. I said Charlie is a *Chinaman.*"

Talk broke out all over the room and the barber plopped back onto his chair. Carl lifted his gavel and had to rap the block of cedar on the table three times before the buzzing voices fell silent.

"Anybody else not up to date on what's happening to this town?"

"Hell, yes," shouted Matt Johnson. In his slow, easy way, the rangy federal marshal got to his feet. "What's the big panic over a bakery?"

"A *Chinese* bakery," a woman shouted.

"Run by a Chinaman," someone else yelled. "We're not gonna stand for it."

Another woman's voice pierced the clamor. "You let one foreigner move in and next thing you know you've got one on every street corner."

The marshal waited for quiet. "I can't see the problem," he drawled. "Unless he bakes bad cakes."

"Siddown, Johnson," Carl snapped.

Matt eyed the mercantile owner and raised one dark eyebrow. "You won't forget it's '*Marshal* Johnson,' now, will you?" he said in his low, steady voice. "Just thought I'd remind you all that this is a peaceable meeting.

Everybody gets to speak his mind but nobody throws a punch."

"Go back to Texas!" someone yelled.

A familiar female voice rose again. "First thing you know there'll be Chinese wives in town and Chinese kids in our school."

Another voice added to the clamor. "The Chinese will take over everything."

Leah sighed. Verena Forester had an abundance of opinions.

"Send 'em back to China!" another woman chimed.

Leah clenched her fists in her lap. This was wrong. Wrong! How could a whole town punish an innocent man just for being Chinese? She had seen it in Luzhou when someone "different" was forced to leave the village. But here, in America? Her father had taught her that America was the land of the free. No one could force Uncle Charlie to leave town.

Could they?

Someone lifted Teddy off his perch and sat down next to Leah.

"Thad!"

He settled Teddy on his lap. "Don't worry about Uncle Charlie," he whispered. "He's safe." He surveyed the roomful of bickering townspeople. "Anybody here get out of line yet?"

"Carl Ness and the barber are the worst so far," Leah murmured. "Marshal Johnson is trying to keep everything legal."

Thad cocked his head. "They all sound crazy to me. Bigoted and uninformed."

A high-pitched tirade poured out of one woman's mouth. "Everyone knows the Celestials bring disease, and God knows what else—inedible food, strange potions, pagan rituals…"

Thad sighed. "Yeah, that's Smoke River, all right. Small towns have their shortcomings."

A man at the back leaped onto an overturned fruit crate. "There's millions of 'em in San Francisco already! The Chinks are gonna take over our towns and cities… our whole country!"

"Ignorant and close-minded," Thad murmured. "I've had just about enough." He set Teddy on his feet and stood up.

"Mr. Chairman?"

Carl Ness boggled at him. "Mr. MacAllister, did you wish to speak?"

"I sure as hell do. Let's get our facts straight before we go off half-cocked and do something we'll regret."

A sullen silence fell over the crowd.

"To begin with, Ming Cha—Uncle Charlie—is just one man. He's only about five foot four and he's way too shy to threaten anyone."

"But there'll be others," someone yelled.

"That's fine with me. We've got plenty of room in this country."

"Oh, yeah? Then let 'em go somewhere else."

Thad raised his voice to reach the back of the room. "We've got bigger problems in Smoke River than one new bakery. With the drought this summer, more than half of us are going to owe the bank more than we like to think about. We should be thinking about real problems, not whether one Chinese man opens a business."

"Well, hell," a male voice shouted. "You're married to a Celestial, so you can't say otherwise, can ya?"

"Sure, I could say otherwise," Thad said in a controlled voice. "But I would be wrong. It's just plain damn wrong to make one of us less important than another, and taking away someone's right to a peaceful life in a peaceful town is wrong."

"Are we gonna listen to the fool of a man who planted *wheat?*" someone else yelled. "Wheat! Now, I ask you, does that make sense?" The speaker waited a heartbeat. "Well, neither does Thad MacAllister!"

"How come Charlie Ming-something came to Smoke River in the first place?" someone called out. "Whose uncle is he, anyway?"

Thad pinned the gaze of the speaker, a gangly man with long arms he was still waving.

"My wife, Leah, is Charlie's niece."

"Don't make no nevermind, MacAllister. It's Charlie we're talkin' about, not yer wife. Besides, she's not so welcome, neither, seein' as how she's a Chinese immigrant, too."

"Hold on a minute," Thad said in a suddenly menacing tone. "What's wrong with immigrants?"

"They don't fit in!" someone answered. "Your wife'll never last in our town. You just watch. She'll bolt and run when the going gets tough."

"Is that right?" Thad said with a laugh. "Then you don't know my wife."

"Miz MacAllister's only half Chinese," a woman sitting in back shouted. "This Charlie person is one hundred percent Chinaman."

"Question is," someone yelled, "what's a foreigner doin' opening his business in our town in the first place?"

Before Leah was even aware of moving, she was on her feet, her teeth clenched, ready for battle.

Thad took one look at her, settled back on his seat and lifted Teddy onto his knees. "Go get 'em, honey," he murmured.

"Yeah," Teddy echoed. "You kin do it, Leah. You're real smart. Go get 'em."

Go get them? Her mouth was so dry she could not swallow.

But her husband and her stepson were right. Someone besides Thad had to fight for Charlie.

She wiped her damp palms on the front of her flounced muslin skirt and faced the crowd.

Chapter Twenty

I pray the Lord will help me. I cannot do this. This was worse than anything she had faced in Luzhai. This wasn't a gang of rock-throwing bullies; it was a whole town full of adults who hated her and Uncle Charlie.

In the front row of the restless crowd opposite her, Leah spotted Noralee Ness seated on an apple crate. The girl's hands were clamped to the edge of the box and her eyes were wide.

Noralee looked back at her, expecting her to say something. The girl's father, Carl Ness, was waiting for her to make a fool of herself. An almost feral grin spread across his narrow face.

Before Leah could unclamp her jaws, Teddy reached out and gave a swift tug on her muslin skirt. She bent down and he cupped his hands and spoke into her ear.

"Remember what you taught me, Leah. Don't let 'em know you're scared." He looked up into her face for a long moment and then gave her a thumbs-up.

Leah gasped out a laugh. *For heaven's sake, what a*

grown-up thing for the boy to do. Thad must have put him up to it.

No, she realized in the next instant. It was Teddy who would remember those words. Not Thad, but his son. *Teddy wanted her to know he was on her side.* Leah's throat ached.

Carl Ness's impatient cough reminded her she was standing before a throng of angry townspeople, some of whom she did not even know. She must speak out, and she must do it now.

Suddenly she was unsure what to say. She knotted her fingers together, sucked in air, began to speak. What came out of her mouth surprised her.

"Were all of you who live in Smoke River born here, in America?"

Her question was met by some hesitant nods and more than a few grumbled no's.

Struggling to keep her hands from shaking, she faced the barber. "Mr. Poletti, where did you originally come from?"

Pleased at being singled out, the barber beamed. "From Napoli. Bee-yoo-tiful Napoli, in Italy."

"You came from Italy to America?"

"I sure did. On a big white ship."

"How about you, Mr. Pritchard? Where do you come from?"

"Amsterdam. Is in Holland. My wife and I, ve are Dutch," he said proudly.

"Mr. O'Brian, what about you?"

The red-bearded man stood up and bellowed, "Ireland, God bless 'er. The Emerald Isle. Came to work on the railroads."

"I am from Chermany," said an older woman next to Mr. O'Brian, her accent pronounced. "Both me and *mein* sister."

All at once eight-year-old Noralee Ness shot to her feet and purposefully stalked over to Leah's side of the room.

"Noralee!" her father snapped. "You get back here."

The girl spun to face him. "I can't, Papa. I'm real sorry, but what Miz Johnson taught us in school is right. In America, everyone is equal."

The mercantile owner's face flushed purple. "When I get you home, I'll—"

"Stop it, Carl," his wife ordered. "She's right."

Taking a deep breath, Leah resumed her questions. "How about you, Mrs. Rose?"

"I sailed from England, dearie. My family had a pig farm in Yorkshire."

Leah turned her gaze on the oversize man who had beaten up Thad and Uncle Charlie. "What nationality are you, Ike?"

"Svedish," he roared. "But my fader, he come from Denmark."

"My husband, Thad, comes from Scotland." She waited two heartbeats. "And I was born in Luzhai, in China."

"Oughtta go back there!" someone yelled.

"What're you tryin' to say, lady?"

"Only this," Leah replied. She waited until it grew so quiet she could hear Thad's breathing behind her.

"Do any of you feel you are better than anyone else in Smoke River?"

"Guess not," a gray-bearded man grumbled. "I got more hair than ever'body else in town, but that don't make me better'n them, just different."

Harvey and Iris Pritchard chose that moment to march across the room to Leah's side, followed by white-haired Granny Bolan. "I come from Russia," the old woman said with pride as she sat down next to Ellie and Marshal Matt Johnson. "My name used to be Bolansky."

Leah nodded. "It must be obvious then that all of us here are different in some way."

Heads nodded and suddenly Leah felt a wave of courage wash over her. She raised her head. "But this is America," she shouted in the strongest voice she had ever used. "We are all kinds of people, with all kinds of backgrounds. We all have the same rights because that is what this country stands for."

"Ya, it sure does," someone interjected in the silence.

Leah squared her shoulders. "And those rights include the right to live where we choose. To live here, in Smoke River."

A sprinkling of guess-so's and maybe's came from her audience.

Leah raised her arms to include both sides of the room. "If you do not believe all of us here in Smoke River have these rights, stand up!"

Not one person moved.

She sucked in a long breath. "Now, about Ming Cha,

my uncle Charlie. Charlie looks different from most of us, and that is because he is Chinese."

"Yeah," someone yelled. "But he sure makes good cakes!"

"So what? He's a Chinaman!" another voice responded.

"What you really mean," Leah challenged in a voice she didn't know she possessed, "is that Charlie doesn't look like everyone else in Smoke River?"

"Yeah, he's got slanty eyes." This came from one of Ellie's students.

"And he ain't white, like the rest of us." This came from the back of the room.

Old Mrs. Bolan next to Ellie banged her cane on the floor. "Well, what of it?"

"By golly," a bent, gray-bearded man spluttered. "I dunno as it makes a lot of diff'rence what color his skin is. He makes the best blackberry pie I ever tasted!"

The opposing sides of the room began slinging comments back and forth.

"No damn Chinaman's gonna show his face in our town!"

"Why not? He's got as much right as anybody."

"Oh, yeah? Prove it!"

"Don't have to," a schoolmate of Teddy's screamed. "It's in the Constitution."

"Sez who?"

"Sez Miz Johnson, that's who."

"No woman speaks for me, you son of a gun!"

"She's the schoolteacher. She oughtta know! She oughtta speak for all of us."

At that point, Marshal Johnson rose to his feet. "Folks, I'm reminding you again that having freedom of speech means everyone can say whatever crazy thing they want, but there's to be no violence."

Leah sank onto the fruit crate. She had said what she had to; now she could only watch and listen.

The heated shouting match went on for another half hour. In the middle of the uproar the Williams family and red-bearded Mr. O'Brian stalked deliberately over to Leah's side of the room.

Finally Carl Ness, his narrow face splotchy with rage, jumped to his feet and banged down his gavel so hard the cedar head flew off and clattered onto the floor. A man grabbed it and raised his arm to throw it into the opposite crowd.

Marshal Johnson heaved his tall frame upright and in an instant complete quiet settled over the room. "Let's keep it peaceful, folks."

Colonel Wash Halliday, Jeanne's husband, rose immediately and raised one hand. "I move we vote on it."

"I second the motion," the marshal said quietly. "That's democratic as hell. Vote no, and Uncle Charlie's bakery goes. Vote yes, and it stays."

"But either way," Colonel Halliday added, "Charlie has a right to live in Smoke River. Right, Marshal?"

Johnson gave a decisive nod. "Absolutely damn right."

Colonel Halliday pinned the mercantile owner with a look that could wither cornstalks. "Right, Carl?"

"Hell, no!" Carl yelled. "I'm never gonna agree to—"

His wife jabbed him in the ribs and he shifted uneasily. "Oh, all right," he grumbled. "When ya put it that way, I guess he's got a right."

"That's real smart of you, Carl," the marshal said with a grin. "I'll set up a ballot box at the mercantile. We'll vote on Tuesday about whether Charlie's bakery stays. That's all. Have a peaceful night, folks."

Thad and Leah mounted their horses in silence and headed back to the ranch. Teddy rode in front of Thad, talking excitedly about the evening's event. Leah, still shaking from her speech-making ordeal, could not say a word.

They rode side by side for a mile without speaking, and then, where the town road split, Thad caught her bridle and leaned his large frame close to hers.

"I'm proud of you, Leah."

A warm flush washed through her. He was really proud of her? For some reason she wanted to cry.

He said nothing more, just rode on. Teddy's chatter brought only an occasional noncommittal grunt from his father.

Leah tightened her hands on the reins. Sharp darts of anxiety were beginning to jump in her stomach. What was Thad really thinking? Finally she could not stand his silence one more minute.

She cleared her throat. "Where did you take Uncle Charlie during the meeting?"

Thad snorted. "You mean where'd I hide him from the tar and feathers? I took him up to Verena's."

"Verena's! *Verena's?* Verena's apartment is right

above the meeting hall!" Angry words bubbled up, but Leah forced them back.

"Thought he'd be safest in the bosom of his enemies, so to speak. Verena never knew he was there. She'd already gone down to the meeting."

Disbelief welled inside Leah. "Thad, how could you?"

"Why the hell not? Charlie loved it. He made tea in her fancy flowered teapot and even scrubbed off her stovetop."

Leah stared at her husband. If she lived ten thousand years, she would never plumb the mysteries of this man. Her mind whirled with questions.

"Why Verena?"

"She's an old friend, Leah. She may be outspoken, but Hattie always liked her."

Hattie! An unwelcome heat flooded Leah's cheeks. She hated to admit it, but she was jealous! Jealous not only of Hattie, but of Verena Forester. Blindingly, stupidly jealous. Suddenly ashamed, Leah felt her face flame. With an effort she kept her eyes on the mare's thick mane.

"There's nothing to be upset about, Leah. Verena didn't know anything about providing a safe haven for Uncle Charlie. Then I took Charlie to the jail."

"The jail?"

"Now, don't get all riled up. The marshal let Charlie sleep there on a cot so he could keep an eye on him."

Leah bit her lip. That would be just like Thad—do something unexpected and think she would understand.

Another question nagged at her. If Verena had been

interested in Thad, why did he not marry her? Was it because of Teddy's dislike? Verena would have made a fine housekeeper. Why had he sent for Leah?

She wanted reassurance from Thad that he wanted *her,* not Verena. Now as never before she hungered for some indication that Thad cared for her, despite his pre-occupation with other things.

If Thad did not care…

But she couldn't think about that now. Instead she pressed her lips together and resolved to keep silent.

For the moment, at least.

Chapter Twenty-One

Tuesday dawned with a sky so blue it reminded Leah of her mother's treasured lapis lazuli necklace, a wedding gift from Father. By breakfast time, the heat in the small house felt as if a prairie fire smoldered under the plank floor.

Teddy poked listlessly at his oatmeal and Thad ate nothing at all, just sat staring out the window, nursing his mug of coffee. Leah tried to eat, but her stomach roiled with such jitters she gave it up after a single spoonful.

Today the townspeople would decide about Uncle Charlie's bakery.

A muscle in Thad's jaw was jumping rhythmically and she wrenched her gaze away. He was obviously troubled. For days now he had slept in the barn.

Suddenly he jerked to his feet and, without a word, strode out the front door. Leah stared after him with a sinking feeling in her stomach. Why could he not tell her what was bothering him?

Hurriedly, she washed the cups and bowls and put them on the shelf, but this morning instead of stacking the china neatly as she usually did, she shoved the pieces in any which way. Her life, she reflected, felt as disordered as her dishes.

What was happening to their marriage?

She shook the thought away, but the question stuck in her brain like a blob of pitch. She stood watching Thad out the window, striding across the pasture with his hands jammed in his pockets.

Then, with a resolute shake of her head, she brushed aside her fear, gathered up her hat and headed for the barn to saddle the mare. It was Tuesday.

Voting day.

Despite the stifling heat, Smoke River's main street was bustling with activity. Leah tied up her mare at the hitching rail and joined the crowd of townspeople jostling each other outside the mercantile door. Thad would ride in later to vote; he and Teddy had stayed at the ranch to dribble what water they could on the sun-seared wheat stalks. But that would not be much, she thought with a stab of unease. Because of the drought, their well was going dry.

Everything was dry! Thad's interest in her was shriveling up like the mudflat in the pasture where the pond used to be. Things could not get any worse.

But she knew they could. What if Uncle Charlie lost his bakery business? Where would he go? What if Thad never returned to her bed? What if the feeling of oneness they had once begun to share had died?

A sharp-edged pain lanced her chest and she caught her breath. What would she do then?

She took her place at the end of the long line of townspeople waiting to cast their ballots. Instantly the loud conversation around her dwindled to an awkward silence. Leah winced. They must have been talking about Uncle Charlie.

Or her.

The line edged forward a step. Behind her she heard Darla Weatherby's high, thin voice. "I think it's purely shameful, having a Chinaman living in Smoke River. Right out in plain sight, too. Mama and I are voting no."

"Me, too," said another voice—Lucy Nichols, Leah gathered from the tone. "My mama's having palpitations whenever the word *Chinese* comes up."

A claw dug into Leah's spine. She kept her face averted.

At that moment a scowling man stomped out of the mercantile and barreled into her.

"S'cuse me, Miz MacAllister." He jerked his head toward the mercantile as he brushed past. "Got a bad smell in there. That damned marshal's pokin' his nose into everything."

Before she could ask, shouts erupted from the store. Men's voices. She stepped out of line to see, but a large figure blocked her view. Ike Bruhn! Thank goodness Thad was not here; the last time Thad and Ike had tangled she had used up the last of the liniment.

When she finally reached the mercantile entrance the first thing that caught her eye was the lean figure of Colonel Wash Halliday, bent over a four-pound tin of Arbuckles' coffee. A slot had been cut in the top to serve as a ballot box.

A grim-faced Carl Ness stood stiff as a broom at one end of the counter. Opposite Carl, Marshal Johnson, Ellie's husband, lounged casually against a display of hoes and axes and snowshoes. *Showshoes?*

Leah studied the odd-shaped wooden objects. They were a reminder that eventually this awful dry, tense summer would be over, followed by fall—harvest season—with crisp air and scarlet maple leaves and, oh, please, God, some rain! And then would come winter, with snow. It did not seem possible these dreadful months would finally be over.

The line swayed forward another arm's length and a tantalizing spicy aroma wafted on the air. Leah peered past the mercantile display shelves to an upturned bushel basket next to the ballot box; on top rested a familiar flower-patterned platter heaped with cookies. Big ones. With raisins.

Her heart flip-flopped. Uncle Charlie might be diminutive and shy and soft-spoken, but he was clever.

People filed by, snagged a cookie and dropped their folded paper ballots into the Arbuckles' tin. Leah clapped her hand over her mouth to keep from laughing. The pile of cookies was diminishing so fast there would be only crumbs left by the time Thad rode into town.

Ellie joined her in line. "I just came from the schoolhouse. Plans are shaping up for the spelling bee."

Four people ahead of them, Leah spotted a woman she had not noticed before. The sadness and resignation in her face tugged at her.

"Ellie, who is that?"

"Elvira Sorensen. She rarely comes into town."

"She looks so unhappy. Do you know why?"

"Not exactly. Her husband grows bush beans, and they have lived on a farm outside Smoke River for years, but there are no Sorensen children at school. I have often wondered why."

The woman kept her head down, but when she looked up to drop in her paper ballot, Leah flinched. Elvira Sorensen appeared dried out, her face lifeless.

Was she mistreated? Or did she have a husband who—Leah caught her lower lip between her teeth—who no longer cared for her?

Leah could not bear to think about it. She shook off the thought, then stepped forward, picked up the offered square of paper and a pencil, and marked her ballot with a big *yes*.

When she turned to leave, she collided with Mrs. Sorensen in the doorway. For a brief instant the woman looked into Leah's eyes. Her face was a mask of desolation.

Leah swallowed over a lump the size of a lemon. Would she end up like Mrs. Sorensen? She tried to scrub the thought from her mind and walked to the hitching rail to mount Lady.

Just as she reined away and headed toward the edge of town, she glimpsed Thad, looking handsome in the new shirt of white linen she had finished yesterday. His battered gray Stetson was tipped down so his face was hidden, but from the set of his shoulders she knew he was not smiling.

His big black gelding moved slowly up the street toward her, its pace unhurried. She stepped her mare forward to meet him.

"Thad?"

He glanced up. "Looks like everybody in town came to vote. How's Uncle Charlie doing?"

Leah gave a short laugh. "Uncle Charlie is unsinkable. He is busy supplying cookies to the townspeople. You had best hurry before they are all eaten."

"In a minute." Thad pushed his hat brim back with his thumb, and his gaze settled on her face. "First, there's something I want to tell you."

A rock dropped into her belly. She could see his eyes now; they were a stormy gray-blue, and the bleak expression in them made her insides go cold.

"What is it? Tell me."

He rubbed his jaw. "The wheat's pretty far gone. The well went dry before we could dump even one bucket of water on the crop, and there's not a goddam thing I can—" His voice choked off.

She leaned forward to touch his arm. "Oh, Thad, I am so sorry."

"I figure I can wait two more days for rain, then I'll have to plow it under." He studied his saddle horn.

Her heart twisted. What could she do to help him?

She gripped her reins so tight the mare jerked. "I thought I would make potato salad for supper tonight, with some cold sliced beef. When you come home, we could eat out on the porch, where it is cool."

"Yeah. Sure." He reached out and squeezed her shoulder. But his eyes had that faraway look she was learning to fear. In silence he moved the gelding on past her, and her chest tightened into an ache.

She blinked hard to keep back the tears, dug her heels into the mare's flanks and galloped down the road until she could scarcely breathe for the dust.

Potato salad was a small thing, but it was all she could think of to offer.

Long after dark Thad started up the porch steps with tired legs and a mind fuzzy with exhaustion. Leah sat on a chair in the shadows, but she didn't say a word, just looked at him. In the pale moonlight her face appeared drawn. Only then did he remember she had expected him for supper.

With a sigh he climbed the last step and shoved his hat back. "I'm sorry, Leah."

He could say he had been jawing with Henry Pritchard and Wash Halliday about the drought. Or that he'd stayed at the mercantile to help tally the ballots. Or...

No, he couldn't. He could never lie to Leah.

"I plain forgot all about your potato salad."

She stood up slowly. "I saved your supper. I will bring it out here."

"I can get it. In the pantry, is it? And I'll bring you some...tea?"

"Coffee," she murmured. She sank back onto the chair. "Good and strong."

The screen door swished shut behind him. Sometimes he hated that calmness she had. It'd be a hell of a lot easier if she laid into him, like most wives would.

He found the plate of potato salad and sliced beef waiting for him under a damp tea towel in the coolest part of the pantry. On his way out, he juggled two mugs of coffee from the blue speckleware pot on the stove and pushed open the screen door with his knee. Lord, the night smelled good—earth and the pungent scent of pine trees.

"Teddy has finished his supper," she said. Thad handed over her coffee and settled himself uneasily on the straight-back dining chair beside her.

"Where is he now?"

A ghost of a smile flitted across her mouth. "Up in his loft, reading the last chapter of *Ivanhoe.*"

Thad raised his brows. "I'll be damned."

"Remember, I stopped reading it aloud just before the joust between Ivanhoe and Front de Boeuf. Teddy wants to see how it ends."

Thad heaved a sigh and forked potato salad into his mouth. "You're a good teacher, Leah. You know how to prick a boy's interest. To be honest, I don't remember where you left off reading."

"You missed a great many chapters, Thad."

"Yeah, guess I have." He knew she was referring to more than *Ivanhoe,* but right now he didn't feel up to tackling the real issue.

"After I left town I couldn't stop thinking about that damn wheat. Just couldn't get it out of my mind."

Leah nodded and sipped her coffee. "You have missed many things because of it."

"Yeah, I have to admit that." From the unsmiling

line of his wife's lips, he guessed he'd missed a lot more than he realized.

Something had changed. She was different, some-how. Almost…what? Not angry, just…distant.

Well, sure she is, you damn fool. You haven't been close to her in weeks. But he'd thought about her. There were nights in the barn when he'd wanted her so much he'd counted the hours until daylight. But something clawing at him in the dark had held him back.

He still dreamed of Leah. Even now, just the scent of her hair floating on the balmy air made him close his eyes with longing.

Leah leaned forward to set her coffee mug down on the porch. "What about your wheat, Thad?"

Her voice, low and controlled, sent a shiver of pre-monition through him. He hunched over his still-warm coffee.

"Have you ever thought about what that field really represents to you?"

"Well, sure. I knew it was a gamble from the begin-ning. I'm known hereabouts as a successful rancher, so growing wheat was a challenge. A matter of pride, too, I guess."

"I think it is more than that," she said quietly. "I think something is twisted around in your mind, that your wheat field represents some kind of control you want over your future."

He could think of nothing to say. He swallowed hard and cleared his throat. "Nah. Growing wheat is an ex-periment. This land is prime wheat country."

"That may be true," she replied. "But there is still more to it."

His shirt collar began to chafe his neck. "What more is there?"

She waited a long minute before answering. "I think it is all mixed up with losing your wife. I think you are afraid it might happen again."

For a moment he couldn't draw breath. "You're way off track, Leah. Besides, what's that got to do with my wheat? I'm just a man trying to do his best for his family."

"You don't want to think about it, I know. Or about me. So you think about your wheat field."

"You're wrong, dammit. You're seeing some significance that isn't there."

She watched his face. "*Am* I wrong? You don't eat breakfast or supper with Teddy and me. You sleep in the barn. You avoid being close to me."

"I—" Thad snapped his jaw shut. Hell, a worried woman could imagine all sorts of things. Some of her words pricked him, but dammit, his wheat field had nothing to do with her. Or Hattie. Or anything else.

He leaned forward and lifted both her hands in his. "Leah, with no rain since last December, any rancher would be worried."

"I know," she murmured. "I understand that."

But she didn't. He could tell by the odd, hopeless look in her gray-green eyes. She didn't understand, not really. He let out a heavy gust of air. But he'd be damned if he knew what to do about it.

Maybe he should have owned up to her right off,

told her how scared he was, not just about the wheat but about losing someone he loved again. Maybe now it was too late.

He released her trembling hands and sank his head onto his palms. The joke was on him. He'd fallen in love with his delicate-looking, industrious, sensible and thoroughly female wife. He loved her, and wild horses couldn't make him stop.

Yeah, he could force himself to stay out of Leah's bed, but now, after weeks of protecting his heart by keeping his distance, he realized he was losing what he most wanted to hold on to.

Chapter Twenty-Two

Leah had just puffed out the kerosene lamp and turned to crawl into bed when an unwelcome thought invaded her mind. She had seen something she could not understand in Thad's troubled expression and the confusion that shadowed his eyes. Something that had nothing to do with his wheat field.

He was not being honest with her. Was it because he did not understand his own mind? Perhaps he was not being honest with himself, either. How could a man as intelligent as Thad MacAllister be so blind to what was happening to their marriage? Did it not matter to him?

She knew she would not sleep, so she padded into the kitchen. A pan of thick cream waited in the pantry to be churned—just what she needed, something to do with her hands. She rinsed out the wooden churn with hot water from the teakettle, dried the interior and poured in the cream. The blurping sounds decreased as the churn filled up; she attached the wooden paddle and began to turn the crank.

As she worked she thought about Elvira Sorensen. The woman was obviously struggling to live with some kind of unhappiness, and Leah felt more than a tug of sympathy. Perhaps Mrs. Sorensen, too, was married to a man who did not love her?

Leah's thoughts turned to Thad and herself. She knew she was not what he had expected when he'd sent for her; he had married her out of decency and kindness. But she had grown to love him and, after that night when they had made love, she'd thought he cared for her, as well.

She tried to concentrate on the sloshing sounds inside the churn, to clear her mind, but her thoughts went roiling on. How could she live with a man who did not care about her?

Would she end up like Elvira Sorensen?

She slapped the paddle against the inside of the churn, and Teddy's face appeared over the loft railing.

"Whatcha doin', Leah? It's gotta be past midnight."

"I am churning butter," she said steadily. "Go back to sleep."

"Can't."

She rested her arm for a moment. "Why not?"

"Someone's trampin' around in the barn. I kin hear it through my window."

"Probably your father. Go to sleep."

Teddy's head disappeared from the railing and then instantly reappeared. "How come Pa's in the barn so late?"

Leah closed her eyes. So Teddy had not realized his father slept in the barn rather than in the bed with her.

"Didja have a fight? I heard voices on the porch, but you weren't yellin' or nuthin'."

"Not a fight, exactly," Leah said over a tight throat. "Merely a…misunderstanding."

The boy's eyes widened. "What about?"

"About…well, about…" What *was* it about, exactly? About Thad's blindness when it came to his wheat field? About her fear that she did not matter to him?

"About grown-up things, Teddy. Things between a husband and wife."

"Huh. I knew Pa shouldn't'ta married you. You're smarter than he is."

Leah gasped. Unsure whether to laugh or cry, she said nothing, and after a long moment, Teddy's voice rose again.

"Hey, Leah? You got any more books like *Ivanhoe?*"

She could not answer. Books like *Ivanhoe.* Oh, if only she did, then she could immerse herself in something more important to her than her day-to-day life with Thad. That must be what sad-eyed Mrs. Sorensen had done over the years—built a separate life for herself.

Suddenly Leah felt cold all over. Tears blinded her. She bent her head so Teddy would not see, and a wave of clarity washed over her, as if a bucket of ice-cold spring water had been dumped on her brain.

She slammed her open hand against the wooden churn and the paddle whooshed to a stop. This marriage might not be important to Thad, but it was important to *her*—more important than anything else.

She lifted her arm, closed her fingers around the

wooden handle and again started to churn. They would need butter for breakfast. But after breakfast, she must decide what to do.

She had two choices: live the rest of her life like Mrs. Sorensen…or leave.

But she must do something—anything—to avoid simply giving up.

Thad lifted his head from the bed he'd made in the straw and sniffed the air. Coffee! What the… He crawled to the edge of the hay-filled loft and looked down.

The barn door stood wide open, admitting a swath of sunshine that reached to his ladder, and in the middle of it stood Leah, her straight black hair gleaming in the light. In one hand she gripped a mug of coffee and in the other she balanced a plate of…flapjacks! Lord bless her!

"Thad?" she called, her voice uncertain.

"Up here. In the loft."

She tipped her head up. "I brought you some breakfast."

"Well, thanks, Leah. I'll come down." He descended the ladder, and at the bottom, turned to face her.

She hadn't moved. Her eyes met his and a fist began to pummel his gut. Jumping jennies, all he had to do was look at her and he wanted to fold her into his arms.

"Leah—"

She didn't let him finish. "I brought coffee, strong like you prefer it."

Thad moved toward her. "That's darn nice of you, Leah."

"I am doing what I can," she said, her voice so soft he could barely hear it. "I am trying to be a good wife."

Oh, Lord. She looked small and defenseless, and his heart was doing somersaults. He clenched his teeth so hard his jaw hurt.

Leah was like no other woman he'd ever known—delicate and resilient at the same time. He prayed it was the resilient side he was seeing now.

"Thad." She looked up at him, her face calm but her eyes suspiciously shiny. "Tomorrow I would like you to eat breakfast at the house. With Teddy and me."

He wanted to. Wanted to watch her flitting about the kitchen, humming the way she always did. But something dark and heavy inside kept him from agreeing.

"I…I'll try, Leah." He cringed at the lie.

"I do not believe you," she said quietly. "I do not believe that you want to be with us. With me."

Something in his chest tightened, then started to crack apart. He couldn't lie to her again.

"I do want to be with you."

She tried to smile. "But no matter what you say, you are *not* with me. And the way you avoid me…well, it tells me something."

"Yeah? What?" He didn't want to hear this. He wanted to tramp away from her, over the pasture to his wheat field, but he couldn't leave it—her—like this.

Her smile faltered. "It tells me that…that our marriage does not matter to you."

His stomach plunged toward his boots. "Leah, believe me, it does matter. It matters so much that I—" His voice went hoarse.

He had to get out of here, away from her small, honest face and the anguish in her eyes.

She didn't say a word, just waited.

He shifted from foot to foot. "I guess we need to talk this through, huh?"

Very slowly, she bent her neck in a nod.

He drew in a shaky gulp of air. "Leah, you think there's enough potato salad left over for supper on the porch tonight? Together?"

Her gaze locked with his and again she tried to smile. "I think so."

Suddenly Leah wanted to wrap her arms around him, ease the worry lines deepening in his forehead. In his eyes there was an anguish that tightened her throat into an ache. She knew she loved this man, but she had not realized how deeply until this moment.

Thad MacAllister had won her admiration from the first hour she had spent on his ranch, watching him wrestle the sewing machine up the porch steps. And oh, the expression on his face that first night when he'd looked down at the plate of *chow fun.*

But did he care about her? She remembered his boyish hunger the night he had made love with her, his strength and gentleness. She remembered his look of pride and concern when she had tumbled off the mare and then finally managed to ride it to the pasture fence and back.

Her feelings for Thad went bone-deep, and nothing, *nothing,* would ever change them. But what about *his* feelings?

"I am riding into town this morning, Thad. I want to

see how the vote on Uncle Charlie's bakery came out, and whether he is all right."

"Charlie should be fine. I gave him my revolver last night."

"You did? You really did?" Leah stepped close, stretched up on her toes and brushed her lips across his scratchy cheek. "Thank you, Thad."

He snaked out an arm and caught her around the waist, then instantly released her. "I thought Teddy and I'd ride over to the Halliday place, maybe see about borrowing—" he hesitated "—borrowing a plow horse. For, um, for my wheat."

He half turned away from her and gazed out the barn door toward the field. Her throat closed. In its dried-up state, the wheat was lost. He would be forced to plow it under, along with everything it represented to him.

Her eyes blurry with tears, she turned toward the stall where her mare waited.

The closer she drew to the mercantile and Uncle Charlie's bakery, the more delicious the air smelled. Her mouth watered at the aroma—something cinnamony with a trace of lemon.

Short, slightly plump Uncle Charlie, clad in his white apron, was working in front of his establishment, industriously sweeping litter off the board walkway.

"Ah, Niece Leah." His round face beamed up at her.

"Uncle Charlie, did you win the vote?"

"I still here. Vote was close, but six more votes for yes. Bakery stays."

"Oh, Uncle, I am so glad." She pried one of his hands off the broom handle and squeezed it hard.

"I glad, too. You bring young Teddy to wash front window?"

Leah's gaze fell on the spotless multipaned glass and she smiled. Uncle Charlie did not need help from Teddy; he simply liked to have the boy around. Of course, Teddy liked sampling the cookies.

"Thad and Teddy rode out to the Hallidays'. Something about a workhorse to plow—" She closed her mouth with a snap. Lord in heaven, she couldn't say it—that Thad was giving up on his wheat.

"What matter, Niece Leah? Your face white as clean apron."

She managed a smile. "It is the heat, Uncle." She dropped her gaze to the ground.

Uncle Charlie stepped forward. "You come inside. Drink water and rest."

Inside the fragrant-smelling bakery, Charlie folded her hands around a glass of cool water, which she gulped down. Then he offered a platter of her favorite cookies, the ones with lots of raisins. She was chewing on a cookie when, through the front window, she spotted Verena Forester bustling down the walkway.

Leah rose and, surprising herself, purposely stepped out into the dressmaker's path. "Good morning, Verena."

The tall, bony woman halted in front of her and peered at the platter of Uncle Charlie's cookies in Leah's hand. "Why, that's odd. That's the same platter

I saw at the mercantile yesterday, loaded with cookies."
She looked closer. "And the same kind of cookies, too."

Verena confronted Charlie, who was hovering in the
doorway. "You were buying votes, weren't you, Mr.—?"

"Ming Cha," Third Uncle replied in a quiet voice.
"But in America, call myself Charlie."

Verena pursed her lips. "I see." She gave the small
Chinese man a thorough once-over. "Come to think of
it, something else is odd, as well. Something that oc-
curred the night of the town meeting."

"No cookies at meeting," Charlie said quickly. "I
hide in secret place with Mr. MacAllister."

Verena nodded. "The night of the meeting," she said
slowly, "I hurried downstairs so I wouldn't miss anything. I was in such a rush I even left my supper dishes
in the sink."

She turned a frown on Charlie, who began edging
backward into the bakery. "When I came home after
the meeting, all those dirty dishes had been washed
and put away."

She pinned Leah with blue eyes hard as stones. "I
don't trust you, Leah. Something is going on that I am
unaware of."

Leah masked her tattered nerves behind a placid expression. "I do not trust you, either, Verena. So we are
even."

"Well, I never!" The older woman lifted her skirts
and marched on down the walkway. "Never in my entire life…" Her voice faded as she stomped up the stairs
to her apartment and slammed the door.

Leah stared after the woman until another voice,

this one soft and hesitant, spoke up. "That woman is rude because she is unhappy. She has no one to love."

Leah glanced behind her. "Mrs. Sorensen!"

The woman inclined her sunbonnet-covered head. "Mrs. MacAllister, isn't it? Leah?"

Leah nodded. "How are you, Mrs. Sorensen?"

"Just fine, I'm sure. And I will be finer after a slice of lemon cake. Such small pleasures make life worth living."

"Oh, but surely—" Leah bit her tongue.

"Sometimes life isn't a happy thing, my girl. An occasional slice of lemon cake can make things tolerable."

"Y-yes, of course," Leah stammered.

The birdlike woman studied Leah with an intent expression, and then a ghost of a smile flitted across her lined face. "You are young, my girl. There is much of life ahead of you. We must all learn to find small pleasures to sustain us."

Leah stared at her in silence.

The woman gestured at the bakery window. "This is what I do to survive," she said. "And now I will bid you good-morning." She swept through the doorway.

All that morning Leah thought about her chance encounter with Mrs. Sorensen, and about her words. The woman was right; small pleasures, like the scent of honeysuckle or the feel of Teddy's curls under her hand when she trimmed his hair—such things were lifesaving.

She did her shopping at the mercantile under the icy glare of Carl Ness, ran her hand over the snowshoes on display and purchased three pairs of winter socks for Teddy.

On her way past Uncle Charlie's shining window, she recalled what Mrs. Sorensen had said, and on impulse turned her steps into the bakery. Thad loved Charlie's lemon cake.

Chapter Twenty-Three

The closer Thad drew to the Halliday spread, the more unsettled he felt. Teddy had wanted to go fishing, but Thad had put him off. He wanted to talk to Wash about his wheat. About Leah. About…everything.

But he hadn't a clue where to begin. It went against a man's grain to talk about personal matters, even to a friend. But he knew he had to do it.

He set his jaw, rode the black gelding up the long lane to the Double H ranch house, and dismounted. Wash Halliday strode out onto the wide front porch.

"Good to see you, Thad. How's that colt working out for Teddy?"

"Colt's fine. Teddy brushes him three times a day and feeds him apples and sugar lumps."

Wash grinned. "Sounds like true love."

Something must have shown on Thad's face because Wash peered at him and frowned. "What's on your mind, Thad? Come to buy another pony?"

"Uh, no. I came to, uh, borrow a plow horse."

"Plow horse! Bit late in the season to plow, isn't it?"

"Yeah, maybe. Trouble is…"

Wash's wife, Jeanne, stepped off the porch and came toward them, a mug of coffee in each hand. Thad touched his hat brim.

"Morning, Jeanne. Coffee sure smells good."

Jeanne Halliday looked into his face with piercing gray-green eyes. "Ah, something is on your mind, is it not? I see it in your face."

Wash touched his wife's shoulder. "Now, Jeanne…"

"She's right," Thad said. "Must stick out all over."

Jeanne glanced from her husband to Thad and back again. Then she nodded and gave them a half smile. "You men have some talk to do, *n'est ce pas?*" Tactfully she turned away, disappeared into the big white farmhouse and shut the front door with a decisive click.

Wash drew him over to the front fence and planted his elbows on the top rail. "What's on your mind, Thad?"

Jumping june bugs, what *wasn't* on his mind? He hooked his boot heel on the bottom rail and leaned one knee into the rough-cut wood. "What's on my mind is, well, mostly it's my wheat experiment." He stopped and swallowed hard. "Nah, that's not it. Mostly it's Leah."

"Trouble comes in brigades, doesn't it?" Wash said evenly. "I've got to tell you, every rancher in the valley thought you'd gone loco when you planted that wheat field."

"Yeah, they made that plenty clear."

"And when you married Leah, every spinster in the county was mad as a wet hen."

Thad worried his boot against the fence rail. "I don't think I'm crazy for either one, Wash. But, dammit, nothing's working out right."

"Something going wrong with Leah?"

"Oh, hell no. She keeps Teddy well fed and cared for, and she keeps the house the cleanest it's been since I built it. I'm damn proud of her. She washes our clothes each week and irrigates her garden with the used water. She's learned to cook dishes I've never heard of, things called cauliflower ah grat-something and beef bour-gone-none. Names are funny but they sure taste good."

He broke off and looked away. "That is, until I stopped eating meals at the house. And started sleeping in the barn."

"That bad, huh? A woman can sure tie a man in knots." Wash shot him a look and chuckled. "Jeanne thinks you're putting your money on the wrong horse."

"She does, huh?"

"Depends on which horse is most important, I guess—Leah or your wheat field. 'Wheat cannot love you back' is the way Jeanne put it."

"Ah, hell, Wash. I've wanted to try wheat for years. Trouble is, it got so important that I—well, I guess I paid more attention to my field than my wife."

Wash snorted. "Maybe you are loco! Now you've gotta decide whether to cut and run…or stay and fight." He slapped the fence rail. "What's it gonna be?"

Thad bit his lower lip. "Wish I knew."

"Kinda chancey, ridin' two horses in the same race, isn't it?"

Thad glanced away from his friend's piercing gaze.

"Yeah. Seems like I'm doin' it all wrong. Maybe Jeanne's right. I put my money on the wrong—"

"Hold on a minute, Thad. It happens I don't agree with Jeanne. I think both the wheat and your wife are important, so I say a man has to put his money on both of them. And then pray like hell."

Thad said nothing, just looked out across the fenced pasture land.

"That's why you want the plow horse, isn't it? You're giving up."

"Yeah. I'm starting to see things clearer now. I'd— I'd rather lose the wheat than lose Leah. And…"

Wash pivoted and put his spine against the fence. "And?"

"And…" Thad groaned. "And I hope like hell it's not too late."

Wash nodded. "Want to know what else Jeanne thinks?"

No, he didn't really want to know. But Wash was already speaking.

"Jeanne thinks a lot of your wife, Thad. And knowing Jeanne, that's saying something. She says Leah is not made of fluff. Leah has a lot more courage and toughness inside than shows on the outside."

"That she does," Thad muttered.

"I think you both have guts to do what you've done, and that includes getting married."

"It didn't take guts for me, Wash. I liked her from the start."

Wash blew out his breath in a sigh. "Maybe. But it takes even more guts to make things work out in a marriage." He clapped Thad on the shoulder. "I'll bring the plow horse over tomorrow."

Thad mounted and rode on down the lane. The last thing he wanted to do was give up on anything; it went against everything he lived by. But right now his back was against the wall. He hated the thought of plowing his wheat under. But when he thought about losing Leah...

He took the long way home to give himself time to think things through. On his way through town he stopped in to check on Uncle Charlie.

"How Niece Leah?" Charlie took one look at Thad's face and propped his hands at his ample waist. "Better question, how Niece Leah's husband? Look like fighting dragons."

Worse than dragons, Thad acknowledged. He was fighting himself.

Leah pumped the last dribble of water from the sink spout into the teakettle and set it on the stove. It was too hot to stay indoors, waiting for her tea, so she stepped through the back door screen and picked up the two buckets of water she'd saved from the washing.

Lugging one in each hand, she walked out to her kitchen garden and plunked them down without sloshing at one end of a row of withered carrot tops. The bush beans climbing on the lath structure she and Teddy had built looked droopy, and the small yellow squash sheltered under the spreading green leaves hadn't grown an inch since she last looked. She had planted potatoes, as well, but the aboveground foliage had not yet sprouted.

The beets and radishes, even the turnip tops, were wilting, but if she waited to water until evening, when it was cooler, she'd lose them all. It would be an uphill battle to save them, but she had to try. Once she decided something was worth saving, she never gave up.

A voice nagged in her brain. Did that apply to Thad, as well? Her feelings of happiness with him and hope for their future together were withering, just like her vegetables.

A single question rang over and over in her head: *What should I do?*

She dribbled another scant cup of wash water onto the row of radishes, then sat back to assess the entire plot.

Everything was dying. Even her heartbeat, inside her tightening chest, was sluggish.

Again she dipped the tin cup into the pail and portioned out the life-giving water, until her temples began to pound under the violent sun overhead. *What should I do? What should I do?*

What did she want for herself in this life? Long ago in China, Father and Mother had decided they wanted each other. For the rest of their lives the two of them had struggled, shunned by her mother's family but unable to desert Father's Christian mission. Still, they had found joy in being together and in raising Leah. But how difficult it must have been.

She emptied the first water bucket and started on the second. Oddly enough, she thought of Mrs. Sorensen. The strained face of that unhappy woman had lodged in her mind since yesterday.

Could she, like Elvira Sorensen, survive without the nourishment of love? If Thad did not care for her, what then?

Leah dipped and poured, dipped and poured, her throat aching. Finally she let the tears come, but even then, she kept on watering. At the end of a row of turnips she sat back on her heels and let her hands fall idle.

I could leave, she thought miserably. Leave Smoke River, and Thad, and go…where? There was no place for her in China now, and she knew San Francisco was too dangerous for a lone female. And how would she live?

What about Portland? She could take the train east and do…what? Teach school?

She swiped her forearm across her wet cheeks. No, she could not. She could not abandon Teddy, as his mother had when she died. Leah could not abandon Thad, either, not after the kindness he had shown by marrying her.

And, she realized with a sigh, she could not do that to herself. She loved Teddy. And, heaven help her, she loved Thad.

Idly she ran her hand over the bean leaves, noting the soft, scratchy feel of the undersides. Even if her husband did not care for her as she cared for him, perhaps she could learn to survive with half a life, learn to make her own happiness.

But she had to let Thad know the cost. She knotted her fingers together so tightly they began to tingle.

Thad dismounted at the pump in the yard to wash up before supper, but a few strokes of the handle brought up only a scant half cup of water. He removed his hat and bent to splash the water over his face and hands; he hated to be near Leah smelling of horse and sweat.

After the afternoon with Wash Halliday, trying to hash out what to do about his wheat, and about Leah, he'd ridden home thinking over what his friend had said. Two things stuck in his brain: first, Thad could borrow the plow horse. And second, he was a damn fool.

Jeanne had been even more blunt. "You are a good man, Thad, but you do not see the big goose that flies right in front of your nose."

He hung the dipper back on the hook and stood up. The early evening light spread a shimmery golden haze over the pasture, and when he gazed at it, his breath caught. At times his land was so beautiful it made his throat hurt.

In the barn he unsaddled the gelding, fed him some grain and brushed his dark hide until it shone. He spent as long as he could with the animal. He'd built this barn, and with its familiar plank walls and earthy smells, he felt safe here.

But dammit, he had to face up to other things that didn't feel so safe. He squared his shoulders and tramped over to the porch.

Leah sat in a tree-shaded rocking chair. He started up the steps, but her voice stopped him. "I watered my garden with wash water this morning," she said in a matter-of-fact tone. "The well is going dry."

"Yeah, I know," he murmured. He settled into the empty chair beside her and stretched his legs out in front of him. "Where's Teddy?"

"He came home about an hour ago. He ate his supper and now he's up in the loft, reading *Last of the Mohicans*."

With relief, Thad latched on to the neutral topic. "Good book. You ever read it?"

"Oh, yes. Father had me read all kinds of books, even the poems of Wordsworth." She blushed prettily and studied her toes. "Are you hungry?"

Thad grunted, afraid to speak for fear his voice would sound unsteady.

"I will bring our dinner plates." She disappeared through the screen door. Before he could stop himself, he found himself beside her in the stifling kitchen.

"Leah, I—"

"I made coffee," she said quickly. She unhooked two mugs from the shelf and handed them to him.

A queer little stab of joy danced through him. He liked this, being in the kitchen with her. He liked it a lot. Maybe too much, but at this moment he felt so worn down he didn't want to analyze it. He just knew he liked it.

"Thanks for making coffee. Guess you'd rather have—"

"I am learning to like coffee," she said quietly. From the pantry she brought two already loaded plates, and snagged a couple of forks from the cutlery drawer. Thad poured coffee into both mugs.

They ate on the porch without talking, listening to the night sounds. A breeze shushed through the two maple trees shading the house. An owl's cry echoed from the barn. In the darkness, the scent of earth and growing things cleansed the air. Thad shut his eyes. The sounds and smells were clean and strong with life.

He snatched up his fork and shoved a huge mouthful of potato salad past his lips. "Tastes different tonight. Better."

"I added a chopped apple from our tree. It makes it crunchy and adds some sweetness—at least that's what Miss Beecher says."

"Who's Miss Beecher?"

Leah laughed softly. "Miss Beecher is our cook. Have you not noticed? Miss Beecher and I are becoming good friends."

Thad shifted in his chair, crossed and recrossed his legs, and drew patterns on his plate with his fork. The connection in his mind between the wheat field and Leah was still fuzzy, but it was growing clearer. One thing he knew for sure—he was damn scared.

"What is troubling you, Thad? You are as jumpy as Teddy's colt."

He couldn't answer because he wasn't sure. Or maybe he was sure, but he didn't know how to say it.

"I—I'm trying to work up the nerve to tell you something."

She looked at him with wariness in her eyes. "Why do you not just say whatever it is? As soon as possible, please. When you get that look on your face, I cannot stand not knowing what you are thinking."

He could tell from her voice that she was trying hard to smile. Thank the saints for that. His wife was not nervous and high-strung like Linda-Lou Ness. Leah might be upset, but she was not a weeper.

"Leah, there's something I want you to know."

"Oh?" She sounded maddeningly calm.

"Yesterday you said, well, that our marriage didn't seem to matter to me. I need to tell you that it does matter to me. You matter to me."

She was no longer trying to smile. "Yet you have withdrawn from me."

He groaned. "I wish I could lie to you and say that's not true, but I can't. Yeah, I guess I have, um, withdrawn."

He edged his chair close to hers and laid his hand on her arm. "Leah. Leah, I swear our marriage is important to me. It's the most important thing in my life, you and Teddy."

Leah laid down her fork, folded her hands in her lap and closed her eyes. "But it does not feel so to me."

A pent-up breath exploded from his lungs. "I love you, dammit. I've loved you ever since you stepped off the train."

Her mouth trembled. "Thad, six months ago I believed that you cared for me. Now I see a man who sleeps apart from me and does not want to be close."

"Oh, hell, Leah, you know I care about you."

"Ah. Do I? It feels to me as if you do not. It is hard for me to say this, Thad, but there is something *you* need to know, as well."

A cold hand reached in and pinched his vitals. "Yeah? What's that?" His throat was so tight he could scarcely get the words out.

She twisted to look into his eyes. "I love you, Thad. I will always love you. And," she continued, her voice still mild, almost detached, "there is something you need to know."

She halted, drew in a long breath and went on. "I cannot go on this way. It is tearing me apart inside."

Jumping jacks! He saw it clearly now; the wall he'd constructed to avoid pain was causing exactly what he feared. He was losing Leah.

Right then he knew the thing that had niggled at him all along: protecting himself from loving Leah all these weeks had come full circle. He'd hurt her. Hell, it had driven her away. Only now did he see the cost.

She reached up and smoothed her fingers over his whiskery cheek. "I know you did not mean to hurt me. But…"

"But I *have* hurt you."

"Yes."

"Dammit, Leah, I wouldn't knowingly cause you pain, but—" He broke off and dragged his hands through his hair. "Oh, hell, I can't believe what I've done."

He shot to his feet and began pacing back and forth in front of her. Suddenly he stopped and bent over her. "I do love you, Leah. And…"

He hesitated so long she repeated the word. "And?"

"And I want to kiss you, but I'm not sure I have the right anymore." He grasped her shoulders and drew her up to him. "Do I have the right?" he whispered.

She did not answer. Instead, she rested her hands on his chest, looked into his eyes for a long moment and lifted her face. With a groan, he caught her mouth with his.

She tasted of apples and salt, and her cheeks and her eyelids were wet with tears. A surge of hunger roared through him. It had been so long, so damn long. He couldn't get enough of her.

He tightened his arms around her small, soft frame and held on like a drowning man. "Please," he murmured. "Please, Leah, for God's sake, stay with me."

In answer she reached around his neck and pulled his face down to hers. "I brought a lemon cake from Uncle Charlie for our dessert."

Then she pressed her mouth against Thad's chin, his cheek, his closed eyelids, and finally, with a tiny moan, she reached his mouth. Thad lost himself in the feel of her skin, the scent of her hair, the welcoming softness of her lips, and then he heard the upstairs window slide up, followed by Teddy's piping voice.

"Gosh, you gonna go on kissin' all night?"

"Maybe," Thud murmured against her mouth.

"Hurry up!" Teddy yelled. "I wanna tell you 'bout this fellow Hawkeye."

The window whapped down, leaving Thad and Leah alone except for the crickets and the whispering maple leaves.

"Tomorrow," Thad murmured when he could breathe steadily. "Tomorrow, come out to the wheat field with me."

Her eyes narrowed slightly. "Why?"

"I just want you with me when…when I have to plow it under. It's important, Leah."

She nodded. "Yes," she said with a sigh. "I think it is time for me to confront my rival."

She turned away. "Sit with me, Thad. We do not have to talk, but I think we should be close together."

Thad lowered his frame to a chair and pulled her onto his lap. They sat quietly together on the porch until the sky turned pink and then flamed crimson and gold with the rising sun.

Chapter Twenty-Four

At noon the next day, Wash Halliday brought the plow horse, roped behind his gray stallion. He found Thad and Leah picnicking on sandwiches and lemonade in the shade of the two maple trees in front of the house, and he sent Thad a speculative look. He received only a silent smile.

"Guess I'll mosey on back to the Double H," Wash murmured. "Jeanne's putting up strawberry jam and I said I'd— Oh, horse feathers, strawberry jam doesn't matter a whit to you two."

He tied the plow horse to one of the trees, reined his mount away and headed back down the road.

By midafternoon Teddy had gone fishing with Harvey Poletti. Leah and Thad crunched across the dry pasture grass and leaned against the split rail fence around the wheat field. Leah wiped her perspiring hands on her white muslin apron, pushed back her sunbonnet and stared at the field.

The wheat stalks were completely dried up. What

should have been tall golden spikes, drooping with heavy heads of grain, was instead three acres of parched, sun-scorched plants.

Beside her, Thad leaned one knee against the fence and put his head in his hands.

"I can't save it," he said, his voice thick. "Dammit, a man feels helpless faced with something like this, when there's nothing he can do. He feels...broken."

"You are not in charge of the rain, Thad. Or the sun, or the wind, or—"

"Yeah, I know, but I wanted this wheat. I wanted it a lot."

Leah eyed him out of the corner of her eye. "I think," she said with a slight hesitation, "that in your mind you have turned your wheat into a magic charm to ward off disaster."

Thad jerked his head up. "What do you mean, a charm?"

"In China, people put their trust in good omens and lucky charms to ward off evil and bring prosperity."

Thad snorted. "Or the reverse, I suppose. If it's a bad omen, something like the northern lights or a shower of stars, it brings bad luck."

"Exactly. The Chinese are very superstitious."

Thad raised his eyebrows and looked away, across the stunted brown field. "Guess that's what I did, all right. I wanted a magic charm." His voice sounded hoarse. He cleared his throat.

"That is very human," Leah said quietly. "But it is not rational. You are thinking like a superstitious Chinese man would. And you are not a Chinese man."

Thad grunted. "I can't stand to look at it any longer. It's time to plow it under."

Leah said nothing. Instead, she stared hard at the brittle wheat stalks nearest the fence. All at once she hiked her denim work skirt up to her knees, set one foot on the bottom fence rail and grabbed on to the top. In the next instant she swung her leg up and over and jumped down on the other side.

Thad watched in disbelief. "What the hell are you doing? You trying to break your neck?"

"I am trying to break an evil spell," she retorted. She waded into the field. The stalks were so dry they clicked softly against her skirt.

Thad shook his head. Leah was always surprising when he least expected it, as if she knew something he didn't. Her uncanny insight had always puzzled him.

She leaned over a bent stalk, wrapped her fingers around the dried-up head and stripped off a handful of brown kernels. She did the same thing to the next stalk, and the next, collecting the bits of refuse in her looped-up apron.

Then she climbed the fence again, one-handed; the other hand grasped the collection of kernels. Once on the ground, she marched up to him with a triumphant grin.

"You are not a broken man, Thad. Just look!" She unfolded her apron. "Seeds! Wheat seeds! For next year's crop."

Dumbfounded, he sifted a handful of the dry bits through his fingers. Leah grabbed his hand and pointed to the kernels in his palm.

"They are not dead, Thad. They are dried out, but they are only sleeping." She lifted dancing eyes to his. "It is a good omen."

He caught her about the waist, spun her around and around until she was dizzy, but she still managed to hold on to her apronful of sun-scorched wheat seeds.

"Leah. My darling Leah, I feel like I've aged twenty years this summer."

Her pleased whoop of laughter made him grin. He set her down practically on his boot tops, wrapped his arms around her and untied her sunbonnet. Then he buried his face in her hair. "Hell's bells," he whispered. "You smell like lemons."

Leah reached one arm around his neck, and he brought his lips near her ear. "Leah, I will regret hurting you for the rest of my life."

A shocking notion poked into her brain. "You could make it up to me...." She made her voice as silky as she could. "Starting tonight."

His eyes widened momentarily and then darkened. "Why not now?" he murmured.

"It's Saturday, Thad. My Ladies' Knitting Circle meets in town this afternoon."

"Damn the meeting. You always come home from those damn things wrapped tighter than new barbed wire."

"Today I will not. I promise." She kissed him until they were both out of breath, then turned toward the house.

The air in Verena Forester's small upstairs apartment was hotter and more oppressive than it was outside. To Leah's relief, a large pitcher of cool lemonade sat on the refreshment table, along with a plate of what must be Uncle Charlie's cookies, with coconut flakes sprinkled on top.

Coconut? Where would Uncle Charlie get coconut? Surely not from Carl Ness's mercantile. Perhaps Uncle had sent away for it.

"It is too hot to knit," Verena announced as she filled glasses with lemonade. Instead, the assembled ladies nibbled on cookies, sipped their lemonade and talked. Gossiped, really, Leah decided after listening for ten minutes. But at least the talk wasn't about *her*.

But then Thad's name came up, and Leah snapped to attention.

"Has to plow it under, I hear," someone remarked in a subdued voice.

"Oh, what a shame." This from Jeanne Halliday. *"C'est terrible."*

"That dratted man. Always a dreamer," Verena sniffed. "His head's been in the clouds ever since—" She broke off and rose to replenish the cookie plate.

"Why, it's enough to break a man's spirit," Darla Weatherby said in an acid tone. "My Henry would never risk growing wheat, of all things."

Leah swallowed a gulp of lemonade and tried to focus on something other than the remarks swirling around her. Verena's wallpaper, for example. Tiny pink roses on a sky-blue background. How oddly feminine for such a…well, soldierlike woman.

Had Thad really wanted Verena?

The answer came like a bolt of lightning. *Thad had never wanted Verena!*

Leah wanted to laugh with relief. It was Hattie who had liked Verena, not Thad.

Not Thad.

Leah's attention shifted to the sound of young Noralee Ness's shoes swinging back and forth against her wooden chair rung.

"My father says Mr. MacAllister is a renegade." The girl looked up at Verena. "What's a renegade?"

"Someone who purposely does something unusual, dear," Verena instructed. "Something different."

"Like planting wheat," Lucy Nichols murmured, straightening her ruffled yellow muslin for the fourth time.

Darla Weatherby leaned forward. "Like marrying a—" Ellie Johnson jabbed her elbow into the young woman's rib cage and she sucked in her breath.

"A renegade is a rebel," Verena finished.

With a quiet groan, Leah went back to studying Verena's wallpaper. The longer she stared at it, the more she understood the stiff-necked dressmaker. Her outer armor might be hard and prickly, but the woman had a soft underbelly.

Then Verena said something that made Leah choke on her lemonade.

"I feel sorry for Thad MacAllister. It cuts a man down to size to be proved wrong."

Leah stifled an impulse to leap to her feet and scream at the woman. But inside her head, she heard her mother's voice. *Wake not the sleeping tiger.*

Her mother had been wise. Leah could fight this battle with a whisper.

"You are mistaken," she stated, her voice quiet. "All of you. Thad has not been proved wrong, and even if he were, his size is not relevant."

"What's 'relevant' mean?" Noralee whispered to Verena.

"Hush, girl."

Leah dug in her skirt pocket. "What is relevant is Thad's wheat field. It is true the sun has burned it almost black. But look."

She held out a scant palmful of wheat kernels. "For next year's crop. The seeds are undamaged; we will simply strip the heads and gather the—"

"How do you know this?" Verena's eyes blazed. "What could you possibly know about wheat farming?"

A pregnant silence descended. Except for the clink of lemonade glasses and Verena's agitated breathing, there wasn't a sound in the room.

"I know this," Leah said calmly, "because I have walked through wheat fields before. We grow wheat in China, too."

She folded her hands in her lap. "Now, Noralee, to answer your question, 'relevant' means 'related.' Pertinent. Which—" she glanced around the circle "—many of our remarks this afternoon have not been."

No one had anything more to say after that, and the gathering broke up early. In awkward silence the ladies replaced their lemonade glasses on the table, thanked Verena and departed.

Ellie caught up with Leah at the bottom of the staircase and squeezed her arm. Jeanne appeared on her other side and hugged her, hard.

"Thank you both," Leah choked out. Her throat was so tight she could not speak another word.

At dusk Teddy came home with a string of brook trout for supper, then scooted back up to his loft for more of Hawkeye.

Thad tried his damnedest to keep his eyes off Leah, who seemed to be having trouble swallowing.

"More coffee?" he offered.

"N-no, thank you. Any more coffee and I won't sleep at all tonight."

He chuckled. "Coffee or no coffee, what makes you think you're going to get any sleep, anyway?"

Her cheeks turned strawberry colored. Amazing. Married almost a year and he could still make her blush. Somehow that made him real happy inside.

He studied every little thing about her—the way her black hair fell forward across her cheek when she bent over the oven; the small pink shell of her ear and the pale skin just behind it where he wanted to put his mouth. The throb of her pulse in the vein that ran down her neck.

As he watched, her heartbeat, visible under her light shirtwaist, began to thump faster. Maybe because she knew he was watching her.

Did she want him? He knew she loved him, but a woman could feel that way and not want a man's body.

Did she want him?

It was agony not knowing. He rose, gathered up the

supper plates and mugs, and plunked them in the sink. Working the pump hard, he managed to draw a scant half kettle of water, which he set on the stove to heat.

She hadn't moved from her chair, but he could feel her eyes on him. Heavens above, this was like their wedding night, when he had been so nervous he hadn't been able to touch her.

The coffeepot beckoned, but he'd put his empty mug in the sink. He grabbed it, anyway, and poured it full. Figured he wouldn't sleep much tonight, either.

"Leah?"

She turned her head toward him. "Leah," he said again, his voice unsteady. He wanted to touch her. Wanted to feel her softness, her warmth. Her strength.

She stood up, untied her apron and walked toward him. His breathing stopped, started, stopped again. She reached around him to hang the apron on the hook over the wood box, and he caught the scent of her hair. Lemon and something musky.

He closed his eyes. Then, with a low groan, he pulled her close enough to feel her breasts press against his chest. She gave a little cry and buried her nose in his shirt front.

"Leah, do you want—"

She lifted her head. "You know that I do," she whispered. How, Thad wondered, could this extraordinary woman be sensible and hardworking one minute, and playful and seductive the next?

The instant his lips met hers, he forgot the question, drugged by her scent. The feel of her body trembling against his made him hard. He lifted her into his arms, puffed out the single lamp and made his way down the hall to the bedroom.

He would always remember how crisp and clean the bedsheets were, how cool they felt against his bare skin.

They made love all night, devoured slices of Uncle Charlie's lemon cake in bed and then made love again. Thad knew he would never forget it.

At dawn, Thad woke to the sound of laughter. And voices. He sat up, then climbed out of bed to peek through the curtained window. He could see nothing but the blush of sunrise.

"What is it?" Leah said in a sleep-fuzzed voice.

"Dunno. Sounds like people."

"People?" She jerked upright, pulling the sheet over her naked body. Thad, too, was naked, and in spite of herself, she giggled. They had slept, *when* they'd slept, skin to skin.

But people? At this hour?

She was dressed before Thad could button his jeans. On the porch she tripped over Teddy, still in his pajamas and popeyed with curiosity.

"What're all those people doin' in our pasture? We havin' a picnic or somethin'?"

Thad banged through the front screen door. "How many people?"

"I dunno, Pa. They're all ridin' horses."

"Horses! Well, let's go and see, son."

Thad and Leah tramped across the pasture, followed by Teddy, hastily dressed in jeans and his pajama top.

When they came within sight of the wheat field, a shiver went down Thad's back.

"Would you look at that," he breathed.

Wash and Jeanne Halliday stood at the fence. Little Manette and her grandfather, Rooney Cloudman, were just dismounting. Next to them, Ike Bruhn came swaggering up to the gate, and—

Thad could scarcely believe his eyes. A trim little black buggy rolled up with Verena Forester, a crocheted lap robe spread across her knees, and Uncle Charlie in the driver's seat!

Thad blinked, then blinked again.

"Heard you had some wheat that needed gleaning," Wash called out. He gestured to the gathering behind him. "We brought bags for the seed. We plan to work straight through this field, strip it right down to the nubs."

Thad was speechless. With numb fingers he opened the single gate and stood back while his neighbors and the townspeople swarmed through and spread out across the field.

"By sundown," Wash yelled, "you'll be ready to plow this field. And by October, you can replant."

Leah reached out for Thad. His blue eyes were wet and shiny, and she bit her lips to keep from crying.

"Leah, honey," he choked out. "What did we do to deserve this?"

She rested her head against his chest, listening to the unsteady thump of his heart. "If I knew," she said, her voice shaking, "I would do a lot more of it."

Her mother had been right, the slow drip had marked the stone.

Thad held Leah away from him, then bent to kiss her wet eyelids. "You are a bonny, bonny lass, Leah. It was a good omen when you stepped off the train in Smoke River."

He took her hand and together they turned toward the open gate, walked through it and joined the gleaners.

Epilogue

The following year, Thad and Leah MacAllister were the toast of Smoke River. At harvesttime, Thad's wheat field brought in twice as much as anyone expected, and the next week the mercantile was flooded with orders for seed.

Even more unexpected was the birth of Violet Marie MacAllister in October. After Violet's entrance into the MacAllister family, nothing was ever the same for Thad's son, Teddy, who had always claimed he didn't like girls.

But Teddy took one look at the pink-and-white creature in the wicker cradle and fell head over boots in love with his baby sister.

That year and all the years that followed, both father and son were the proudest males in town.

* * * * *

COMING NEXT MONTH from Harlequin® Historical
AVAILABLE AUGUST 20, 2013

THE BALLAD OF EMMA O'TOOLE
Elizabeth Lane
On trial for his life, the stakes for gambler Logan Devereaux have never been higher. But then he's offered a shocking form of restitution... marriage to Emma O'Toole, his victim's beautiful sweetheart!
(Western)

MISTRESS AT MIDNIGHT
Sophia James
Haunted by rumors following her husband's death, Aurelia has withdrawn from society. To secure her family's future, there's only one man who can help. And he demands payment—with a kiss!
(Victorian)

RUMORS
Louise Allen
Lady Isobel Jervis has been exiled to Wimpole Hall to avoid further scandal...but then she meets arrogant architect Giles Harker and their growing attraction could cost them both their reputations!
(Regency)

THE RUNAWAY COUNTESS
Bancrofts of Barton Park
Amanda McCabe
Hayden Fitzwalter longs to win back the only woman he has ever loved—his wife, Jane. But first he has to convince her that this rogue is ready to be tamed....
(Regency)

HHCNM0813

REQUEST YOUR FREE BOOKS!

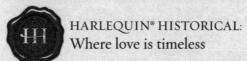

HARLEQUIN® HISTORICAL:
Where love is timeless

2 FREE NOVELS PLUS 2 **FREE GIFTS!**

YES! Please send me 2 FREE Harlequin® Historical novels and my 2 FREE gifts (gifts are worth about $10). After receiving them, if I don't wish to receive any more books, I can return the shipping statement marked "cancel." If I don't cancel, I will receive 6 brand-new novels every month and be billed just $5.44 per book in the U.S. or $5.74 per book in Canada. That's a savings of at least 16% off the cover price! It's quite a bargain! Shipping and handling is just 50¢ per book in the U.S. and 75¢ per book in Canada.* I understand that accepting the 2 free books and gifts places me under no obligation to buy anything. I can always return a shipment and cancel at any time. Even if I never buy another book, the two free books and gifts are mine to keep forever.

246/349 HDN F4ZY

Name	(PLEASE PRINT)	
Address		Apt. #
City	State/Prov.	Zip/Postal Code

Signature (if under 18, a parent or guardian must sign)

Mail to the Harlequin® Reader Service:
IN U.S.A.: P.O. Box 1867, Buffalo, NY 14240-1867
IN CANADA: P.O. Box 609, Fort Erie, Ontario L2A 5X3

Want to try two free books from another line?
Call 1-800-873-8635 or visit www.ReaderService.com.

* Terms and prices subject to change without notice. Prices do not include applicable taxes. Sales tax applicable in N.Y. Canadian residents will be charged applicable taxes. Offer not valid in Quebec. This offer is limited to one order per household. Not valid for current subscribers to Harlequin Historical books. All orders subject to credit approval. Credit or debit balances in a customer's account(s) may be offset by any other outstanding balance owed by or to the customer. Please allow 4 to 6 weeks for delivery. Offer available while quantities last.

Your Privacy—The Harlequin® Reader Service is committed to protecting your privacy. Our Privacy Policy is available online at www.ReaderService.com or upon request from the Harlequin Reader Service.

We make a portion of our mailing list available to reputable third parties that offer products we believe may interest you. If you prefer that we not exchange your name with third parties, or if you wish to clarify or modify your communication preferences, please visit us at www.ReaderService.com/consumerchoice or write to us at Harlequin Reader Service Preference Service, P.O. Box 9062, Buffalo, NY 14269. Include your complete name and address.

HH13R

*Sophia James takes you on a delicious journey of scandal,
deception and overwhelming desire in*
MISTRESS AT MIDNIGHT

"And what is our full story, my lord?" Alone, Aurelia felt
braver, their history built up in layers, one upon the other
and all beginning with the kiss at Taylor's Gap.

"Our story?" He turned the words so that each one
of them was carefully pronounced, his eyes grave. "Our
story is unfinished and ill concluded, any hint of what
might have been between us buried beneath duty and lies."
She stood very still.

"Debts of ill repute and payments for silence are things I
am trying to rid myself of, Mrs. St. Harlow, and if the reasons
for my cousin's death are going to be pegged to any future
problems then I would rather not know of them. For years
deception has been my companion, you see, and now I find I
need something different altogether."

"You need honesty?"

The simple question was quietly asked, a pledge that she
knew she would never be able to give him with her mother
and her father and the faithless arrogance of her dead husband.

"I do."

Honesty and innocence and pure, untainted goodness.
Lady Elizabeth Berkeley.

She suddenly and clearly understood why Lord Hawkhurst
had chosen the girl and all hope was lost.

"Would you dance with me again, Mrs. St. Harlow?"

"Yes." She had heard another waltz strike up, the first

chords of Strauss drifting about the room. Aurelia placed her fingers upon his offered arm and they walked onto the floor, the lights dim here and the glow of candles evoking some nighttime grotto far from London town. She hoped that he would not feel the rapid beat of her heart as he brought her into his arms, closer than she expected, farther apart than she wanted.

No one else existed in that room as the music swirled about them and he led her into the steps, the smell of soap and brandy vying for an ascendance, his body hard beneath his superfine jacket.

They were hardly strangers. Not quite lovers. There was a danger in it Aurelia found exhilarating and forbidden. Pushing against him so that he might feel the curve of her breasts, she watched his expression change.

Feminine power was surprisingly easy, the potency of her own body something she had never considered before because Charles had left her so very damaged.

"Keep doing that and I will drag you off home before you know what has happened to you and you will not have a chance to change it."

Look for Sophia James's
MISTRESS AT MIDNIGHT
Coming September 2013
from Harlequin Historical

SADDLE UP AND READ 'EM!

This summer, get your fix of Western reads and pick up a cowboy from some of your favorite authors!

In September look for:

STERN by Brenda Jackson
The Westmorelands
Harlequin Desire

COWBOY REDEMPTION by Elle James
Covert Cowboys Inc.
Harlequin Intrigue

CALLAHAN COWBOY TRIPLETS by Tina Leonard
Callahan Cowboys
Harlequin American Romance

THE BALLAD OF EMMA O'TOOL by Elizabeth Lane
Harlequin Historical

Look for these great Western reads and more available wherever books are sold or visit
www.Harlequin.com/Westerns